# Purranormal Activity

*St. Martin's Paperbacks Titles*
*by Cate Conte*

CAT ABOUT TOWN
PURRDER SHE WROTE
THE TELL TAIL HEART
A WHISKER OF A DOUBT
CLAWS FOR ALARM
GONE BUT NOT FURGOTTEN
NINE LIVES AND ALIBIS
SHOCK AND PAW
CLAWS OUT
PURRANORMAL ACTIVITY

# Purranormal Activity

CATE CONTE

St. Martin's Paperbacks

This is a work of fiction. All of the names, characters, organizations, places, and events portrayed in this work are either products of the author's imagination or used fictitiously.

First published in the United States by St. Martin's Paperbacks, an imprint of St. Martin's Publishing Group.

*EU Representative*: Macmillan Publishers Ireland Ltd., 1st Floor, The Liffey Trust Centre, 117–126 Sheriff Street Upper, Dublin 1, D01 YC43, Ireland.

PURRANORMAL ACTIVITY



For information, address St. Martin's Publishing Group, 120 Broadway, New York, NY 10271.

www.stmartins.com

ISBN: 978-1-250-43518-7



Printed in the United States of America

St. Martin's Paperbacks edition / August 2026

10 9 8 7 6 5 4 3 2 1

*In memory of Bill Stanley, whose passion for history and the telling of it, along with his big heart, made him a force of nature*

# Acknowledgments

I can't believe this is book ten in this series. I am so grateful to everyone who fell in love with Maddie, JJ, Grandpa Leo, and the crew and their adventures on Daybreak Island. Without you, the readers, these books wouldn't exist. Thank you for your loyalty.

A huge thank-you to my agent, Jill Marsal, for shepherding the next season of these books into the world.

I'm grateful for the amazing crew at St. Martin's for believing in the books and championing them for all these years, especially my editor, Claire Cheek, whose sense for the characters and keen eye for plot holes always make the final product so much better. There are so many people—Olya Kirilyuk, my cover designer; the tireless publicists; marketers; editorial and production team—working behind the scenes to bring these books to life.

Despite being a mermaid at heart, I have very little actual knowledge about marine science. Much gratitude to marine biologist Shelly Wanamaker for sharing her insights with me so I could capture the essence of the work.

Thank you to Jason Allen-Forrest, my beta reader, for always making these books better. An early reader is so important to make sure everything is holding together, and you are incredible at catching all my errors!

Last but definitely not least, thank you to my husband, Alan, for always believing in me, even when I'm having a hard time believing in myself. I love you.

# Chapter 1

*Wednesday*

My hands were full of cat food bowls when the JJ's House of Purrs cell phone blared the opening riffs of "Stray Cat Strut" from the check-in desk, the vibrations sending the phone dancing along the surface and pens rolling dangerously close to the edge.

I didn't remember setting the volume this loud. It was probably Adele. My cafe manager liked to make sure she didn't miss anything, but she hated carrying the phone around. Said it made her feel like a millennial. I figured she probably meant a Gen Zer, but didn't bother correcting her. Adele liked things her way.

I looked around to see if anyone could grab the food or the phone, but aside from JJ—my orange cat and the cafe's namesake sprawled across the counter—the closest person to me was my mom, and she was holding a bag of cat litter.

"I got it," I told her, nearly bobbling a couple of the bowls before setting them down so I could grab the phone, grimacing as the chorus started again for the fourth time. I used to like that song.

"JJ's House of Purrs, Maddie speaking." Saying the words made me smile. If anyone had told me five years ago that I'd be back home on Daybreak Island, living in my Grandpa Leo's house that we'd turned into a cat cafe, I'd have accused them of being the worst kind of delusional. Moving home had never been on my bingo card. And yet, here I was.

"Yes, hello, I'd like to book an event." The female voice on the other end of the line was strong and confident, more of a command than an ask.

"Sure thing, what kind of an event?" I glanced around for the iPad we used for scheduling all our cafe visits and now our parties.

My mom's ears perked up and she dropped the cat litter and rushed over, flashing me a thumbs-up. She loved being a part of the action. After we decided to add a new piece to our business model—mobile cat parties in our new cafe truck—she'd decided she wanted to run them. I'd known it was only a matter of time until this business, which I owned with my Grandpa Leo and my longtime business partner Ethan Birdsong, became a true family affair.

It had been creeping that way slowly, starting when my sister Val accidentally fell in love with Ethan after I convinced him to come back here with me to take our shot at running a cat cafe. Ethan oversaw the food part of the business. Since my sister Val ran an event-planning business, it seemed like a natural fit for her to become our consulting party planner. Then more recently my sister Sam became a barista at the food cafe, which we'd created inside our former garage. Now with my mom's inclusion, the only holdout was my dad. Although I didn't see him finding much spare time given his duties as the CEO of Daybreak Island Hospital, one never knew in this family. Everyone always had time to get up in everyone else's business, something that I used to find annoying. It was one of the reasons I'd hightailed myself off the island for college and didn't look back for more than a decade.

Now—even though I wouldn't admit it often—I found it endearing. As for my mom, working the parties gave her another way to be out and plugged into the community, which she loved. So we'd had more bonding time lately. It was nice. Most of the time.

"It's a birthday party," the woman on the other end of the line said. "A dual birthday party, actually. My daughter's and granddaughter's birthdays. They're the same day."

I could hear the smile in her voice. "That's so cool. Okay, what date were you looking for?" I finally spotted the iPad hiding under an adoption application and snatched it up, hoping it was charged. I breathed a sigh of relief when it powered on.

"Saturday," she said.

"Saturday? This Saturday?" I asked, sure I'd heard wrong. That was in three days.

"Yes, this Saturday," she said, a bit impatiently. "We're planning a themed party—the Enchanted Cat Garden. We'll have tea with the cats—plushies, of course—and then a fairy woods setup. Fairy lights, fog, a princess or two, the whole deal. Our backyard is perfect for it, and having real cats there too will be such a great surprise for the kids. I'm so glad I heard about you in time."

In *her* time, maybe. July was our busy season, when Daybreak Island, our little paradise off the coast of Massachusetts, beckoned to all the tourists and summer residents. This year, news of our mobile truck had spread fast, and our schedule had quickly become jam-packed for most of the weekends all summer long. I'd had to turn away double bookings for several weekends already, which I hated to do but I couldn't clone our operations to be in two places at once. And we still had the actual home-based cafe to run.

I pulled up the calendar for this weekend. We already had a party at the library Saturday afternoon—just cats, no actual food in the food truck—and an event here at the cafe on Sunday. Nothing else had been added, thankfully, since the last time I looked, but it was still shaping up to be busy.

As if she could sense my hesitation, the caller said, "I know it's very short notice and I'm sorry for that. But I really want you—the other option just wasn't cutting it, and I want this to be a special event. I'm prepared to double your fee."

*Other option?* I registered the words but didn't quite understand them. I was also more focused on that last bit that she'd said. "Double my fee? Well—"

"Triple, then," she insisted. "I have my credit card here right now to give you a deposit. I just need a yes."

I pondered this. It would mean a super busy day staffing both the cafe and the parties. Not to mention, rushing from one party to another—cutting it close depending on how long the library party lasted—was never ideal. But also, who was I to turn down an influx of cash? That would be more cats saved, so of course I would say yes. I recited our fee to her.

"Great," she said. "Triple it, and here's my card number."

"I do have something that afternoon, so it would need to be later in the afternoon or early evening," I warned her.

"Even better. A nighttime party might be even more magical for Tess and Piper's Purr-Day Bash. My daughter is Tess and my granddaughter is Piper," she added.

I agreed a nighttime Purr-Day Bash would be fun. It would be a long day for the cats, but I could switch out our feline attendees so no one had to be at both events. We agreed on a two-hour block from six to eight that night. I created the calendar event. "You're in. What's your name?" I hadn't managed to get it from her before now.

"Olivia McAllister," she said.

I added it to the calendar listing, took the credit card

number, and finalized the booking. "You should get an email confirmation shortly," I told her.

"Great. How many cats will you be bringing?"

"How many kids do you expect?" We still staggered the amount of people in the truck at once, and with kids we had to make sure there were enough supervising adults, but we liked to have a 2 to 1 ratio of people to cats.

"I think we'll have about seven or eight," she said. "We don't live here permanently—yet—but my granddaughter has been visiting a local camp when we come over to the island, and she's made some friends there. We've also been taking her to story time at the library, and she's met children there as well. It will be small, but fun."

Small sounded good to me. I finished entering the info and got her address. "We'll probably take a trip by over the next few days to scope out where we'll put the truck and setup," I said. "Is there a time that works for you?"

"No problem," Olivia told me. "Come by anytime."

Even better. She didn't seem concerned with meeting me, or maybe she already had and I just didn't recognize the name. We were getting so many visitors to the cafe these days it was hard to keep track. Which was a great problem to have. Still, I was curious. "Where did you hear about us? Have you been to the cafe before?"

"No," Olivia said. "Not yet. But I heard about you through the grapevine. Your business came so highly recommended. It was my top choice, no question. The other place just didn't seem to have the resources you do. No mobile option, specifically. And everywhere I go here someone tells me something about your cat cafe. It's on our list to get there."

*The other place.* That was the second time she'd mentioned that. And unless something had changed literally overnight, we were the only ones on the island with a cat cafe, let alone a mobile one. What was she talking about?

But before I could ask, she said, "I must run, Maddie, but thanks for your time and flexibility. Can't wait!" And she hung up.

I must have been frowning because my mother, who had come to the counter to await details, waved a hand in front of my face. "Everything okay?"

I adjusted the volume on the phone so it didn't blast us out of the room the next time it rang, then put it back on the desk. "Yes, fine. Just thinking." I made a mental note to ask Olivia about this "other place" when we met her, then focused on my mother.

"So, what's the story?" she asked. "A party?"

"A double birthday," I said. "Mom and daughter. That was the grandmother calling. You in to work it with me? It's Saturday night."

"Of course," she exclaimed, whipping out her own phone to mark the date. "And I heard you say something about doubling the fee?"

"She offered. Tripled it, actually, since I was going to decline because of the other booking." I was still pleasantly surprised by that.

"Excellent!" My mom high-fived me. "Whose party is it?"

Since she and my dad knew just about everyone on the island, I'd expected the question. I'd only been back a couple years after a decade away, so I wasn't as in tune with the Daybreak Island locals roster as I used to be. But my mom and dad knew literally everyone. Partly because of my dad's job, and partly because of my mom's personality. And because she'd grown up here. "Not a resident. Sounds like she visits on summer weekends. Her name is Olivia McAllister."

I wasn't prepared for the reaction I got. When she didn't answer, I glanced back up from the iPad where I was adding a few notes. And saw she'd gone so white I had to look behind me to see if perhaps a ghost had appeared in cat form or something. But there was nothing there. "What is it?" I asked, alarmed.

"Olivia . . . McAllister? Are you sure?"

I checked the details I'd typed into the iPad. "Yep." I handed the device to my mom.

She went even paler when she looked at it. "One fifty-six Cliff Walk Lane," she murmured. "I can't believe it."

"I take it you know her," I said, curious now.

Lost in thought, she didn't answer me until I prodded her again.

"Yes," she said finally, handing me back the iPad. "We were best friends in high school."

I stared at her. "Seriously? She used to live here?" She hadn't mentioned that.

"Yes. Until one day she just . . . poof! . . . moved away. Without a word. Her whole family. It was right after they had a family tragedy, to be fair, but it was all very abrupt. And we've never reconnected."

"Yikes," I said. "What kind of family tragedy?" I was always intrigued by stories like this. Not only because I liked a good mystery—Grandpa Leo's policeman genes were in my blood—but because it involved my parents' early lives. I always jumped at the chance to know more about them. I'd made it a recent practice to ask my parents and Grandpa Leo for all the stories I could get out of them. It was something I'd learned when my grandma died a couple of years ago, and pretty much every day since, I'd thought of something I wished I had asked her and never gotten around to.

"Her aunt Delia went missing. She lived here too. At that address," she said, nodding toward the iPad. "I can't believe Olivia's there. Anyway, the whole family lived out here. They go back generations. Delia was such a cool lady. It was really sad. No one ever did find out what happened to her."

"Yikes," I said again. "That is sad. I take it you didn't know Olivia was back?"

She tucked some unruly curls behind her ear as she shook her head. "No. I didn't. Which is surprising, because usually I would hear about that kind of thing. You said we're going to scope out the area for where to put the truck?"

I nodded. It was a practice of mine, so I didn't get surprised by a tiny driveway or a street so small the truck barely fit. I was still learning how to maneuver the thing and hated getting caught off guard. Especially when Harry Timmins, our volunteer who'd procured the truck, wasn't around to drive it for me.

"Can we go today?" My mother clasped her hands under her chin, watching me earnestly, as if she were now the child and I was the mom.

I glanced at my watch. I hated disappointing her, but the day was almost over and I had promised to cover the evening shift at the cafe tonight so Grandpa could meet his friends for a card game. "Can it wait until tomorrow?"

A glimmer of disappointment flashed across her face, but then it was gone. "Of course," she assured me. "I'm just excited—I haven't seen her in ages. And I've missed her so. I wonder why she didn't call me to tell me she was back?"

I had no answer to that. "Maybe she just hadn't had a chance yet?" I suggested. "Why don't you call her? She probably had no clue who we were when she called, otherwise of course she would've said something." I hoped that was true.

My mom thought about it, then shrugged it off. "Maybe you're right. Or else she probably felt bad about leaving the way they did," she decided. "It's been such a long time I imagine it might be awkward. I'll just wait until we go over. It will be a good surprise, I hope." She smiled, looking like a little kid again. "I can't wait to see her tomorrow. I hope she's as excited to see me."

# Chapter 2

*Thursday*

When JJ and I rolled into the kitchen the next morning around eight—after he had insisted I get out of bed and feed him by patting my cheek insistently with his paw—my mother was already there, huddled up with Grandpa Leo. We were supposed to go to the McAllister house today, and apparently she was ready to go. It also looked like they were having a serious conversation. Mugs of coffee sat untouched in front of them as they talked in low voices, trailing off when I walked in.

"Good morning," I said, giving them curious looks.

"Morning," they replied in unison.

"And no, we didn't drink all the coffee," Grandpa Leo said with a grin, getting up to bring his mug to the microwave to warm it.

"Thanks for that." I got JJ's breakfast while he supervised from his usual perch on the counter, tail swishing, making sure I did it correctly and didn't skimp on portion size. When I'd finished preparing the bowl and he approved, he hopped down and followed me to his food station and attacked it with a vengeance. He loved the fish "topper" I put on his food for added nutrition. I needed to remember to stop by the Lobstah Shack to get more. Our friend Damian Shaw owned the restaurant down near the ferry docks, and he generously kept JJ's menu stocked with any fish remnants he had.

"I assume you want a cup," Grandpa teased, grabbing a mug for me.

"You bet. Did you see Lucas and the dogs this morning?" I asked. My boyfriend—who lived here with us, another wildly unexpected but awesome result of my moving back home—ran a pet grooming salon on the island, and he often left super early to do some admin work before the clients started getting dropped off.

"I did. He left maybe an hour ago," Grandpa said.

"Took the dogs with him," my mother added. "He knew you had a busy day. He's such a thoughtful guy."

That was certainly true. "I didn't even hear them leave." I made a mental note to text him once I'd woken up a bit more. Lucas always let me sleep if he left early. He knew the hours I kept, so he always wanted to make sure that if I had a chance to rest, I took it.

Once JJ was set and Grandpa had returned to the table, I perused the fridge for something semi-healthy to eat. While I could sustain myself indefinitely on Ethan's muffins and other baked goods, my wardrobe couldn't.

"Ethan made quiche," my mother said. "It's in the oven. Spinach and feta, with vegan butter so it's not fattening." She grinned at me. "It's to die for despite that decision."

"As is everything Ethan makes," I said, and I meant it. Even when my business partner and new brother-in-law made things that were vegan and gluten-free and all other kinds of healthy and allergen-free—which he did regularly to make sure we had something for everyone at the cafe—his food was untouchable. Ethan could make anything vegan taste as good as something that had four pounds of butter in it. I kept waiting for him to wake up and realize that he belonged in a Michelin-starred restaurant in Paris or New York rather than on a tiny island cooking and baking for a cat cafe. But he loved it, and now he loved Val, so here we were. Lucky us.

I opened the oven door and took the casserole dish out. Even the smell was heavenly. I noticed nearly half of it was gone, and the empty plates on the table in front of Grandpa Leo and my mother gave a clue why. I cut my own generous slice and joined them at the table, gratefully picking up the hot mug Grandpa had put at my place. "You're here early," I said to my mother once I'd sipped my coffee and it had hit my system.

She nodded. "I'm excited to go see Olivia." She glanced at Grandpa.

I didn't miss the look that passed between them. "Is that what you were talking about when I came in?"

"It was," Grandpa said.

"Were you surprised to hear that she was back?" I asked him.

"I certainly was. I usually hear things long before they happen, so this was an anomaly."

I could tell he was taking it as a bit of a personal affront, or perhaps using the opportunity to chastise himself for not being as on top of things. "You were close to her too?" If she was my mother's best friend, it would've been inevitable.

Grandpa nodded. "She and your mother were always together. She spent a lot of time here at the house." He glanced around the room, maybe remembering a time forty years earlier, with his daughter and her best friend giggling at this table over cookies. "It was a huge shock to all of us when the family up and left the island without a word to anyone. But there was a family tragedy that made it hard for them to stay, I guess."

I nodded. "Mom mentioned that. The missing aunt. Did

you work on her case?" I took a bite of the quiche. It was as good as it smelled.

"I did. I was still green then—just made detective when it happened. It was never solved. Never found a trace of her, and there were no signs of foul play. Olivia's dad, Delia's brother, ultimately told us that she'd been having some mental health issues. The family became convinced she'd left the island on her own and didn't want to be found." He shrugged. "Others thought she'd possibly committed suicide, but that never really sat right with me. Especially since no body was ever found. It made no sense."

"So, they closed the case," I said, looking from him to my mom.

"We kept it open for a couple of years, but the family requested we close it after that. Sounded like they wanted to accept she was gone and try to move on."

"And you did?" I was surprised at that. Grandpa had no quit in him. Then again, he hadn't been the chief then.

He smiled, a little. "We couldn't officially close it because we had no answers, but the chief at the time had us stop actively investigating to placate the family. We thought it was weird, but we couldn't go against the directive, especially without the family's cooperation."

"And you never heard from Olivia again?" I asked my mom, scraping the last bite of quiche into my mouth. I glanced longingly at the oven, debating another piece.

"No," my mother said. "And I had no way to reach her. We didn't have Facebook back then for me to send a message, you know? Eventually I went to college and moved on. But I always thought about her. I probably should have tried harder years later."

"How come you didn't look her up?" I asked Grandpa. "You probably knew how to get in touch, right?"

Grandpa looked like he was pondering how to answer

that. "The family was being handled by another detective, and we were told that they were requesting privacy, didn't want their business spread around the island, basically. So, I had access to Delia's parents' info, but even if I had used it, I'm not sure they would've responded. They made it clear that they didn't want to be affiliated with this place anymore."

"Where did they move to?" I asked.

"Cape Coral, Florida," Grandpa Leo said.

"But Olivia's back now, booking parties and bringing her granddaughter to camp. Seems like she might be back for good, no? Or does it seem weird, given the history?"

"I don't know if it's weird," my mother said. "They still had Delia's house here. That was the one thing that still belonged to the family. Eventually someone would've had to deal with it. Maybe they want to sell it." She shrugged. "Who knows? I hope I find out when we go there, though. I'm excited for a chance to reconnect." She eyed me. "So, when are we leaving?"

I took that as a sign that I wasn't going to get to linger over my coffee and another piece of quiche. "I need to shower real quick," I said.

"Okay. I'm going to go visit the cats." She rose and left the room, leaving her coffee mostly untouched.

I turned to Grandpa. "Is Mom okay?"

"I think so. She's nervous about seeing her friend again. Understandable."

"Why do you think Olivia never got in touch?" I asked him.

"I couldn't say, Doll," he said, glancing at his watch as he drained his own coffee cup. "But I hope they have a nice reunion. Your mother deserves that."

# Chapter 3

After Grandpa left the room to start his day, I refilled my coffee and went upstairs to get ready. I didn't bother drying my long hair—it was going to get curly as soon as I stepped outside anyway. It was a beautiful day here, if not a little humid, which meant uncooperative hair. I sprayed some extra anti-frizz product in it, put it in a ponytail, and hoped for the best.

Before I went downstairs, I called Lucas. He answered right away.

"Sleep well?" he asked.

"Better than I thought. I didn't even hear you get up."

"I was quiet," he said. "The dogs, not so much."

"Thanks for taking them. I'll stop by later and visit?"

"That would be nice. You and your mom are going to check out the new party location, she said?"

"Yep. And I didn't even get to tell you about it. Turns out, the lady is her old best friend from school."

"No way."

"Yeah. And she had no idea she was back. So this should be interesting."

"I can't wait to hear about it," he said. "My first client is here though, so I have to run. Kisses."

"Kisses," I said, and I couldn't hold back the grin. Yes, it was super sappy. No, I didn't care.

I grabbed JJ and headed downstairs. My mother was still in the cafe, so I figured I could take a minute to check in with Adele and see what was going on today.

When I entered the cafe through the French doors off our living room—we'd remodeled the house last summer to make it cat cafe–friendly—my mother was at the counter chatting with Adele, who looked like she was barely tolerating the distraction. I hurried over. "Morning," I said cheerfully.

Adele turned to me, cutting my mother off mid-sentence. "You scheduled two parties in one day?" she demanded.

I should've known I'd get some heat for that.

Adele Barrows had started out as a volunteer when we first opened the cafe, and I'd quickly realized she was indispensable and hired her as our first (and currently only) paid staff. Adele was one hundred and fifty percent devoted to the cats. Humans, however, she was less keen on. I knew she liked me enough because she worked here, and she and Grandpa got along well. She'd met her beau here also—our very own Harry. Another retired cop like Grandpa, he came to the cafe to volunteer and met Adele, and the rest was history. Now they were inseparable. But aside from us, she barely tolerated people. Which was funny because she spent most of her days here dealing with the public and somehow hadn't scared anyone off yet.

Although lately I'd been thinking that it might be time to put a few more people on staff. As our manager, Adele handled all the scheduling and the adoption requests, and she also worked in the cafe most days. And now we had the party truck, as I was calling it, which added even more to her load.

I was starting to worry that people would think I was overworking her. The reality was that she was loath to give up any control over most of the operations to anyone, especially potential adoptions, except for me.

But that was a problem for down the road, after the busy season.

"I did," I said. "But don't worry, I've got it covered. My mom is helping me with them."

"Happy to," my mother chirped. She really wanted Adele to like her.

Adele sniffed. "You're going to tire the cats," she said.

"I thought of that. I'm going to take different cats," I said.

"Are they both kid parties?"

"They are."

"Well, then you don't have a ton of options," she said. "You don't want to bring the shy cats."

She did have a point. "The party at night is small," I said. "That gives me more options. Don't worry, I'll figure it out. And who knows, Katrina could have a whole new batch of cats for us by then." I was being a little facetious, but it was true. Katrina Denning, the town animal control officer, my former babysitter, and ultimately my longtime friend, was never without a supply of cats for us. One might think that on an island our size, where Katrina and I had really revitalized the animal rescue efforts, that we wouldn't have so many cats needing homes. One would be wrong.

"Well, don't take on too much," Adele said, still clearly not thrilled. "You don't want to dilute your brand."

I covered my giggle with a cough. I had no idea where Adele had picked up that phrase, but I was quite sure she didn't give a hoot about our brand. "I promise," I said solemnly.

My mother turned to me, her face anxious. "Almost ready to go?"

"Yes. Ready. Unless Adele needs anything first?"

Adele waved us out, looking relieved at having her kingdom back. "Go," she said. "And don't schedule anything else this weekend."

My mother, JJ, and I piled into her car. My car—really my grandmother's old car that I'd commandeered when I moved home—was not doing well. Most days I had to just pray it would start, and about half the time, my prayers went unanswered and I had to borrow Lucas's or Val's car. We were all avoiding the reality that we were probably going to have to let it go soon. Yes, it was just a car, but it was a connection to my grandmother. And no one wanted to suggest taking it to the scrapyard. In the meantime, my wheels situation was getting desperate.

But I was more than happy to let my mother drive. And judging by her level of anxiety, she needed something to do. I watched her clench the steering wheel, lost in thought. She had dressed up for the reunion with Olivia. She loved to wear flowy, colorful skirts and dresses that gave her an ethereal aura, and today she'd outdone herself. Her baby blue chiffon skirt was piped with gold, and her top was black with lace sleeves. She'd straightened her normally wildly curly hair, which surprised me. Her curls were her signature. But this look was pretty too, and I told her as much.

"Oh, you like it?" Her hand flew up to touch it. "Thank you. I did it myself. Olivia and I used to do all kinds of fun things to each other's hair. I found some old pictures when she'd straightened mine. She always told me she loved my hair straight, so I figured I'd do it in her honor. You really think it looks okay?"

"It looks great," I assured her. I felt sorry for her. I tried to imagine what it would be like if my best friend, Becky Walsh, had ditched me without a word years ago, even if she didn't do it purposefully. I couldn't imagine the loss I would have felt. Also, I felt guilty imagining Becky herself may have felt some of that when I'd left the island for a decade. Granted, she had been away at college too, and we had still talked almost every day. We'd also had the benefit of technology far more advanced than my mother and Olivia had access to back then, but I was still all the way across the country when she returned to Daybreak, and I stayed away much longer. I realized now that it couldn't have felt good for her. I made a mental note to stop by and see her at the paper later today.

Becky was executive editor of the *Daybreak Island Chronicle*, the island's daily newspaper—a job she'd coveted since she was about seven years old. She'd started out as a reporter right out of college, and worked her way up to the top position. And even that job had expanded recently when the paper went through some ownership turmoil. Between that and my own expanded cat cafe responsibilities, we hadn't spent that much time together in the past couple of months.

My mother and I had both fallen silent, each of us thinking about the friends we had and the friends we'd lost. I shook off my thoughts and turned to my mother as she made the right onto Cliff Walk Lane, the address Olivia McAllister had given me. The address of her long-vanished aunt Delia.

Was that creepy? I realized I hadn't gotten much intel about the actual disappearance—like if she'd vanished from this very house or somewhere else. Maybe it didn't matter, but if it was the house, I felt like we were visiting the scene of a crime. I didn't want to fixate on it and make my mother sad, but a good mystery always intrigued me. Becky and I had recently found ourselves in the middle of a similar cold case—a maid who had gone missing from a local hotel many years ago—and had actually been involved in solving it. Something about that experience had stuck with me. I wondered what Aunt Delia's story was, and if it would ever get a proper ending.

I turned my attention to the windy coastal road we were climbing. Cliff Walk Lane looked as romantic as it sounded—one of those streets on the outskirts of Daybreak Harbor where houses sat far enough apart that you barely knew you had neighbors at all. Nine or ten homes stretched over a couple of miles, each with its own private beach. Some had been in families for generations; others belonged to newer arrivals who'd turned island living into a profitable side hustle. The combination of privacy and proximity to downtown made it one of the most coveted stretches on the island. The only comparable spot was Fishermen's Cove, clear on the other side—beautiful, but far enough away to feel inconvenient. Here you got quiet, space, and an easy ride into the center of things.

It was so silent, in fact, that when a car tore past us in the opposite lane, going way too fast, it scared the crap out of me. I whipped my head around to see the tail end of a lime green Hyundai SUV disappearing around the bend, dangerously close to the center line.

My mother didn't seem to notice. That was how focused she was on getting there.

"Jeez," I muttered. "Can you drive a little faster?" I turned back to my mother. "Did Olivia live nearby?"

"Her family lived in Turtle Point," my mother said. "Not far from where we live now. But Delia's parents owned this house first. They gave it to Delia when they wanted something smaller. They'd bought it when they first got married and then it got too big for them. They bought a house down the street, a smaller rehabbed cottage."

My mother slowed her car to a stop in front of the driveway. My mouth dropped open in delight as I took in the large pink house trimmed with teal and the little turret on top.

"I remember this place!" I exclaimed, sitting up straight. "Grandma used to take us by here when we were going to the beach sometimes to look at the houses. I loved this one!"

My mother smiled. "Really? I didn't know that."

"It has a name, right?"

She nodded. "Mermaid Cottage. Although it's clearly not a cottage."

It certainly was not. It wasn't a sprawling estate, but it was big enough that it had needed caretakers and all that back in the day.

"It came with the name when Delia's family bought it, and they wanted to preserve as much of its original state as possible. It's one of the oldest houses on the island. Said to have been owned by one of the original families that landed here back in the 1600s. Very historic. It's why Delia's parents didn't want to deal with it when they got a bit older. Lots of meddling from the town.

"But honestly, it's worth it to keep the charm intact. It's so adorable and it has all these nooks and crannies, and just so many rooms! And we spent so much time here. Olivia was close with her aunt, and Delia let us have the run of the place. Oh, the stories we concocted in these walls," she said with a small smile. "We used to come up with all kinds of fantastic tales. We'd go up to the lookout tower"—she pointed to the part of the house that extended up at least two floors from the rest, shaped like a turret—"and pretend we had to defend the castle. When we were really young it was from typical monsters, but as we got older and more creative, we made up all these stories about the pirates coming in on boats trying to take us all hostage and take over the island. Or we'd pretend that there were secrets hidden in the walls of the house from the original owners and we had to solve the mystery before someone came to kill us all."

I laughed. "So that's where this desire to write mysteries comes from," I realized as a long-missing piece clicked into place. My mother had decided in the past year that she wanted to write a mystery novel and had been working on it for a while. None of us really blinked an eye at the declaration, as my mother was the free spirit in our family who managed to do exactly as she pleased while still keeping the entire island charmed in her role as the hospital CEO's wife. But it sounded like she'd always had the love of a good mystery in her.

"I think so," she said. "Olivia was certainly creative. She wanted to be an actor. So I'd make up the stories and then we'd act them out. She was always better at the acting part. And definitely the directing part. She loved to oversee everything."

"Fun." I glanced at my mother, who still hadn't moved the car closer. "Should we figure out where to park the truck or do you want to go to the door first? I don't see any cars, though." I wondered if they were home.

"Maybe in the garage," my mother said. "There's a three-car garage in this place. Let's go to the door first. I don't want them to be wondering who's creeping around their property."

"Good idea."

She took her foot off the brake and we drove up the long driveway. As we got closer, the house came more into focus and I remembered my own delight at the stories my grandmother used to tell us about it. Nothing as dark as what my mother and Olivia had cooked up, but she'd tell us that anyone who lived in the house for a certain period of time became a mermaid and that's why they had to live right on the beach—so the mermaids could have easy access to the ocean. Since our house was also technically on the ocean—although we didn't have as easy of an access point to the beach—I'd convinced Val at the time that we were both mermaids too, and we'd made our parents get us mermaid tails we could wear all summer long. Since it was impossible to walk in them, the novelty wore off quickly.

My mom pulled off to the side of the driveway and put the car in park. As I opened my door, I caught a flash of white out of the corner of my eye, a streak that vanished around the side of the house. I blinked, trying to focus, but it was gone. My imagination, probably. Or just a trick of the morning sunlight.

JJ, sensing an adventure, perked up, his nose already going a mile a minute. I put him down as I stepped out of the car, wrapped his leash around my hand, and waited for my mother. JJ immediately began sniffing around, ears up and eyes alert. He loved scoping out new places.

I followed my mom through the whimsical little gate, down a stone path surrounded by grass and gardens, and up the porch steps to the door. The teal blue sign proclaiming the Mermaid Cottage still hung over the front door. I paused for a moment to admire the wraparound porch with the swing. It looked like one of those porches that went all the way around the house, which made sense given the water view that must be commanding top rental dollars, especially in the summers. Off to the side of the porch, a small bistro table and chairs waited for the occupants to come enjoy a meal. A vase of daisies sat on the table.

My mom's hand went to the bell, then paused. She glanced back at me, uncertainty in her eyes.

"What's wrong?" I asked.

She stepped back and gestured to the front door, which I could now see was ajar.

# Chapter 4

I studied the door. It looked like maybe someone just hadn't pushed it all the way shut. "Knock?" I suggested. "Maybe they saw us and opened the door to let us know they were here."

She did, once. Mostly silence from inside, although I could hear the echo of voices coming from somewhere far away. She knocked again, harder and louder. Still nothing. I stepped up and pushed the bell, wincing as the sound reverberated much louder than I'd anticipated.

Still nothing.

Mom pushed the door open a bit more and leaned in. "Hello? Olivia? It's Sophie," she called out. "Sophie Ja—Mancini," she corrected herself, referring to her premarried name.

No response. The voices were louder now, and I realized it sounded like a TV was on. I frowned. Despite the whimsy of the place, something about this felt off. And my gut had been in enough "off" situations to know what it was talking about. "Mom, maybe we should—" I started, but my mother had already shoved the door open the rest of the way and stepped inside.

I guess she wasn't about to be deterred. I followed, trying to swallow my growing feeling of unease.

My mother paused in the doorway, calling out tentatively. "Olivia? Anyone home? Hello?"

No reply. The TV chatter grew slightly louder as we moved inside.

"It's Sophie," she repeated, taking another brave step. "You hired my daughter's mobile cat cafe for your party. We just came by to see where to park the cat cafe truck."

Still no reply. I listened for sounds of live people—water running, chatter, utensils scraping plates. Nothing. Maybe they were just very intent on whatever they were watching.

I pulled my phone out, found the number she'd called me from yesterday, and pressed send. The phone rang a couple of times, then went to voice mail.

"No one's answering the phone," I told my mom.

She didn't answer, just moved farther inside. Well. Guess we weren't waiting. I hoped we didn't scare the bejeezus out of them if they were in here and just hadn't heard us.

I followed my mother into a small foyer that opened up on both sides—one side to a living room, the other to a smaller parlor room. The first thing I noticed were shoes, scattered right inside the doorway: flip-flops, slip-on sneakers, kid and adult sizes, strewn around like people had come inside and kicked them off, not caring where they'd landed. I stepped over them as JJ stopped to sniff.

The house was furnished in a style that made me think I'd stepped back in time, and I imagined it hadn't changed since the days my mother had played here as a kid. I could see from her face as she looked around that I was right about that—this place was full of memories for her.

The TV noise wasn't coming from the living room. That room to our left was quiet, if not messy. Books, toys, and blankets were tossed on and around the couch, and a sippy cup sat on the stately coffee table in front of it. The TV on the wall, the only item that looked modern, was blank and silent.

In the parlor, there was no TV. Just a few comfy-looking chairs and a love seat, with bookshelves built into both walls filled neatly with books. The room ended in a circular nook overlooking the gardens outside to the right of the house. The built-in sitting area in front of the windows would be the perfect place to curl up with one of those books.

The house was decked out in mermaid and sea decor, as expected. What I loved was that the whimsy of the outside was just as present inside. Each room was painted a vibrant, oceanic color. The parlor was emerald green. The living room was a sea foam, a bit tamer but still on brand. The parlor ceiling, I noticed when I stepped inside, was painted with a beautiful mural of what I envisioned it looked like under the sea, with sea grass, smiling sea creatures, shells, rocks, and sparkles from the sun overhead. This room was immune from the family debris cluttering the hall and living rooms. It didn't seem anyone had spent time in here of late. Maybe it was reserved for more formal events or dinners.

My mother was already onto the next room. I trailed behind. A dining room, with the table set as if guests were expected. Beyond the dining room, what I assumed was the kitchen. And it was bright, at least from where I stood. The wall I could see was painted a teal blue, and there was a mermaid mural on the top half. The TV sounds seemed to be coming from that room. I headed in that direction, leaving my mother in the dining room where she studied photos propped up on the cabinet that held some china.

On my way out of the dining room I almost stepped on a large, plush gray and white cat stuffie lying forlornly in the middle of the floor, forgotten in some kind of rush.

It was one of those with the bright blue piercing eyes, a whiskered mouth set in a small smile. It looked just worn enough to tell me it was well-loved, and I wondered if it had been left behind accidentally when the family had gone wherever they'd rushed off to. I picked the cat up and carried it into the kitchen with me.

I was assaulted immediately by the sapphire blue walls, similar to the piercing eyes of the stuffed cat. I stood for a moment as JJ strained at the leash, sniffing madly, then remembered I was still holding the stuffed toy. I placed it on the kitchen island next to a notepad, which I glanced at. The header said Randall Renovations. The name sounded familiar to me, but I couldn't quite place it.

This was the room where it looked like they'd spent a lot of time. And recently, from the looks of it—even aside from the TV, which was tuned to the local news station—the source of the voices I'd heard from the foyer. I glanced at the TV and recognized Mila Daindridge, a local personality who had been covering the island for a couple of decades. She seemed very serious, talking about some public hearing about eelgrass restoration and some town fight.

I turned my attention back to the room. Two coffee mugs, coffee still in them, sat on the island. I leaned over and touched one. Cold. A plate with egg remnants sat next to one of them, the orange of the yolk congealed into a sticky mess. The coffee machine on the counter's red light signaled "on," which meant the coffee had been poured long enough ago to cool, but the machine's auto shutoff hadn't kicked in yet. Out of all the appliances, this machine looked pretty new—I respected people who prioritized their coffee—and I knew from my extensive experience with coffee machines that it took around two hours before they shut off on their own. Next to the coffee machine a burnt piece of bread had popped up in the toaster and sat there, also cold, the singed-bread smell still in the air.

I checked out the table at the back of the room. There was a kid's bowl of cereal on it, spoon still submerged in milk that had turned the pinkish color of whatever sugary treat had been served. Next to it was an iPad that had never locked. Some kind of children's game—a puzzle of some sort—was visible on the screen, abandoned in mid-play.

Where was everyone? And why had they left breakfast everywhere, half-eaten or, in some cases, untouched? I couldn't shake the "off" feeling.

"Nothing, huh?" my mother said, coming up behind me.

I jumped. I hadn't heard her coming, and this place was giving me the creeps. I turned to her. "You think they're upstairs? There are two more floors, right? Maybe they just can't hear us. The place is big. Or maybe they went outside?" I wondered if this was the moment, if we were in a movie, that the audience would be yelling, *Get out of the house, you idiots! Don't you dare go upstairs/downstairs/wherever you're thinking of going next!*

My mother apparently hadn't seen that movie. She was still focused on seeing her friend. "Good idea. Let's check out back. There's a back door, and a big yard. She could be outside. Maybe they went down to the beach. Or maybe Olivia's in the shower and everyone else went to the beach."

In the middle of breakfast? Without the toast they'd just toasted? It seemed weird to me. Also the last thing I'd want to find were people in my house as I was getting out of the shower, but I kept my mouth shut for the moment, very aware of how much this meant to her.

I motioned for my mother to lead the way. JJ was straining against his leash, sniffing wildly around. Usually he only did this if he'd come across another animal.

I wondered if Olivia had pets, and thought about that white streak I'd seen racing behind the house. Did she have a cat that had gotten out? Maybe they'd all left to go find him or her.

Either way, I wanted to just do what was necessary to get out of the house faster. I followed her through another doorway off the kitchen, which led to a giant four-season porch off the back of the house. It was perfect for year-round nights looking out at the ocean in all the different seasons, with a fireplace, multiple comfy couches and chairs, and even a built-in wall of books.

The perfect room—except for the fact that the door was also wide open. And just beyond the fluttering curtains, on the top step, was a child's sandal.

# Chapter 5

As an island kid, I remembered what it was like being in a rush to get outside and live the beach life. Summers were so enticing and there was so much swimming to do, friends to play with, wild berries to pick. When I was very young, we lived at Grandma and Grandpa's house, and they didn't have direct beach access despite our waterfront property—we'd had to go down the street and through an access point to get there. But I'd had plenty of friends who lived right on the water. Shoes were not a priority, especially if the beach was close, or right through your own yard. I could remember as a kid barely finishing getting dressed to get outside.

Still, the abandoned shoe seemed ominous. And I'd learned to not ignore my gut.

I scanned the yard and the beach below. The McAllister house towered over the water, with one of those cool staircases built into the side of the cliff leading down to the beach. I could see boats out on the water—a fishing boat, one that looked like a pleasure boat a bit farther offshore, and another smaller boat in the cove to the right of the house—but couldn't see anyone on the beach itself, at least from this vantage point.

"Can you call her again?" my mother asked, turning to me.

I nodded, hitting redial. I still had the phone in my hand—partly because I figured I'd keep trying her number but also to be able to call 9-1-1 quickly if we found a serial killer. We should have just left a message the first time and saved ourselves from this tour, but apparently that wasn't the way we rolled in the James family. A trait passed down from Grandpa Leo, no doubt. We always had to see for ourselves what was going on.

With one last glance at the shoe, I followed my mother back into the house. She had moved far ahead of me with apparently some memory of where she should go next. I kept a firm hold on JJ's leash—I definitely didn't want him taking off on me—as I pulled up the number and hit the call button.

Immediately, I heard the faint tones of the phone coming from somewhere in the house. My heart sped up as I tried to imagine what that could mean. Maybe Olivia *was* here in the shower, blissfully unaware there were people strolling through her house. Maybe she was napping.

Or maybe something was wrong and she'd run out without her phone.

*Don't be an alarmist, Maddie*, I admonished myself. I'd never been one of those until a series of events after I'd moved back here had changed my reaction default to worst-case scenario. But this was my mother's best friend whom she hadn't seen in decades, and I didn't want to scare her.

She'd heard the phone, though. She turned back to me. "You hear that?"

I nodded.

The ringing had stopped now as the phone went to voice mail. I called again. My mother paused, listening, then took an abrupt right turn toward a set of stairs. "The bedroom's upstairs," she said.

"I don't know that we should do that," I said, the horror movie trope still lingering in my brain, but she'd already started up the steps.

Muttering dissent under my breath, I followed, my finger poised over the emergency call button on my phone. The ringing stopped again as we reached the top of the steps. We were in another long hallway, with doors on either side. All of them were open.

"Call again," my mother said.

I did.

The now-familiar ringtone sounded just a few feet away. My mother turned into a bedroom two doors down on the right. Holding my breath, I followed cautiously.

The phone in question sat on a hastily made bed amidst an open suitcase vomiting a pile of clothes. Nothing was folded or tidy. Things looked like they were in the process of being shoved inside. A purse lay next to it. A glass lay on the floor, next to a puddle on the worn gray rug. Drawers from the bureau against the far wall hung open, more clothing peeking out of some of them. On the dresser, an open laptop—locked—sat next to an AirPods case. A candle still burned next to it. I went over and picked it up. White linen scent. The wax had burned down low, giving off a faintly smoky odor—another red flag. Unless Olivia was super forgetful, leaving a candle burning didn't seem like a good sign. I blew it out, returned it to the table where a book lay facedown, open to mark a page. I leaned over it to see the title: *The World Is Blue: How Our Fate and the Ocean's Are One.* Not your typical light beach read, but I guess it was on brand for island life.

The door leading to an adjoining bathroom was open. There was no shower running, although the light was on.

I took a step closer, praying no one would jump out at me with a knife, and risked a glance inside.

Empty. Makeup and toiletries cluttered the sink. A blush compact sat open, the brush next to it.

"I hope nothing's wrong," Mom said, her voice tinged with worry. "Maybe there was an accident and they had to leave in a rush and go to the hospital. Should we check there? Dad can find out."

"That's a good idea," I said, relieved that we might be able to leave. "You should call Dad. From outside."

She nodded, her face brightening at the thought of a task, something to do besides wonder what was going on here.

I followed her to the stairs. Something made me pause to take one more look around. I noticed JJ standing at attention at my feet, staring at something behind me.

The hair on the back of my neck stood up as I slowly turned all the way around, praying some dude with a butcher knife wasn't standing there.

There wasn't, thankfully. But there was a cat.

A longhaired, gorgeous white cat with gray ears and gray paws, sitting in the doorway of a room at the end of the hall, staring back at me, eyes piercingly blue and steady, much like the stuffed cat I'd found downstairs. JJ's tail swished as he regarded this potential new friend.

Part of me felt some relief—I'd been worried about a cat, if there was one, being lost outside. But if that had been the cat I'd seen, how did it get back *inside*? We'd closed the door behind us. And even though the windows were open, they all had screens. And I'd closed the back door we'd found gaping open—a habit of mine so bugs wouldn't get in.

I needed to make sure the place was secure until these people came home.

I turned back to the cat. He—or she—was beautiful.

I especially loved the tail. Longhaired cats had the best tails, even though I wouldn't dream of telling JJ that. JJ led me toward the kitty, straining at the leash, sniffing furiously. The cat turned and disappeared into the room, where the door was ajar. My mom and I hadn't made it to this end of the hall in our search—we'd called it quits when we'd found Olivia's stuff in the primary bedroom and bathroom.

I'd had a friend once out in San Francisco whose cat had taken advantage of a slightly pushed-out screen on the second floor to make an escape, which prompted a week-long recon effort. Miraculously, we found the cat unharmed and a little put out that his food choices during his escape hadn't been more robust.

Even if this was where the open window was, I could understand the cat getting out, but not back in. I knew from experience how resourceful cats were, but still, I was eager to figure out the mystery and make sure the cat wasn't in danger. Even though we lived on an island without predators, it still made me super anxious when cats were outside running around. Especially in the summer, when tourists brought their big SUVs over on the ferry and drove around like our narrow, windy beach roads were their own personal NASCAR tracks. Like that awful lime green car we'd passed on the way up here.

I felt a little chill as I remembered that car now. They'd certainly been in a hurry to get away. Had it been Olivia? Or her daughter? What were they rushing away from?

*Stop creating stories*, I scolded myself. *There's probably a reasonable explanation for all of this.*

And until I figured out what that was, I felt like it was my responsibility to make sure this kitty stayed at home, at least until we figured out what had happened to the humans.

Ignoring the anxiety now roaring in my stomach, I

walked as confidently as I could toward the room. My fears about open windows grew when I stepped inside. It was set up as a cute little library and reading room. It was also empty. No cat in sight.

I'd just seen him go in here, though. My eyes immediately went to the one window in the small room, but it was closed and locked.

I surveyed the room. A built-in bookcase that spanned the whole back wall, which I allowed myself a moment to fangirl over—I loved a good reading nook—and a comfy-looking rounded chair with an ottoman that would be the perfect place to curl up with a book. The room wasn't exactly overflowing with hiding places. It didn't look like even the chair had any room underneath to hide. I checked just to be safe, but nothing. Strange. But, as I knew all too well, cats were slippery creatures, able to perform disappearing acts worthy of the most clever magician. With all these strangers in the house, what had to be Olivia's family's cat was probably spooked.

"Where did he go?" I asked JJ, looking around curiously.

JJ remained in the doorway, unmoving. I wasn't sure what his problem was, but he didn't seem to want to join me in the room.

I turned to go, figuring I'd check the windows in the other rooms up here, when I heard a faint meow. Since JJ had a very distinct squeak—that he didn't like me or anyone else pointing out—I knew it wasn't him. I took another look around the room.

And jumped nearly a foot when two books went flying off the bookshelf, landing on the floor with a crack that sounded as loud as a gunshot.

# Chapter 6

"Jeez!" I pressed my hand to my heart, trying to keep the pounding to a minimum as I realized what was going on. The tuft of white hair peeking out from between the books tipped me off. The cat had somehow wedged himself—I'd decided it was a him, based on all this trouble he was getting into—behind some of the books and was throwing them down, another typical cat behavior. Well, aside from JJ. He didn't typically engage in such activities—they were beneath him. He had much bigger fish to fry, like running the cat cafe and overseeing the sale of his merch.

I started toward the bookshelf, but JJ refused to move from the doorway. I gave his leash a tug, but still he resisted.

"Why are you being so stubborn?" I asked, exasperated. He looked at me and squeaked.

I gave the leash a little tug, forcing him to come forward. He dug his paws in, but I wasn't having it. I was not letting him loose in this house if he could escape on me somehow.

"Sorry, but you're coming with me." I moved over to the bookshelf, JJ still straining at the leash behind me, literally sliding across the floor in protest. I reached down to pick up the two books that had already hit the floor and glanced at the titles as I did. One, *Haunted Cape Cod & the Islands*, was a hardcover, which explained the loud noise. The other was the latest Thursday Murder Club mystery. I had to remember to buy this one—I'd heard it was a delight. I was behind on my reading, though, what with my newest gig of hosting cat parties every weekend.

I scooped the books up and paused before replacing them on the shelf, peering into the space where the books had sat. The cat . . . wasn't there. Unless he'd somehow wedged himself behind the row of books so expertly that I'd never see him unless I took them all out.

"This is not the time to play games, kitty," I scolded as I started tipping books to check. I went through the whole top row, but nothing. I reached for the last book on the right, a hardback classic version of an Agatha Christie title. But the book didn't easily tip backward. I had to grip it and pull it, like something was holding it from the other side. When I did, it moved, but slowly. A horrible squeaking sound grated against my eardrums and sent JJ skittering away, as far in the other direction as he could go still being attached to the leash wrapped around my wrist.

I jumped back with my own actual half shriek when the whole shelf started to move.

*What the?*

It took me a second to realize this was a hidden door, and this book was the door-opening mechanism. If it hadn't scared the crap out of me, I'd be exclaiming over how clever it was. I'd only cracked open the door, but I could see that there was something behind it. I pushed it a bit more, fascinated when I realized what I was actually looking at.

This had to be one of those secret rooms that were rumored to be in some of the oldest houses on the island. I'd never actually seen one myself, but I'd heard plenty of stories about them. They'd been used during Prohibition days to hide smuggled goods like molasses that would be used to make illegal liquor. Sometimes they'd even be used to hide people during times of conflict, or at least those were the rumors. The coastal areas around Cape Cod and the islands were ripe for smuggling, so rooms like these had been the subjects of a lot of historical legend and lore out here on the island.

But to have one right in front of me seemed really cool.

I reached for the book "handle" again and tentatively pulled it a bit more. The door creaked open slowly, like it was a huge burden on its old hinges. I finally got it open enough to reveal an entire doorway. Leading into . . . a legit black hole. There was no speck of light beyond this door. I felt around inside on the wall for a light switch on either side, but there was nothing. I suddenly felt exposed, standing here in the light and hurried to press the flashlight button on my phone and shine it inside.

The room was tiny. There was just enough space for a small, old-timey desk pushed against the wall farthest from me and a short bookcase on the opposite wall.

But I couldn't focus on either of those things, because once I dropped my light a bit lower I saw something else.

Or rather, some*one*. As in, someone on the floor in the middle of the room. A woman with shoulder-length dark hair spread out on the floor like a puddle. Her back faced me, and one arm seemed to be bent underneath her, the other splayed out to her side. She was dressed in jeans and a blouse, but her feet were bare.

And she was definitely not moving.

Then I realized it wasn't just her hair that looked like a puddle on the floor under her head.

It was blood.

# Chapter 7

I jumped back from the doorway with a gasp, almost dropping my phone in the process. I had to do a mad juggle to keep it in my hand and not send it skittering across the floor straight into the pooling blood.

Was it still pooling? Had this just happened? *What* had just happened? The thoughts raced through my brain, interspersed with a panicked *ohmigod* and a *not again* and one big *please don't let that be Olivia McAllister.* My mother would be devastated.

*But who else would it be?* that annoying voice inside my head badgered me.

Behind me, JJ squeaked. He was still sitting as far away from me as his leash would allow. I felt his pain. I needed to get out of here too. I needed to call someone. That woman definitely did not look responsive, but maybe she just needed help.

*Yes. Help. Good idea. Go get some*, my annoying voice said in that what's-wrong-with-you tone. My ever-present inner critic could never just take a day off.

I grabbed the book handle of the hidden door and slammed it closed again, then raced out of the room, JJ leading the way. He hadn't wanted to be in there at all.

Which also gave me the chills. We all knew animals instinctively knew things we didn't, and knew them well before we even had a clue anything was wrong. I trusted JJ's and our dogs' reactions to people and places more than I trusted my own. And his reaction right now told me everything I needed to know.

I didn't want to be in this house. I hoped my mother was still outside and hadn't run into . . . anyone on her way.

I scooped JJ up and bolted down the stairs, nearly tripping over the part of his leash that dragged on the floor as I stumbled to the door, intent on calling 9-1-1.

But I couldn't tell my mother I was calling 9-1-1. She'd want to know why. And I couldn't tell her about the woman in the room. Not yet, not until I knew more.

That thought stopped me short at the front door. I saw my mother standing at the car, talking on her phone. Relieved, I turned to race through the house to get to the back door, where I could still get outside and make the call without my mother hearing. I just hoped she stayed put and didn't go back inside.

I stepped onto the back porch, over the child's sandal, and with shaking hands dialed 9-1-1 and told the dispatcher I needed help with an unresponsive person. It seemed to take forever to explain, get her the address, and answer the questions they were trained to ask to keep you on the line. Once she had what I knew she needed to get someone there, I disconnected and made another call, this one to Grandpa, praying he would answer.

He did. "Hey, Doll. How's it—"

"I think Olivia McAllister is . . . hurt. Really badly," I blurted out. "I haven't told Mom yet. I just called the police. Can you come here?"

"On my way," he said, and disconnected. I loved that about Grandpa Leo. No questions asked.

I hung up and tried to do some of the deep breathing

that I'd learned from my mentor, Cass Hendricks, when he tried to teach me Tai Chi and all those peaceful-type practices. They'd kind of stuck, because I was able to do the breathe-in-for-four, hold-for-four, breathe-out-for-four thing he'd showed me and got my heartbeat to slow down a little bit, which enabled my brain to start working a bit more effectively.

Still, I wasn't getting any good answers despite the swirling questions: Was it Olivia in the room? What had happened to her in there? Was she dead? Dead or not, she wasn't looking good. There was a lot of blood. The visualization of it popped back into my mind unbidden, and I had to swallow back a wave of nausea. Lieutenant Mick Ellory, our head murder honcho on the police force, wouldn't like it if I threw up on his scene.

Because what I'd seen had to be murder. Attempted murder? Maybe she wasn't dead. *Please don't let her be dead.*

JJ sat stock-still on the porch, no longer straining against the leash. Instead, he watched me curiously, probably wondering if I was okay. I tried to pull it together and took another look around the yard. It was quiet. The nearest neighbor was maybe half a mile down the road, and I couldn't even see over the privacy shrubs on either side. The only uninhibited view was the ocean, directly behind me. The boats were a bit farther out now, but still visible. I scanned the beach again. Still looked empty, but I couldn't see all of it.

I felt like I waited there forever, not wanting to go face my mother and have to tell her about this, until I finally heard sirens. A quick glance at my phone told me it had been eight minutes since my initial 9-1-1 call. The ambulance must have been nearby. Which meant it was going to pull up any second, and I needed to give Mom a heads-up.

I scooped JJ up and cut around the side of the house that would put me closest to the driveway. My mother still waited next to the car. She sent me a questioning look that I didn't have time to answer before the siren noise overpowered everything on the quiet street and an ambulance roared into the driveway. I watched her face pale.

"I'll fill you in," I told her, giving her arm a squeeze. "Can you hold JJ?"

I handed him to her. She started to say something, but I had already walked away to meet the EMTs. I had no idea how long it would take the police to get here, and if there was any saving that woman, they needed to get inside fast. When the door opened on the passenger side and a tall, handsome dude with spiky black hair tipped blond at the top hopped out, my mouth dropped open. "Adam?"

Adam DeSantis looked as surprised as I felt. "Maddie!" he said. "What are you doing here? Did you move? Nice house!"

Adam worked at the hospital as a nurse. We'd crossed paths last year when his super famous boyfriend had turned up on the island with another celebrity and gotten involved in some drama. As a result, we'd hit it off and since become friendly. We had my dad and the hospital in common, and we also both loved to hang out at Jade Moon, the local bar run by my ex-boyfriend Craig's new girlfriend Jade. Lucas and I double-dated with Adam and Marco Moore, his boyfriend, a few times when Marco made a rare appearance out in public. It was kind of wild to me that I was now friends with a major movie star, but that's the way it was on an island this size. Now that people were used to Marco, he was just one of us. In the summer, though, when all the tourists were here, he kept a lower profile. I felt like I knew them both well at this point, but I'd had no idea Adam was an EMT too. Then again, he got involved in tons of things around the island already, including running programs at senior centers. He just loved to help people.

"I didn't move. It's a long story," I said.

He laughed, pushing up his sleeves against the heat. I could see the snake head tattoo peeking out from under one sleeve. "Why am I not surprised?"

"Same question for you! Did you change jobs or something?"

"Nah. Just took up a new hobby. Marco's away for a movie and I needed to keep myself busy." He shrugged. "Figured picking up a second gig was a good way to do that, and this is in my wheelhouse." He gestured toward the house. "Someone needs help?"

I nodded. "Second floor, last room on the left. The police aren't here yet, but should you go in and see?"

"If someone's hurt, yes, let's go. Lead the way." Adam motioned to the other EMT, a woman with a large copper-colored Afro who'd just climbed out of the driver's side of the ambulance. I didn't recognize her and she paid me no attention as she headed to the back of the rig and wrenched open the door. They pulled a gurney out and started toward the house.

My mother finally made it over to me. "What on earth is going on?" she demanded. "Why is there an ambulance? Did you find . . . something?"

"There's someone inside on the second floor. I don't know who yet," I said, cutting off the question as it formed on her lips.

She looked like she might cry and I hated that I had to leave her like that, but time could be of the essence. There was still no sign of Mick—I presumed he'd be the one coming, likely with my ex, Craig Tomlin, a newly minted detective—by the time we reached the door. Adam and the other EMT dropped the gurney at the base of the stairs and followed me up to the second floor and all the way down the long hall, past all the closed doors. I prayed there was nothing in any of the rooms we hadn't checked reminiscent of what I'd found in the secret room.

When we got to the study, Adam paused. "I thought you said there was someone in here." He scanned the empty room, eyes questioning.

"There is." I strode inside and wrenched the book-handle on the secret room's door and pulled it. The door yawned open again, just as slowly as the first time.

The two of them stared in fascination. "Wow," the female EMT said finally. "Is that . . . a secret room?"

"It is." I flicked the flashlight on my phone on again and shined it inside. Unfortunately, the scene hadn't changed. Adam turned on his own flashlight and took a cautious step forward, scanning the room. He spied a lamp that I hadn't seen before on a small table next to the bookcase and moved in to turn it on. The small room suddenly flooded with light.

Which made the scene even uglier.

I stepped back as they rushed in to see if there was anything that could be done for this woman.

"Ma'am?" I heard Adam's counterpart call out. "Can you hear me?"

No response. I wasn't surprised.

Adam knelt beside her, pressing two fingers to her neck, then leaning close to listen for breath. "Nothing," he murmured. He glanced at his partner, who was checking for a carotid pulse on the other side. She gave a slight head shake.

He turned back to me. "I'm sorry," he said, his voice full of the compassion that made him an exceptional nurse. "Do you know who she is?"

“I have an idea, but I don’t know for sure,” I said. “Do you have . . . any idea what happened?”

“Head injury,” Adam said, stating the obvious. He stood, careful not to step in the blood. “Let’s get out of here and wait for the cops. They’ll want this room preserved as much as possible.”

# Chapter 8

We left the room with its terrible scene and headed for the stairs. The closed doors all along the second-floor hall combined with the knowledge that there was an unexamined third floor above us made me antsy, and I wished someone would get here who could check the rest of the house and make sure no one was hiding inside somewhere.

As we stepped out onto the porch, I saw Mick's undercover car pull in, followed by two patrol cars. Mick parked haphazardly next to the ambulance, shoved his door open, and stepped out of the car. I saw a second head in the passenger seat and realized it was Katrina. Then I realized Mick was not wearing his usual slacks and button-down outfit. I took in his Bermuda shorts and T-shirt that had a picture of the famous *Jaws* shark on it and tried to hide my surprise. I'd never seen Mick in shorts before, but I wisely didn't comment. The *Jaws* shirt felt apropos, though.

"I should've known," he said by way of greeting. "You couldn't give me one day off? I can't remember the last time I had one."

"It was your day off?" I felt terrible, even though it wasn't technically my fault that he'd been called away.

That also explained why Katrina was in the car. I glanced her way. She waved at me.

Mick had been dating Katrina for about a year now. Since her ACO position was part of the police department, they'd gotten to know each other through work and they'd hit it off. Which had been beneficial to me as well. Before Katrina, Mick and I had a complicated relationship, mostly because I tended to stumble on problems—like the occasional dead person—and with my type A personality, it was hard to let go of the need to be part of the solution. Which meant I continually inserted myself in places where I didn't always belong, much to Mick's chagrin.

But we were in a good place now, partly because of Katrina's influence and partly because I'd shown him just how helpful I could be. He even sought out my input now, which felt good. But sometimes, he still marveled at how much trouble I could find without looking.

Today would be one of those days.

"Yes, it was my day off," he said. "I was at the beach. Which normally I don't really care about, but Katrina loves it, so . . ." He shrugged, indicating that meant now *he* loved it too. "What's the deal?"

I jerked a thumb over my shoulder at Adam and his partner. "The EMTs already checked it out and we thought it best to leave and wait for you. The woman upstairs is . . ." I shook my head.

"Deceased," Adam confirmed. "Seemingly unnatural causes."

Mick glanced up at the house in front of him. "How big is this place?"

"Big." I gave him a rundown of the layout and where my mother and I had already been. "There's a ton of rooms on the second floor we didn't look into and a whole third floor."

"And you've all been running around here without a care? There could be someone inside, Maddie."

"That's why we came out," I said.

"Stay here." He motioned over my shoulder to the patrol guys. Four of them emerged from the two cars and followed him inside, weapons in hand.

I stood on the porch, not sure what to do. I didn't want to have a conversation about this with my mother. I'd already told her what I knew, which wasn't much. Thankfully, more people were arriving. I watched Craig's unmarked pull into the driveway, right behind Grandpa's truck. Followed by a van. Channel Six's news van, to be precise.

I felt my stomach plummet. How on earth had they gotten tipped off already? TV crews were not common here. We had a local community channel, but our journalism was largely delivered through Becky's newspaper. The major TV news people from Boston only came out for a big story, and they could only be here as fast as the next ferry.

"I'll be right back," I told Adam, then rushed down the porch steps, past Craig's and Grandpa's cars and over to the van, where a guy and a woman had just exited from. The woman, I saw with a sinking feeling in the pit of my stomach, was Mila Daindridge, the Channel Six reporter who had been on the news earlier.

"Excuse me," I said. "Can I help you?"

The guy, who'd just reached into the van and emerged with a camera, glanced at me, unfazed. He wore dark glasses that made his eyes unreadable and had a goatee the likes of which I hadn't seen since my last encounter with the San Francisco tech bros. "I don't know," he said. "You part of the interview?"

"What interview?"

Mila Daindridge pushed past both of us, her eyes lighting up as she took in the police cars and ambulance. "What's going on?"

The camera guy ignored her, still focused on me. "The Scientology thing," he said, answering my question.

Mila heard this and whipped around. "It's not Scientology, genius," she snapped. "It's science. Maybe you've heard of it?" With a head shake, she stepped over to me. "Mila Daindridge with the Channel Six affiliate."

I nodded to let her know I was aware of who she was but didn't introduce myself. "Who are you here to interview?"

She studied me now, curious. "Did something happen out here that the residents should know about?"

"You can't be here." I wasn't sure I could say that—it wasn't even my property, and to be fair, they were on the street—but I squared my shoulders and kept my chin up. Mostly because I was thinking about the McAllisters' privacy, but also because I was thinking about Becky and how she would feel if Mila caught this story before she did. I believed *homicidal* would be the most positive way to describe it.

But from the way she was smiling at me with a glint of challenge in her eye, I guessed I wasn't going to be able to help it.

"I'm sorry, I didn't realize this was a private road," she said, barely covering the snark in her tone. "We're interviewing Neil Caldwell, who's in charge of the shoreline water-quality monitoring and eelgrass restoration pilots that are all over the news these days. We're filming in multiple locations this morning because of the proximity to one of the coves where the eelgrass restoration project is happening." She peered over my shoulder again. "But maybe there's a bigger story?"

Before I could say anything else, Craig appeared next

to me. "Nothing to see here," he said. "Can you please move the van and the cameras away from this property?"

"Depends," Mila said with a wink. Gross. "Can you tell me what's going on?"

"No," Craig said. "And I'm going to have to ask you again to back up. You're blocking the street."

Mila and her camera guy didn't move. Neither did Craig nor I.

# Chapter 9

As I wondered how long this standoff would continue, a sleek black Jaguar pulled up, narrowly missing scraping the side of the van. An older, bearded man wearing an orange-and-black plaid scally cap jumped out and hurried over, slightly out of breath like he'd been rushing to get here.

"My apologies," he said to Mila. "I got stuck behind some tourists. Thanks for changing locations." He shook his head, shoving his wire-framed glasses back up on his nose with his middle finger. Then he saw me, and a flash of recognition ran across his face.

"Maddie James," he said, beaming white teeth at me that looked unnatural for a dude his age. "Well, I'll be. Haven't seen you since junior year, when you got sick on our expedition boat. Remember that?" He laughed. "It took three crew members to mop it up! I'd heard you were back."

I could feel Craig's amused eyes on me and resisted the urge to outwardly cringe. That was the problem with this island. As much as I loved it, there was no escaping your past. Most people who were born here never left, so chances were very good that the people who knew your most embarrassing childhood memories were still running around eager to remind you of when you'd gotten your training potty stuck on your head (which had happened to my sister Val) or, in my case, remind me of a mortifying moment of seasickness.

But I did remember Neil Caldwell too. His company, Caldwell & Emmett Marine Enterprises, had been involved in the community forever. The island was, of course, a prime locale for marine biologists. His firm had been around for decades, working on shellfish conservation and other things I didn't know much about. They were funded by grants and heavily embedded with leadership in all the towns. And part of their appeal was their dedication to cultivating young scientists. That was what their presence in the schools was all about—they did elective classes for students in eighth grade and up in hopes of getting students interested in marine biology.

The one I'd signed up for was in my junior year. I'd done it because it involved spending time on the water and because anytime we got to leave the classroom felt like a field trip, not so much because I was interested in science. They'd taken us out on boats and showed us experiments and how research was done. It had been fun—until the day I got seasick and threw up all over the boat.

Neil Caldwell had personally taught the class I'd taken, which I remember my science teacher being over-the-top impressed with. Maybe I'd been too young to fully appreciate it, but he hadn't seemed that impressive to me. Mostly, I remember him talking to the female students a heck of a lot more than the male students.

Now, I forced a self-deprecating smile. "Yep. Good thing I have better sea legs now. Although in my defense, the water was super choppy that day. Nice to see you." Aside from his blindingly white teeth, he had aged well—better than I'd have expected for a guy who spent so much time outside in the elements. Maybe marine biologists who had to be public facing did a lot of Botox. Or maybe he'd just found some excellent sunscreen over the years. But he'd been doing this decades ago, and he hadn't been a spring chicken then. He had to be in his seventies, I calculated, but could easily pass off early sixties.

"What's going on here?" he asked Mila with a nod to the house. "Did we pick an inopportune time to do our segment?" Turning back to me he said, "We're discussing our summer restoration project. Maybe you've heard? We're expanding eelgrass beds, boosting scallop habitats, and protecting water quality at the same time." He beamed a camera-ready smile at me. "Ensuring the island's fishing heritage for generations, essentially."

Craig was losing patience. "Great. But you'll need to move along." He pulled his radio out and said, "I need a perimeter set up out front."

Caldwell's perfectly groomed eyebrows rose. "That sounds very official. I hope everything is okay with the house. The family would want to know immediately if there was a problem."

I opened my mouth to ask how he knew that but never got to.

"Something you need help with, Neil?" A stealth Grandpa Leo appeared at my side, holding out a hand to Caldwell, a smile on his face that didn't quite reach his eyes. I hadn't even heard him come up behind us, but even Craig looked relieved to see him. Grandpa's presence still held weight.

"Leo! Or excuse me, Chief Mancini," Caldwell said, reaching over and pumping his hand a little too enthusiastically.

"Not anymore," Grandpa said. "But I think I heard Detective Tomlin ask you all to please not be filming here."

We all turned to the camera guy, who was calmly filming all of this.

Before Mila could interject, Neil held up a hand, face earnestly contrite. "Sorry about that. We were going to do this on the actual beach, but then I thought the view from up here would be even better. We won't be too long, right, Maya?"

"It's Mila," she said through gritted teeth that she tried to hide behind a smile. "And no, not terribly long."

"Great. If you go around the bend right up here a ways, you have an unfiltered view of the ocean from a higher elevation," Craig said, pointing. "Either way, you're going to have to move along."

Mila let out a dramatic sigh and muttered something about this being her third setup today. Then with a flick of her wrist, she snapped at both Caldwell and her cameraman, "Let's go."

With a shrug, the cameraman stopped filming and headed to the van. She followed. Caldwell hesitated a second. "So good to see you both," he said. "Make sure to come to the town meeting next week where we'll report on our project. I promise you it's fascinating." With another nod, he headed to his fancy car.

We waited until they drove slowly up the street, then Craig turned to Grandpa. "Thanks, Leo."

"No problem," Grandpa said. "But I'd suggest you get some patrol officers set up so the lookie-loos stay away."

"On it," Craig said.

As we followed Grandpa back toward the house, Craig glanced at me. "I'd say I'm surprised to see you here, but I'm not really."

I wrinkled my nose at him. I wasn't in the mood for jokes. Although he wasn't wrong. If mayhem made an appearance on this island, you usually wouldn't have to look too far to find me. "Hi to you too."

"Someone's dead?"

I nodded. "Yep."

"And you're here why? Or do I even want to know?"

"I just got hired by them to do a party. We were here to do a site visit."

Craig looked like he had questions, but he resisted. Instead, he motioned to the street. "And that creepy old guy?"

I shrugged. "You heard him. Filming his TV segment."

"More like being nosy," Craig said.

"That too."

Craig's phone buzzed. He glanced at it, then at me. "Mick wants to see you."

# Chapter 10

We headed to the front porch, where Mick had just emerged from the house. His face was grim. He was speaking to Adam and his partner, who were nodding. Then they went inside.

When we reached him, he said to Craig, "We cleared the house and I assessed the victim. Go up and take a look as well. We'll need to get more photos. I got a few. Second floor, end of the hall. Weird setting. You'll see."

Craig nodded. "I need to send the patrol guys to barricade the area. Press was already by. Seemingly by chance, but who knows."

"Great," Mick muttered. "Send Bellamy and Hemsworth and call in more if you need them. I can't let this become a circus."

"On it," Craig said. With one quick glance at me, he headed inside.

Mick turned to me. "Want to tell me how you're involved in this?"

I nodded. "Do you know who she is?"

"I'll need official ID from a family member, but it appears to be Olivia McAllister," he said. "There's a purse with an ID in the master bedroom."

I'd been expecting this, but it still hit me like a punch. I resisted the urge to look over at my mother, figuring she'd be able to see the truth in my eyes even from all the way over here.

"What happened?" I asked.

"Medical examiner has to do their thing, but appears to be blunt force trauma to the head."

"Like maybe she fell and hit her head?" I asked.

He shook his head. "Definitely not. A fall wouldn't have done that much damage. And also, she's face down. The wound is on the back of her skull."

"Someone killed her." I had to say it out loud, just to be sure.

"Looks that way." His tone was grim. "So. The full story about why you're here," he said. "And what's the deal with that room?"

"The secret room?" I remembered that he wasn't originally from the island.

At his nod, I said, "It's kind of an island lore thing. I'd never seen one myself until today. They're tiny rooms with hidden doors built off other rooms, or sometimes underneath a room or behind some stairs. Usually in really old houses where they used to hide stuff during Prohibition, or even people during the Underground Railroad times."

"For real?" he asked.

"Yep," I said. "I've never seen one before but I've heard of them."

"Well, aren't we lucky," he said. "Now tell me what happened."

I told him the story, starting with the phone call and my mother's desire to come out here and see her friend again, to the open front door and our horror-movie search of the house, and finally about following the cat into the room and accidentally finding the book-activated door.

He listened without comment, but I could see the skepticism settle at this last part. "You're kidding, right? A cat? Is there something you're not telling me, Maddie?"

"No! I swear," I protested. "The cat was in here and that's how I found it. I can't find the cat now, though." Where *was* that cat? I hadn't seen him again since the book-throwing incident.

He decided to let that go. "So, you said her daughter and granddaughter are supposed to be here too? You didn't see any sign of them?"

I shook my head.

"Your mother been back in touch with her for long?"

I shook my head. "No. She didn't even know Olivia was back until yesterday. She hasn't heard from her since she left the island with her family when they were in high school. When I told her who'd booked the party, she looked like she'd seen a ghost."

"Did they know you were coming over today?" he asked.

"Not really." At his questioning look, I explained. "I asked her if she had a preference for when we should stop by, she said whenever. Mom wanted to come as soon as possible and see Olivia again."

"So you just wandered through their house? Hoping to, what? Surprise them?"

I was taken aback at his tone. For the most part, Mick had dropped his posture about me getting involved in incidents like this. He knew that I was only trying to help, and I'd proven myself to be a valuable partner on a few occasions. Today, though, he was acting weird.

"No," I said. "The door was open a crack when we got here and no one answered the bell. My mom thought they might be out back and just didn't hear us at first. Then we called and heard her phone ringing, and she got worried."

"Okay. I'm going to need you to give a statement. Why don't you head to the station. I'll be there soon." He turned to go back into the house, but I put a hand on his arm.

"Mick. What's up?"

"I have a dead woman in a secret room."

"I know but you seem . . . extra tense."

"I just need to deal with this," he said. "You might want to get your mom out of here before they bring out the victim."

And with that, he slipped inside and shut the door behind him, leaving me alone. I watched him go for a moment, not sure why I felt like he was avoiding my question.

I turned and went down to where Grandpa, my mother, and Katrina were all standing together. Katrina was holding JJ. Never mind Mick's beach outfit, I hadn't seen Katrina outside of her typical ACO uniform in—well, I couldn't remember how long. She wore a pair of shorts and a tank top, bathing suit straps peeking out from underneath. Her hair was wrapped in a messy bun on top of her head, and she was a little tanned for the first time that I could remember since moving home.

She looked relaxed—and that was definitely different.

My mother, on the other hand, looked stricken. She grabbed me as soon as I got close. "What's happened?" she asked. "I know you know something."

"I'm sorry, Mom. Really. I didn't want to say anything before I knew for sure." I took a breath. "There's a secret room upstairs. Off that study at the end of the second-floor hall. The cat led me in there . . . Anyway, I found the door and there was someone inside it. She was . . . passed away." I took a breath. "Mick checked the victim against an ID and thinks it's Olivia."

My mother's face went actually white. She clutched

Grandpa's arm for support. "No," she whispered. "It can't be."

Katrina, wide-eyed, stepped away with JJ to give her some space.

"They still have to do a formal ID," I said helplessly. "Maybe . . ." I trailed off. "I'm sorry, Mom."

"Oh my God. I can't believe this," she said, looking around frantically like she thought Olivia might appear in front of her and tell her it was all a misunderstanding.

"I'm so sorry, honey," Grandpa said, pulling her into a hug.

I could see her shoulders shaking as she hid her face against his shoulder. I wondered if she'd cried like that on his shoulder when Olivia moved away without saying goodbye all those years ago.

"I'm going to take you home," Grandpa was saying. "You shouldn't be here for this. Maddie, you'll take her car?"

I nodded. "I have to go to the station to give a statement, but Mick only told me to come. He didn't say he needed Mom. You should go."

Grandpa nodded and, without another word, led my mother to his truck. When they'd driven away, Katrina and I looked at each other. She let out a breath. "That was intense."

"Tell me about it," I said.

"You found the woman?"

I nodded.

"How awful."

"Yeah. Is Mick okay?" I asked. "He was acting a little weird."

She shrugged. "I think he's fine. Just maybe stressed about this. It's high profile, yes?"

"What do you mean?" I said.

"I don't know. The chief called him personally after the call—your call, I guess—came in. I couldn't hear what he said, but Mick got a little tense. He'll figure it out."

The chief had called him directly? After, what, getting briefed on a 9-1-1 call? That seemed odd, but before I could ask any more, a movement by the line of shrubs at the edge of the yard caught my attention.

"Are you kidding me," I muttered when I caught a glimpse of the now-familiar white and gray fur of the cat I'd been following around what seemed to be all morning. How did he get out here when I'd last seen him at the bookshelf? There had to be more than one cat.

Katrina followed my gaze. "What?"

"Right there." I pointed. "The cat. I may need you to help me trap it if I can't grab it."

JJ saw him too. I could tell, because he was hyper focused on where I was looking, tail poised straight up.

Katrina squinted. "Can't see a thing. I really need to get a new prescription," she muttered. Katrina wore contacts most of the time. Unless she forgot them, which happened regularly. "I'm wearing them now," she said defensively, as if she could read my mind. "I just haven't been to the eye doc in a while."

I sighed impatiently. "There's a cat running around. I'm assuming it's theirs and not sure it should be outside. Although I've seen it both inside and outside so I'm wondering if there's two. I'm going to go try to catch it." Without waiting for an answer, I headed toward the side of the yard where I'd seen the flash of white fur. Of course, now I didn't see it. Was this cat taunting me? It almost seemed like it at this point, but I wasn't one to give up easily. The last thing I wanted was for this family to come home and find their cat missing on top of a dead relative.

I was going to save the cat if it was the last thing I did today.

# Chapter 11

"Be right back," I told Katrina and took off around the back of the house. Once I got to the backyard, I shaded my eyes from the blaring sun and paused to scan the lawn.

And then I saw the cat. He gazed imperceptibly at me, the fluffy tail swishing behind him. When he realized he'd gotten my attention, he turned and began a leisurely stroll toward the wooden stairs leading down to the beach.

"Shoot." I felt in my pockets to see if I had any treats. Sometimes I remembered to put some in, other times I had treats stashed in so many pockets of things that I often found them later—but not today, unfortunately. I'd gotten a little out of the habit when I was out with JJ because people just gave him treats wherever we went, so it didn't seem necessary. But then I remembered that I often found myself in situations where I had to lure stray animals over to help them. Like this kitty.

Looked like my only choice was to try to scoop him up.

I followed, hoping the steps were in good shape. It was a feature of the big houses that jutted out over the ocean—not only were their views high enough to die for, but they had access to the private beach below via their own staircases. They had to be rebuilt every decade or so because of the saltwater beating the crap out of them, but it made beach access a breeze. As long as the stairs didn't collapse or get washed away in a storm. And if this house had been empty for all these years, there was no telling the shape they were in.

I made some kissing sounds, trying to get the cat's attention. I didn't want him to run down the steps and take off. I headed toward the cat as fast as I dared to move, trying not to spook him. My efforts were unsuccessful. As soon as he saw me coming, he turned and headed down the stairs in a graceful hop, tail still swishing majestically.

"Crap," I muttered, picking up the pace. The smell of salt was overwhelming in the humid air. I could taste it on my lips and feel it in my hair, which was starting to do that wavy thing it did in this weather even in its ponytail.

I made my way down the uneven stairs as fast as I could without falling and breaking my neck, because we didn't need another emergency. When I hit the beach I paused, trying to see the cat in the tall sea grass around me. I couldn't catch a glimpse of the white and gray fur. But I did see a spot of color farther down the beach, rooting through the tall grass. I squinted for a better look.

And gasped when I realized it was a little kid wearing something bright pink. She was squatting, hunched around a pail and shovel, intent on something in the grass. The way she sat made it hard for me to make out what I was seeing, but once my mind wrapped itself around the sight, I raced toward her. I didn't see any other people around, just her, alone on this giant beach. Aside from some boats bobbing over by the nearby cove, the place was eerily deserted. Odd for the summer months.

"Hey," I called out as I got closer.

She turned, regarding me curiously, before going back to whatever she was digging.

"Hi," I said when I came up behind her. "I'm Maddie." She was a cute little thing, with long, tangled dark hair and green eyes. Her pink dress, the one spot of color I'd seen, had fuzzy caterpillars on it. On one foot she wore a pink sandal. I recognized it as the mate to the one on the back porch and was relieved that there hadn't been anything terrible associated with that lone shoe. Her other foot was bare. "What's your name?"

The little girl threw one more shovelful of sand into her pail before she stood, assessing me suspiciously. "Piper." She squinted at me. "You're a stranger. I'm not s'posed to talk to strangers."

Piper. Olivia's granddaughter. I recognized the name from our brief phone call the other day. I felt immense relief at this before the next worrying thought struck me. Why was she down here alone? What had happened to her grandmother? And her mother?

Piper was still watching me, her face more curious than anything. She seemed unfazed that she was out here alone on the beach, with a strange woman talking to her.

"I know, but I promise I'm not a bad stranger. I know your grandma," I said. It wasn't technically true, but that was a nuance a four- year-old didn't need. "Where's your mom?" I felt woefully underqualified for this conversation. I didn't really know how to talk to kids. I hadn't spent much time around them. Not sure I even liked them, if I was being honest.

Piper shrugged. "She went out. My Grammy's home. She said I could go play."

"That's your home?" I asked, pointing at the house at the top of the stairs, just to be sure. Last thing I needed was to try to "rescue" the wrong kid.

But Piper nodded.

"Why are you out here alone?"

"I had to find Puck," she answered, as if I was stupid.

"Who is Puck?" I asked cautiously, figuring it would be an imaginary friend or something.

"My cat!" She sounded exasperated with my lack of information. But my ears had perked up now. The same cat I'd been chasing around all morning? Had to be. "The white and gray cat," I confirmed.

Another nod.

"Are you looking for it in the bushes?" I gestured around us.

Piper frowned at me. "It's a *boy*."

"Sorry. Him," I amended.

Piper sighed. It was a hefty sigh for a kid her age. "He ran away again. But I saw him come this way."

I looked around, but there was no cat in sight. And not many places to hide on the beach. I'd have to leave that quest for later.

"We should probably go find your mom," I said to Piper.

Piper pondered this for a moment, then said, "Okay."

Relieved that she wasn't going to put up a fight, I held out my hand. She regarded it for a second, then thrust the bucket full of sand and shovel into it. "Carry my cake," she said, and skipped ahead to the stairs, leaving me holding the proverbial bag. I had a moment of panic as I followed her. She couldn't go in the house, of course. And since I had no idea where her mother was, I felt like a big fat liar right now.

Well, nothing to be done about it now. I would worry about that when we got up to the house. The most important thing was not letting this kid get swept out to sea or something. I wished we could have found the cat too, but I could always go back and look. One emergency at a time.

When we got up to the backyard, I redirected Piper from the back door, where she'd been headed, around to the front. The ambulance was still there, lights still flashing long, lazy strobes around the driveway, along with all the police cars and another official-looking van parked off to the side near the porch. Everyone was seemingly still inside. I had a fleeting moment of panic that we'd come out front right in time to see Olivia's body being carried out of the house, but that wasn't the case. Although I couldn't be sure it wouldn't happen any second now.

Piper, who had skipped ahead of me, stopped now and was staring at the lights in fascination. I realized that this might have not been the best idea either. She could get freaked out and start to cry or something, but she just stood there, taking it all in.

She looked at me again, those intense eyes searching mine. "Can I have my game?"

"Your game," I repeated. "Where is it?"

"Inside. On the iPad."

The iPad we'd seen in the kitchen. "Sure. In a few minutes," I said, relieved when Katrina appeared at my side. "This is Piper," I told her. "She was on the beach. Alone." I raised my eyebrows to convey that this wasn't good. Katrina used to babysit me and my sisters. She'd be better with kids, right? And maybe she'd be able to tell if Piper was actually okay, or if she was having some kind of trauma response right now. Or was she just going about her day with no idea what was going on around her? I sincerely hoped she'd already been out chasing the cat when whatever happened inside had happened.

"Hi, Piper," Katrina said, kneeling in front of her. "I'm Katrina. And this is JJ. Would you like to play with him for a bit?"

Piper nodded. Her eyes darted around the yard at all the chaos, and I could almost see her weighing the choice in her head: Freak out, or play with the cat? Luckily for me, she chose the cat by reaching out her hand to JJ.

"Let's go over here," Katrina suggested, leading her

toward my mother's car. As they walked away, I heard her ask Katrina, "Is my mommy coming home soon?"

"Maddie!" A shout from the porch caught my attention, and I turned to see Mick and Craig standing there. Mick beckoned, his arm an angry slash through the air.

I hurried over.

"I thought you headed to the station?"

"I just found the missing granddaughter," I said, nodding in Piper's direction. "Props might be in order?"

He ignored this. "Where was she?"

Why was he acting so weird? "On the beach. Said her Grammy was home. But has no idea where her mother is."

"Yeah. Well, that's getting more curious by the moment," Mick said. "I found another cell phone in a bedroom that I'm guessing is the daughter's. Wherever she is, she didn't take her phone either."

# Chapter 12

I felt my stomach pitch with this news. Piper was all alone on the beach. Her grandmother was inside their house in a secret room, dead. And her mother was nowhere to be found, without her cell phone.

Things weren't looking good for the McAllisters' homecoming.

"Do you think something happened to her too?" I asked.

"I don't know," Mick said. "We didn't find a trace of anyone else in the house, no signs of foul play anywhere but in that room where Olivia was. Now, if there are other rooms like that . . ." He let the thought trail off. I thought of Tess being stuck in a secret room that no one knew how to access and shivered.

"Is your mom okay? I heard she knew our victim," Craig said. He and my mom had always liked each other, a sentiment that continued long past our breakup. On an island this size, it was harder for it to be any other way. Also, I thought it was sweet.

But I could feel Mick's eyes on me at the question, and I got the sense there was more here than him simply being concerned about my mother. "She's not," I said. "Grandpa took her home."

Craig nodded. "Understandable," he said. "Please give her my condolences." He turned to Mick. "I'm going to go get the patrol guys canvassing. More units are on their way, yes?"

Mick nodded. "We need to keep the curious out. Don't want the news getting out ahead of us."

My phone started to buzz. I pulled it out and looked at it. Becky was calling. "Too late," I told him. "I bet Mila Daindridge already did her damage." I turned away to answer.

"How the hell did Mila Daindridge get first dibs on a story you're involved in?" Becky snapped without even bothering to say hello. "And why am I even surprised you're involved?"

"Hi to you too," I said dryly. "I take it she published something." That was fast. She had left here less than an hour ago.

"Yes! It's not much, but she's the first to report on *major police activity* at the old McAllister house. What's going on and why are you there? And why was *she* there?"

I could feel Mick's eyes boring into the back of my head and walked away a little so he couldn't hear me. "Long story. She was in the area for something else but saw all the commotion."

"Commotion at the old McAllister home," Becky confirmed.

"Yes."

"And what was this commotion?"

"If I tell you, you can't break the story yet," I warned her. "It's complicated."

"Am I going to get it first?"

"I mean, I can't promise you that Mila doesn't have any contacts herself, but I'll try to make sure Mick gives you a heads-up before he confirms publicly," I offered.

"Fine," she said, slightly pacified but still clearly agitated. Becky hated to lose.

I gave her the thirty-second version.

"Whoa," she said, stunned out of her rant.

"I know."

"Your mom's best friend." Becky sucked in a breath. "God. I'm sorry."

"I know. I feel terrible for her."

"Were they close?"

"She hadn't seen her since the family moved away."

"And her daughter is missing."

"As of right now, she's nowhere to be found," I said.

"Well, this is interesting, because when I heard Mila's report, I did a quick look into the McAllisters. I remembered seeing something come across my desk recently."

I frowned. "You did?"

"Yeah. I just read an op-ed that came into the paper a couple days ago. My editorial page editor flagged it for me. It was by the Town Historian, Helen Holloway. And it was all about historic properties that need to be preserved. It seemed to be a rant about them in general, but she mentions that house specifically. Mermaid Cottage, right? But it's not a cottage."

"Right," I said. Helen Holloway. I knew the name. I had a vague recollection of a tiny, fiery woman with tightly permed white hair and bright red glasses who never seemed to age. She held court in our main historical society office here in Daybreak Harbor, but her work encompassed all five towns on the island. But as far as I knew, she'd been old back when I was still in school—and that was a long time ago. "What about it?" I asked.

"That 'homes in desirable residential areas'—this is where she mentioned the cottage—'should not be capitalized upon to enable greedy landowners to make use of them when they abandoned the island and their heritage itself.' And about 'bad actors trying to ruin the fabric of the island's historic homes and buildings in an effort to pillage our appeal for all that it's worth.' She's passionate about this place, I'll give her that," Becky said.

"Why was it flagged?" I asked.

"There wasn't context about why she was saying this. There was nothing mentioned about doing anything specific to any of these properties that triggered the rant. My editor wasn't feeling it but wanted to make sure we wouldn't get backlash by not publishing it. You know, make the town mad, that kind of thing." I could hear the smile in her voice. "I told her that's not the way we do things here. If it's not relevant, it's not relevant. I asked around to see if anyone knew anything about the property, or any developments on the old case—I know the owner vanished a long time ago. Nothing there, but I did find out that the McAllisters gave some big endowment to the paper a long time ago. It still funds some scholarship or something. So our legal department is wary about mentioning them in any negative way."

She sounded like she couldn't care less about the legal department's thoughts. "I'm sure that sat well with you," I said.

"Oh yeah. Made my day. I'm going to do a little digging on land records and permits," Becky said.

"Good idea. Can I call you back in a bit?"

"Yeah. I'll be waiting," she said.

I pocketed my phone and turned back to Mick.

"Done?" he asked sarcastically. At my nod, he continued, "I need you to go to the station and wait for me. I'm leaving here in ten minutes, maybe less. Take Katrina and the kid. You understand?"

He did not want me hanging around here. I nodded, trying not to feel hurt by his attitude. He was under a lot of stress, I reasoned. And on his one day off in forever too. "On my way," I said.

Katrina, Piper, and JJ were already sitting in my mom's car as I slid into the driver's seat. "We're going to go downtown," I said, trying to sound like we were going on an adventure.

Piper didn't even seem to notice. She was sprawled across the back seat, snuggling with JJ and talking to him softly.

Katrina turned to me. "You never found the cat, did you?" she asked in a low voice.

I shook my head. I didn't want to upset Piper by talking about it. "No trace."

"I think I know why," she said, a little triumphantly.

I'd been backing out of the driveway, but now I stopped and glanced at her. "Why?"

"Because it's not real!" She sat back with a smile.

"What are you talking about?" Annoyed, I let my foot off the brake and continued down the sloping driveway.

"I mean, I don't think it's real. This is one of the places the Ghost Cat frequents," she said in a stage whisper. "I've never seen it. But if you have, that's wild."

I had to hit the brake again so I could stare at her in disbelief. "Ghost Cat?" I repeated, not sure if I was hearing right.

"Yes, the Ghost Cat! You can't tell me you've never heard of it."

I shook my head. "Nope."

She threw her head back against the seat melodramatically. "You've gotta be kidding me. It's, like, an island legend."

"If it's a legend, why don't I know about it?" I asked.

"I don't know," she said. "You weren't paying attention, maybe?"

She could be right about that, I reasoned. Although I'd always been interested in anything related to animals. "Maybe. But I know there's a cat here. I saw it with my own eyes and she even mentioned it." I gestured with my head toward Piper. "She saw him too. That's why she was on the beach."

"Whatever you say," she said in a singsong voice. "But then why couldn't you find it?"

"Because cats are good at hiding," I retorted. But at the same time, I couldn't help but think about the odd circumstances every time I'd seen the cat. Here one second, gone the next in every instance. Was he really that good at hiding, even in the bookshelves?

"So what is this legend, then? Is this cat, like, an evil spirit that's predicting bad things or something?" I asked, still trying to speak softly. I could hear Piper singing to JJ in the back seat, so I hoped she really wasn't listening.

"No, he's not bad! Remember, there are no bad cats. Well, mostly," she amended. "Some of them can be little brats for sure. Like the one that scratched my eye that time."

I hadn't heard that story, but now didn't seem the time for it. "Then what's the story?"

"The legend is that he shows up for people who are at a turning point. Like one of those sliding-door moments from that movie? And he usually appears in doorways, speaking of."

I felt a tiny chill. I had seen the cat in the doorway of the study—it's what led me there. Was that an irreversible turning point for me somehow? Finding a dead body was heavy. Or was it strictly related to Olivia?

I'd also seen the cat outside, though. Katrina brushed it

off when I pointed that out. "It doesn't just sit in a doorway the whole time," she said, her tone suggesting I should be able to figure this out.

"What kind of turning point? Do you mean, like . . . death?"

"No, not necessarily. At least I don't remember *that*," she said, thoughtfully tapping her chin with her finger. I think it's like if someone is going to find out about a betrayal, or something else life-changing. I'm sure it could be death but doesn't have to be."

"Whose cat was it? Before it was a ghost."

"The rumor was it was a fortune teller's cat," Katrina said.

"For real, or was she a scammer?"

Katrina shrugged. "No idea. The sailors would come ask her if they would make it back from expeditions or die at sea. She made a killing off them."

"And was she right?"

Katrina grinned. "About half the time. The other half didn't come back to say."

"Of course," I said, pointing the car toward downtown. "You want me to drop you at home, or bring you to the station?"

"My house, please."

Katrina's house was on the way to the police station. When we pulled up, she said goodbye to Piper, then turned to me. "Thanks for the lift. Sorry about . . . today." She got out, then leaned back into the car. "Stay away from doorways," she added with a wink.

"Cute. Thanks," I muttered.

"I'll be by tomorrow with those kittens," she added.

"Wait, what kittens?"

She just grinned and shut the door.

# Chapter 13

Instead of driving straight to the station, I made a pit stop to pick up coffee and doughnuts from Bean. The cops would like that, because even though it was cliché, they loved doughnuts. And I, for one, needed more coffee. In fact, there wasn't enough coffee on the island for this day.

As Piper, JJ, and I waited in line—I was letting her pick out the doughnuts—I couldn't stop my brain from trying to make sense out of today's events. Was there any sense to it, though? Who would have wanted to murder Olivia McAllister? Who even knew they were here? If my mother or Grandpa hadn't known, it seemed unlikely that a large sampling of people had. And out of those people, who wanted her dead? And where was her daughter? I was terrified I'd hear from Mick that they'd found another secret room and an equally grotesque discovery inside it.

Once we got our doughnuts and coffee and an orange juice for Piper, we headed back to the car. I waited until Piper was again preoccupied with JJ before I called Grandpa.

"I'm heading to the station to give my statement now," I told him.

"I'm already here waiting for you," he replied.

"How's Mom?"

He hesitated. "Not great. She wanted to lie down. Told me not to stay."

"I have Piper with me," I said.

"The granddaughter?" He sounded surprised.

"Yeah." I explained how I'd located her on the beach.

"Well, that's positive," he said. "But no sign of her mother."

"No. So, what's the story with Neil Caldwell?" I asked. "You didn't seem to care much for him."

"I don't," Grandpa replied immediately.

"Why?" I was pulling into the police station parking lot and saw him leaning against his truck.

"Long story. I'll tell you later."

I disconnected and pulled up next to him. We didn't have a chance to debrief, though, because Mick's car pulled up right behind me. He paused and rolled down his window. "Park out back," he instructed.

Grandpa and I glanced at each other, but Grandpa got in the car and I drove slowly around back to where the officers and personnel parked.

Mick took us inside through the back door, straight to his office, not even letting me dispense the doughnuts first. He took them himself, along with Piper (and JJ to keep her company), and went out front, leaving us alone in his office with the door shut.

I looked at Grandpa. "He's acting weird."

Grandpa nodded. "To be expected."

"Why?"

"This case is going to be complicated."

"What do you mean?"

"Lots of eyes on it. The McAllisters always had a lot of clout. I'm sure that remains, even though they're mostly long gone."

Before I could interrogate him further, Mick shoved the door open and entered the room. He looked tired. He'd changed out of his beach outfit too—he must have a backup detective's outfit in his locker. He looked way more comfortable in his work clothes, which told you everything you needed to know about Mick Ellory.

"What a morning," he said grimly, dropping into his chair behind his desk. "What do you know about this family, Leo?"

That was the beauty of Grandpa's longevity on Daybreak Island—he knew everything about everyone who'd lived here for any length of time. Added to that institutional knowledge was his tenure with the police department, and he was singlehandedly the most sought-after person on the island in times like this. He lived for this stuff. And he'd be all in on this one. Someone had murdered his daughter's childhood friend. He would take that very personally.

Grandpa recited the now-familiar story about the McAllister clan, the aunt's disappearance and the remaining family members' abrupt departure from Daybreak.

Mick had pulled out his notebook and was taking notes. "And your daughter. What was her involvement with them?"

"She and Olivia were friendly when they were kids," Grandpa said.

I thought his word choice was interesting. According to my mother, they were not just *friendly*. They were besties.

"And after they moved?"

"She hasn't had any contact with her," Grandpa said.

Mick's eyes met his, stayed a moment too long before dropping back to his notebook. "Maddie said Olivia was here with her daughter, as well as the granddaughter. Have either of you met the daughter? What's her name?"

"Tess," I said. "And no, we haven't met her."

"Haven't even seen Olivia since she was a teenager," Grandpa said. "No sign of her, then?"

"No," Mick said. "Which could be alarming but could also be something else."

I frowned. "What do you mean?"

Mick tilted his head and studied me. "Her mother winds up dead in a secret room in the house and she's nowhere to be found. Either something happened to her, or . . ." He let the sentence hang.

While I'd been wondering if Tess was okay, Mick's mind had gone somewhere darker. "Wait. You think she killed her mother, and left her daughter there with the dead body?"

He inclined his chin in a not-quite-yes, not-quite-no gesture. "Just working through the possibilities," he said. "She was the only other person in the house."

"That we know of," Grandpa said.

"Right. Regardless, we need to find her. She could be in trouble."

"Agreed. Also, someone could have been watching the house and saw an opportunity with her gone," Grandpa said.

Before Mick could respond to that, a woman I'd never seen before stuck her head in the doorway of Mick's office. "I've got her downstairs. Preliminary findings—blunt force trauma to the back of the skull, causing a fracture and associated bleeding." Then she paused, as if realizing we were in the room too. "Oh. Sorry," she said, wincing a little.

I had to smile at her wrecking-ball energy. She appeared to be in her early forties, a compact, pixie-shaped woman with chin-length dark hair and cat's-eye glasses that perched precariously on her nose, as though they were always on the verge of escape. She gave them an impatient shove back into place and turned to Mick.

"Jeanette," Mick said. "Thanks for coming by. This is Leo Mancini. He used to be the chief here. And his granddaughter Maddie. She found the room. And the body."

Recognition dawned on her face and she marched over to Grandpa and held out her hand. "Chief Mancini! Good to meet you. Jeanette Winters. I work with the medical examiner's satellite office on the mainland."

Grandpa rose to shake her hand. "Lovely to meet you as well."

Jeanette turned to me and shook my hand too. "Bad day?" she said sympathetically.

I wasn't sure how to answer that. "It was worse for the victim," I said. "Did you say satellite office?" I'd never heard this before.

Jeanette nodded. "Yes, we cover the Cape and islands. Made sense with the uptick in crime in the area the past few years. I'm usually out on the islands once or twice a month, and they finally gave us some space. We have a designated ME suite inside the station." She smirked as she said the word *suite*.

Mick grinned. "They have a corner of the basement. They turned it into one small exam room, a freezer space, and a desk."

"Four-star quarters," Jeanette agreed. "It's just a preliminary assessment place. We still ship any guests over to the mainland for the full autopsy. And you all are lucky, because I was already out here when this . . . unfortunate event occurred." She waved a hand to indicate Olivia's case.

"It appeared someone came up behind her and she didn't see it coming," Mick said. "Do you agree?"

Jeanette nodded. "Appears so. Not to mention you said the door was closed from the outside."

Mick nodded, then turned to me to confirm.

"Yes. I found it . . . accidentally," I said.

"Someone was hoping she wouldn't be found, at least for a while." Mick blew out a breath. "I didn't know those rooms actually existed."

"I've seen a few. More like secret little passages," Jeanette said without missing a beat.

We all looked at her. "You have?" Most people who weren't from here didn't know about these rooms.

She nodded. "I spent summers out here with my aunt. She took me to a lot of historic houses."

"Who's your aunt?" Grandpa asked.

"Helen Holloway. Official title, historian. Unofficial title, town busybody." She winked as she said it.

"Is that so!" Grandpa exclaimed.

She nodded. "I spent a few weeks here with her every summer as a kid. Absolutely loved it. It always seemed like a Hallmark movie, living out here. When I found out about this position, I jumped on it. Needed to get out of the city and it seemed like fate. So I moved here. It's different having to ferry to work most days, but it works. And I get a couple days out here a month, so . . ." She shrugged.

"Well, welcome," Grandpa said. "I hope it's as magical as you hoped. *I* certainly think it is." He glanced at Mick. "Aside from a few unfortunate incidents, but I guess that's true for anywhere."

Jeanette inclined her head in a nod. "My job is a lot different now than when I worked out in New York," she said, then glanced at her watch. "I've gotta get back. I'll get you my full report in the next couple of days, Lieutenant. And nice to meet you both," she added with a nod to me and Grandpa, then turned and headed out.

"Helen Holloway's niece," Grandpa mused. The Town Historian who had been on the job long enough to be called *historic* herself.

I didn't mention the op-ed Becky had told me about.

Something about the vibe in here told me to keep quiet and talk it over with Grandpa first.

"I don't know her personally," Mick said. "Our cases aren't usually that cold. So back to our victim and her family. Anyone know why they were here? Other than this party they hired you for?" He turned to me. "Were they staying out here, visiting, what?"

"When Olivia called me, she mentioned spending some weekends here," I said. "Said Piper has been going to camp. So, at the very least, they've been meeting people."

"It's something." Mick made a note. "Do you know what camp?"

"I don't."

Mick nodded. "Okay. I checked the daughter's phone at the house. The emergency contact is her mother, so that's no help. I also called the number for 'Dad' in Tess's phone—left a message there too to get in touch. Olivia didn't have an emergency contact in hers. Do you know if she's married? Or if the daughter is married?"

Again, neither of us knew.

"You said Olivia has a brother. What do you know about him?" Mick asked Grandpa.

"I don't know anything about him present day," Grandpa said. "Haven't seen him since he was eighteen or nineteen."

"Who else would they be in touch with out here?" Mick asked. "Was the family still close to anyone? Friends, other relatives?"

Grandpa shook his head slowly. "No relatives. Friends, again, not sure. Our family lost touch with them."

"I'm not used to you not knowing everything about everything, Leo. Gotta say it's throwing me for a loop," Mick said.

"You and me both," Grandpa agreed.

"Well, someone had to know they were here," Mick

said. "You didn't see anyone else around? No cars parked on the street, nothing like that?"

"There was no one around," I said. "That area is pretty isolated. Except for the news showing up to do that story."

"Yeah. That was a cluster," Mick said. "What was that about again?"

"They said it was related to some restoration project," I said. "They're doing work in the cove or something nearby and were filming a segment." I waited for Grandpa to chime in, but he stayed quiet.

Then I remembered the car and sat up straighter. "You know what, I did see a car driving really fast down the road when we were heading up there. It was lime green. The color really stood out."

"Driving in what direction?"

"Back toward town."

"License plate?"

I shook my head.

"Can't be too hard to find a car that color," he said. "But I want to talk about the missing aunt. You think this could be related?"

Grandpa spread his hands wide. "No idea, since we don't have a clue what happened to her."

"What was your theory?" Mick asked. "I'm sure you had one."

Grandpa shrugged. "There was never any real evidence of a crime, or at least not that we ever found for the short time we were allowed to look at it. Lots of rumors, but no facts to back them up. I'd like to think, if anything, she just up and left. Who knows what families are really like? Maybe she'd just had enough of hers."

"They were that bad?" Mick asked.

"Who really knows?" Grandpa said. "People only show what they want to the public. It's very different at home. Bottom line, I knew Delia well enough. She and my wife had worked on a very early version of the Island Grown food service together for several years, and my wife was a fan. Always said D had a good head on her shoulders and a good heart in her chest."

I felt a pang at my grandmother's familiar saying. I'd heard that more than once. And I'd also heard her opposite opinion of people whom she didn't look upon as favorably: *They're not the right sort.*

Mick considered this. "If she left because of her family, why do you think the family would've left?"

"I don't know. They were gone within a month, not even a goodbye. I can't imagine that losing your daughter or sibling and the only place that's ever been home at the same time would've been an option. But people are different."

"They sure are," Mick agreed. He was quiet for a moment, then said, "So what if there was foul play? Was there ever any conversation about who it could have been, even if it was just theoretical?"

"Like I said," Grandpa repeated. "Our hands were tied."

The two men watched each other. I got the feeling that something was going on here that I knew nothing about. And it wasn't necessarily positive.

"And the house? Why did no one sell it?" Mick asked finally.

"It was a family house. It was paid off, as I understood it, so no bank could seize it. The family likely didn't want to deal with it. They had Arthur Randall taking care of the place. They paid him nicely too, I remember him telling me. He could've easily had that one job to float that side of his business on if he was so inclined."

"Arthur Randall," Mick repeated, writing that name down. "He still taking care of it today?"

"As far as I know," Grandpa said.

Mick leaned back again, drumming his fingers on the arms of his chair. "I'll talk to him. It would be great to find out why Delia's niece and her family came back. Hopefully it helps inform what happened when they got here."

"Well," Grandpa said, "maybe he can help."

They did the staring thing again, then Mick scribbled something on his notepad. "I'll put him on the list," he said, then stood. "Maddie. You can do your statement now if you want, so we're not keeping you." He handed me some forms. "You can use the conference room out in the lobby. I'll come find you in a few."

# Chapter 14

I tried to linger a minute or two to see if Mick and Grandpa were going to say anything else, but they were clearly waiting for me to leave. Finally, I headed down the hall to the door leading to the lobby.

A few of the cops who saw me walking by waved, then came out to say thank you for the doughnuts. Most of them knew me. Some just waved or shouted hello, while a couple stopped to chat and catch up. Almost all of them knew Grandpa and either wanted to know how he was doing or wanted to tell me about how they'd seen him at some crime scene or another. It made me laugh. Grandpa certainly kept himself busy and found ways to offer his stellar investigative services to the island long after his civic duty was technically done.

"You know he showed up at that bust out in Duck Cove?" This was from Sergeant Bogart, head of the patrol unit, who leaned against the door to his office. He glanced surreptitiously around, probably to make sure the current chief wasn't nearby. The chief had kind of a grudge against Grandpa. He didn't love that Grandpa's reputation often had more impact on the department than his own—even now.

Most of the department, especially the OGs, knew about the one-sided feud and tried to not fan the flames.

Bogart was a tall, lanky Irishman who always looked like he needed to buy new clothes that weren't drowning him. "I'd gone out there to interview this guy it took me weeks to track down for a burglary out here in the harbor," he continued. "Leo was already there. He'd gotten the guy pegged on an assault!" Bogart shook his head in wonder. "We got the collar for both, thanks to him." He grinned slyly. "I didn't tell the chief. Figured it would potentially cramp your granddad's style."

"I'm sure he appreciates that," I said. I enjoyed hearing the stories about Grandpa in retirement. He had so loved his work. Almost as much as he loved my grandmother. After he retired, he had her. And when she'd left us, he'd been so lost. Starting the cat cafe and the PI businesses had been literal lifelines for him.

Finally, the guys drifted off, and I continued on my way. I caught a glimpse of Piper in the dispatch office, still playing with JJ. It appeared I was going to have a hard time getting my cat back.

I went into the "conference room" Mick had directed me to. The description was generous. It was a small room with a tiny window, a banged-up table, and two mismatched chairs. Usually when people came in off the street to talk to an officer, they were handled in here. I gingerly sat in one of the chairs, trying not to let my bare legs touch too much of it, and started writing.

It didn't take me very long to give my statement. It helped that I left out the Ghost Cat version of the story—I just said that I'd heard noises from that room and the cat had led me to the hidden door. No need to go into more detail than that, I reasoned. I'd already told Mick how I'd happened upon the handle of the door.

I signed the bottom of the statement, then sat back in the chair. Before I could help myself, I pulled out my phone and googled "Daybreak Island Ghost Cat," then sat back in astonishment as the hits poured in. I scrolled through, trying to get a sense of what I'd been missing all this time. The first hit was an excerpt from a book that, interestingly, was written by Helen Holloway, our Town Historian. The one who'd penned the op-ed that Becky had pulled.

> *The legend of the Daybreak Island Ghost Cat says that he belonged to Temperance Puckett, a midwife who served the island. One winter, Temperance demanded an oath from a prominent trader who needed help. He had been accused of cheating a struggling family out of their land. He vowed aloud that he would set the matter right in exchange for her help. He never did.*
>
> *Days later, he was found at the foot of the bluffs, his face frozen in terror. Locals swore that a white and gray cat had been seen on the rocks that night, staring out to sea.*
>
> *In the years that followed, strange sightings were recorded:*
>
> - *A dark shape perched on windowsills where no cat lived.*
> - *Paw prints appearing on frost-hardened stoops.*
> - *A cat's distinct meow heard when a truth was finally spilled.*

I tapped the table, thinking. Temperance Puckett. What was it about that name? I racked my brain for why it was sounding an alarm, but was jolted out of my concentration when the front door of the police station flew open and a man raced in, eyes wild, looking from right to left. He was young, maybe around my age, and looked like a disheveled college professor with his wire-rimmed glasses, longish dirty blond hair, and scruffy beard. His faded T-shirt had a dinosaur on it and the words "Let's eat kids. Let's eat, kids. Punctuation matters." When he caught sight of the woman behind the glass, he marched over and, even though she could clearly see him, rapped on the glass.

"I need to speak to a detective," he said loudly. He sounded desperate.

I moved to the door of the little room so I could hear better without attracting attention. I didn't hear what the woman behind the glass said since her voice was muffled, but I clearly heard his response.

"It's about Piper Gallagher, my daughter," he said tersely. "An officer at my ex-mother-in-law's house said she was here? What is going on? Is she okay? Is my wife okay?"

Piper's dad? I stepped out of the room, ready to answer the guy—and start asking him questions. But hearing her name, Piper popped her little head up in the window, a half-eaten doughnut in one hand and JJ in the other. She looked perfectly content, laughing as JJ tried to sniff out the doughnut. A beaming smile hit her face. "Hi, Daddy!" She waved the doughnut at him, then pointed at JJ. "I borrowed a kitty!" Unable to pronounce the Rs in the words, it came out like "bowwowed."

Relief coursed over the man's face and his whole body sagged with it. "Piper!" he cried. "Can I see her?" he asked, approaching the glass.

The dispatcher again said something I couldn't quite hear, then paged Mick to the lobby. I waited with interest to see what happened next.

When Mick appeared, the guy turned and pounced on

him. "I really want to see my daughter. Have you made sure she's okay? Does she need to go to the hospital? What happened?"

Mick held up a hand. "One step at a time, sir," he said in his most no-nonsense voice. "Your name?"

"Dean," the guy said. "Dean Gallagher. And that's my daughter." He pointed at Piper, still behind the glass watching this unfold. "And my wife . . . well, my ex-wife . . . I can't reach her. I went to the house they were staying at—her mother's house—and some officers told me to come here. I have no idea what happened. Do you know?" His voice and his face pled with Mick. He raked a hand through his hair, causing it to jut out in multiple directions from his head.

"Mr. Gallagher. Hold up a minute, please." Mick held up a hand, his voice softer than when he'd first addressed him. "I'm going to need some identification, and then I'm going to need to speak with you for a bit."

"Sure. Yes. Here." Dean reached into his pocket and pulled out a wallet. He flipped it open and showed Mick what I assumed was his driver's license.

Mick perused it, then nodded. "Thank you. Please come with me."

But Dean Gallagher stood his ground. "I need to know what happened," he insisted. "Tess. Is she okay? Did something happen to her? Why was my daughter brought here?"

Behind the glass, Piper watched this whole exchange, and her face had started to crumple. I couldn't tell if she could even hear him, but she could certainly feel the energy he exuded. And it was upsetting her enough that she'd forgotten about both the doughnut and JJ. She let him down on the desk, where he proceeded to nuzzle against the dispatcher.

"It's almost Piper's birthday, and we're all here to celebrate," he went on. "It's not like Tess to be out of contact. So I'm concerned—"

Before he could continue, the front door flew open again with such force that it banged off the wall behind it and a young woman about my age raced in. She wore black Athleta leggings, a pink sports bra, and sneakers. She looked even more distraught than Dean. Mascara-colored streaks were visible under her eyes. Her hair was falling out of a messy ponytail and she clutched a water bottle like it was her last lifeline.

She looked frantically around the station lobby, then faltered when she saw Dean. She looked from him to Mick, then focused on Mick. "Piper. Where's Piper? I'm looking for my daughter," she cried. "Somebody, please tell me what's going on!"

# Chapter 15

I stopped in my tracks. Piper was her daughter—which meant this had to be Tess, Olivia's daughter. Alive and well, thank goodness, and not lying in a secret room somewhere bleeding or worse. This was confirmed when Piper jumped up and down behind the glass shouting, "Mommy!"

But where had she been while her mother was being murdered and her daughter was wandering the beach alone?

Tess turned toward the sound, relief flooding her face when she saw her. "Oh, there you are! Hi, baby!" She made a move to run toward the room but realized she couldn't get in there. She whirled back to face Mick, a question on her face.

Mick stepped forward, trying to speak in a soothing tone. "Ma'am. What's your name?"

"Tess. Tess McAllister," she said. "I went home and there were police there. They told me to come here. Why is Piper here? Where's my mother? What's happened?" Her eyes were welling up with tears again. I saw her trying hard not to look at Piper's dad, though he was staring at her with pure relief on his face.

"Do you have identification?" Mick asked.

She touched her pockets as if trying to remember, then shook her head. "I—I went out running. I didn't bring anything with me."

Mick studied her, then Piper pressed against the glass, beaming and seemingly ecstatic that her parents were here. "I'll have them bring her out," Mick said, motioning to the dispatcher.

"Oh, thank God!" Tess burst into tears. Dean went over to her and tried to awkwardly hug her, but she pushed past him and dropped to her knees to hug her daughter when she ran out. Ainsley, the dispatch officer, followed, holding JJ, who she deposited in my arms. He smelled like doughnuts.

After Piper got hugs from both Tess and Dean, Tess stood. "Where's my mother?" she asked again. "And why were the police at our house? They wouldn't let me in."

"Why don't you come with me," Mick said to her. To Dean he said, "Wait right here, please." Dean's crestfallen expression said he didn't like this plan, but Mick pushed past it. "I'll have another detective come out to speak with you shortly. Piper might want to go back behind the desk to finish her snack?" He raised his eyebrows at Tess to convey that he thought this might be best.

I could see the dread settle on her face as she digested the reasons for this, then nodded.

"I'll take her," Dean said.

"You'll need to talk to a detective too, Mr. Gallagher, so why don't we just wait on that," Mick suggested. "I'll get someone out here in a minute."

Dean didn't like that, but he didn't fight it. He dropped into one of the grimy chairs that probably hadn't been replaced since the days when Grandpa Leo had been a detective and rubbed his hands over his face, knocking his glasses askew.

Mick gave me a look that said, *Show's over*. I held up the statement, showing that I was done.

He motioned for me to bring it to him. I stepped forward and handed it over. He glanced at it then nodded at me. "You're free to go," he said before leading Tess away.

I looked at Dean. He was sitting in the chair in the far corner of the room, clearly trying not to cry. I went over and sat next to him. "Hi," I said. "I'm Maddie James."

He glanced at me, clearly too polite to say, *So what?* Instead, he gave me a nod.

"You're Piper's dad."

He nodded again, eyes narrowing. "Who are you?"

"My mom is an old family friend of the McAllisters," I said. "They booked my cat cafe for the birthday party."

Now he sat up straight. "Seriously? You're JJ's House of Purrs?"

I nodded, pointing to JJ. "Well, I own it. And this is JJ."

"Wow. We were so excited," he said. "That type of party, well, it's Piper's dream to be surrounded by cats. We were all committed to making this party great, and then they found your place and it just seemed, well, perfect."

I smiled. "You all spend a lot of time out here, then?"

"Oh, no. Well, Tess has been spending a fair amount." His eyes darkened a bit at that. "At her mother's behest. We . . . split up last year and Tess is trying to figure out where to live. I think her mother wants her to come out here and work with her on some new venture. They've been coming out to visit a lot. I only came out for the party."

*So, Olivia had been planning to move back*, I thought. Although whatever venture she had in mind probably wasn't coming to fruition now.

"What kind of venture?" I asked. "We always love to hear about new entrepreneurs coming out to the island," I added when I saw a suspicious frown crease his forehead.

I should probably not be too eager in pumping him for information.

He studied me for a second, then let out a sigh that said it didn't matter anyway. "I don't know, a hotel or bed-and-breakfast or something. Which is funny because neither of them like to cook." He smirked. "Maybe they'll call it, McAllister's Bed and Make Your Own Damn Breakfast."

It seemed like the wrong time to giggle at that, although it was funny. I thought of the burnt toast popped up in the toaster at the McAllister home this morning. Maybe it hadn't been a clue after all. "How far along were they in the planning?" I asked, trying to sound casual. I was thinking of what Becky had told me, about Helen's furious op-ed that talked about preserving historical properties. And the Randall Renovations notepad I'd seen on the McAllisters' kitchen counter. And felt a tingling in the back of my neck.

"I have no idea. She wouldn't tell me much. Said she'd talk to me once it was figured out and she'd made a decision on her role." He slumped farther down in his chair, rubbing his hands over his face.

Before I could ask anything else, Craig appeared at the door with Grandpa close behind. He opened the door and motioned for me, then turned to Dean. "Mr. Gallagher?"

Dean nodded, springing up from the chair.

"Come with me," Craig said, leading him inside.

He held the door for me too. Grandpa and I had to go out the back way, so we trailed them down the hall until Craig veered off into a room, then we continued out the back.

"Tess showed up," I said, as soon as the front door shut behind us.

"I heard," he said. "So did her ex-husband." He nodded toward the parking lot. We walked out to where I'd parked my car. I drove us around front and pulled up next to Grandpa's truck, letting the engine idle.

"Something wrong?" I asked.

He shook his head and motioned for me to continue. "You talked to the ex-husband?"

I nodded. "He said they were all excited about the party. He also said that Tess had been coming out here, scoping out a business opportunity with her mother. Hotel or bed-and-breakfast, he said. No other details, at least not that he'd share with me. But get this." I told him about the op-ed and the Randall Renovations notepad I'd seen in Olivia's kitchen.

Grandpa's bushy eyebrows shot up. "Randall Renovations. That's Art Randall's son Cliff's arm of the business. They worked on our house when we did the remodel for the cafe, remember? And Art has been the caretaker for Delia's house all this time."

"I knew I recognized the name," I said, giving myself a figurative head smack. I couldn't believe it hadn't hit me sooner, although I hadn't really been involved in the renovation part of that whole process. Grandpa had mostly handled that since it was his house and he was very cautious about keeping the integrity of it despite the changes we needed, while I focused on the business side of things. Aside from input into the design, I hadn't interacted with the contractors at all. Mostly I tried to keep myself and the cats out of the way, even when the job ran long, as inevitably happens with contractors. "So you think she was going full-on renovate? And trying to keep a low profile because she knew that she'd get pushback because of the historic designation?"

"Quite possibly," Grandpa said. "It seems like the most obvious reason."

"Doesn't seem like it worked," I said thoughtfully. Then I had another, more sobering thought. "Do you think . . .

that has anything to do with her death?" It seemed a wild reach to me, but people have killed for less than houses and property before.

"The only way to know is to do some digging," Grandpa said. "Speaking of which, I think we'll be on our own for that this time."

"Meaning?"

"I think we should be prepared to be kept in the dark on this one," he said. "I have a feeling our help won't be welcomed from official channels."

That surprised me. Mick was all about using us to help him with cases. "Why?"

"Because of the history. And because of who this family is."

It took a moment for me to start putting the pieces together. "You mean because of Delia? And you working on her case back in the day?"

"Partly," he said. "But there's more to it."

"What kind of more?"

But his eyes had gone over my shoulder. I turned to see what he was looking at.

Tess McAllister had just emerged, gripping Piper's hand as she walked. She moved slowly, like she was in a fog. I saw her stumble on the steps, catching herself right before they both went tumbling down them.

Grandpa moved faster than I'd seen him move in a while, jumping out of the car and rushing to her. He had already reached her before I snapped to and followed. He put out a hand to steady her.

"Are you alright?" he asked.

Tess eyed him warily through red-rimmed eyes, tightening her grip on Piper, who looked like she'd been crying too. "Yes. No. Not really." She squinted at him, as if trying to bring him into focus. "Who are you again?"

"Leo Mancini. Former police chief of the island." As I

reached his side, he added, "And my granddaughter Maddie. She's the cat cafe owner. The one you called about the party."

At this bit of info, a flicker of interest crossed Tess's face, but it was brief as the misery of the moment hit her again. "Did you know my mother?" she asked in a choked voice.

Grandpa nodded. "I did. My daughter was her best friend growing up. I'm so sorry for your loss, Tess."

At this, Tess almost crumpled. She started crying in earnest, which made Piper start to cry, and soon the two of them were sobbing uncontrollably. I looked at Grandpa, alarmed. I was a little out of my depth here. But years of dealing with grieving families put him completely at ease. He led her to the bench in front of the building and sat her down. I trailed behind, feeling useless. When Tess finally got it together, she looked up at him again. "I had to go downstairs and . . . identify her." She swallowed. "I still can't believe it. I can't go to the house. They won't let me. I mean, I don't even want to go in anyway. But I don't know where to go," she said through hitching breaths. "They said they'd give me a ride, but I said I'd call someone. But I don't have my phone. It's at the house and I don't know how to get it." Her voice rose to a near-hysterical pitch. "Do you know a hotel? I guess I could ask my friends. They're here for the party—oh God, my friends are here somewhere." She looked around frantically, like they might pop up in front of us.

Grandpa put a reassuring hand on her arm. "Whoa. Easy," he said. "We'll figure it all out. Look, why don't you come stay with us?" he suggested. "Our house is plenty big enough, and the cat cafe will keep Piper occupied."

My head snapped up at his offer. Was he serious? I tried to meet his eyes, but he was focused on Tess. My mind kept returning to Mick's question: Could she have had something to do with her mother's death?

She shook her head uncertainly. "I . . . I couldn't impose like that."

"Nonsense. It's not an imposition. It's the least we can do to help your family right now," Grandpa said firmly. "What do you say?"

Tess still hesitated. "I do need to get my phone and some things—"

"We can take you."

She seemed to be thinking about his offer and finally nodded. "Okay. Thank you. I'm . . . very grateful." Her voice wavered again as a fresh bout of tears hit her.

"Happy to help." Grandpa stood and offered his hand. Before we could make it to the truck, Dean Gallagher burst out of the police station. When he spotted Tess, he veered toward us. He looked shocked and even paler than when he'd first arrived, if that was possible. He must have been told about his ex-mother-in-law's death. And maybe even more troublesome, that his daughter had been home when it happened.

When he reached us, he looked like he wanted to embrace Tess, but she stepped out of his reach, taking Piper with her. He shoved his hands into his pockets instead. "Are you okay?"

"Of course I'm not okay," she snapped. "Would you be?"

He took a step back. "No. Of course not. Do you want me to take Piper while you . . . get things sorted out?"

"No," she said.

Tess's answer reverberated in the silence. I could see Dean turning over in his head how to respond. Finally, he said, "Okay. I'll call you later. But call me if you need anything."

She turned away without acknowledging him.

With one more nod at me and Grandpa, Dean walked toward a rental car parked haphazardly in the front row of parking spots.

She let out a sigh of relief when he'd gone. "Exes," she said with a weak smile.

I had to laugh at that. "I hear you, sister." I turned to Piper. "JJ's waiting for you," I said, pointing to the window of the truck where JJ's head stuck out, watching us closely. "How about we go play with some cats?"

# Chapter 16

The drive back to the McAllister house was a little awkward, partly because we were crammed up against onc another in Grandpa's old pickup truck—I wasn't the only one who needed to go car shopping—but also because none of us really wanted to go back to the scene of the crime. Piper sat in the tiny back seat, which wasn't really a back seat, holding JJ. It was probably breaking some law about how children should ride in a car, but that seemed the least of everyone's problems right now.

I checked my messages and saw that Lucas had called a couple of times and sent me a few messages. He was probably wondering what had happened to me. I sent him a quick message saying I'd be in touch soon and not to worry. I figured he'd hear the news any minute anyhow. Word traveled fast on this island. I could wait until later to tell him about my part in the whole drama.

Tess was silent most of the ride. When she finally spoke, her voice was so low I could barely hear her. "I feel like this is a terrible dream," she said to no one in particular, resting her head against the window. "Like, is this actually real? How could this happen?" Her voice started to wobble again and she squeezed her eyes shut. I could see a tear slip through and slide down her cheek. "My mom said it was safe here. It doesn't feel very safe to me."

I glanced at Grandpa. It seemed odd, given that her own aunt had disappeared under mysterious circumstances, that she would be touting the safety of the island, but what did I know. If she wanted her daughter to move here, she'd be a fool to say otherwise. For the most part it *was* safe, relatively speaking. And who knew what the family narrative around Delia had been?

"Is there anything you can think of that would help us figure this out?" Grandpa asked her gently. "Did anything out of the ordinary happen this morning?"

"No. Everything was normal. I went out for a while. . . . Running," she added.

I clocked that it was the second time she'd mentioned this, as if it wasn't obvious by her attire. Also, running without a phone or anything seemed strange to me. Most people liked to listen to music while exercising. Also, if she wasn't familiar with the island, it was helpful to have a phone or at least a maps app in case you got lost. Or was I just nitpicking now, because of what Mick had said? Of course he had to look at everyone close to Olivia. That didn't mean Tess had done anything.

Still.

"I left my phone. Mom said she'd watch Piper," she continued, trying to keep her voice low so her daughter wouldn't hear. Luckily, Ainsley at the police station had given her a game that had been in the lost-and-found bin and it had headphones. After she'd cleaned them, Piper had been allowed to wear them. She had the headphones on and was busy playing with JJ as well as the game. "I didn't really keep track of how long I was gone. When I came back . . ." She trailed off.

"Did you know about that room your mom was in?" I asked her.

She looked at me. "No. The detective mentioned to me that it was one of those rooms inside a room. My mom never showed it to me. Or mentioned it. I had no concept of it. I was living in New York City. We barely had rooms, let alone secret ones. So I had no idea what he was talking about."

"But you've been out to the island before?" Grandpa confirmed.

"We've been coming out on some weekends for a while now," she said. "My mom was working on the house. I work remotely and I just moved to Florida to be near my parents—that's where my mother lives—lived—full time, and my dad just moved out there. They're divorced," she added. "Anyway, I said I'd come out here and work for a few weeks while she did her thing."

"What kind of work was she doing on the house?" I asked innocently.

Tess hesitated. Since she was basically pressed up against me, I could feel her body tense. But then all the air seemed to deflate out of her as she remembered the current situation. "She told me not to tell people about it, but I guess it doesn't matter anymore. She was thinking of turning it into a bed-and-breakfast. She wasn't ready to tell my grandfather yet. Or anyone in town, for that matter. But she especially wasn't sure how our family would feel, given the history. Her aunt—my great-aunt—used to own the house, but she disappeared a long time ago."

"I remember," Grandpa said. "I worked the case."

Tess's head snapped up. "You did? My mom never wanted to talk about it. I guess it was painful because they were close. But I always wondered. Did they ever close it?"

Grandpa thought about how to answer before responding, "Not officially."

I could tell Tess was waiting for more, but that was all

he said. I turned the conversation back to the house. "Was she renovating?"

Tess nodded. "She's been talking to a contractor. Cliff Randall."

Grandpa had been right about that.

"How far along in the planning were you all?" Grandpa asked.

"I'm not really sure," Tess admitted. "She was running that show. I didn't really want to get involved."

"Did your mom know a lot of people out here?" I asked. "I mean, anyone who remembered her?"

"No! She really did her best to keep her identity low-key. She still used my dad's name for a lot of stuff. That's why I can't even . . . wrap my head around this." Her voice choked with tears again. "She told me living here would be idyllic." She let out a sharp laugh. "That's certainly not the way I would describe how all this turned out."

Grandpa turned into the driveway leading up to the house, edging past the police vehicles blocking it. Tess took a sharp breath as she looked up at it.

I watched her carefully, trying to see if there was any air of acting or fake grief. I had a pretty good BS meter and I wasn't picking anything up. She looked overwhelmed, confused, and scared.

If she was just an innocent daughter, I couldn't imagine what she would be feeling. I couldn't help feeling sorry for her and hoped I wasn't wrong. So even though the last thing I wanted to do was go in this house again, I heard myself ask, "Want me to go in with you?"

She looked at me gratefully. "Please. Thank you."

"I'll stay with Piper," Grandpa said, catching Piper's eye in the rearview mirror and winking at her. She grinned shyly back at him. She was snuggling JJ, squeezing him so tight I worried he might not be able to breathe.

I got out and followed Tess to the door. "She needs to

get her things," I told the two cops stationed outside. Unfortunately, I didn't know either of them.

The bigger one looked reluctant. "I'll have to call in—"

Tess seemed like she was about to start sobbing again. She looked at me helplessly.

"Can't you just have someone come with us?" I asked. "She needs clothes for her and her kid."

"It's fine, Reg," the other one said. "I'll just go with them." He motioned for us to follow him and escorted us upstairs.

Tess didn't take long. She went straight upstairs and into the room she'd been using.

I waited in the hall and tried to take in any details I might have missed before, but nothing new was jumping out at me. I wondered how the killer had gotten in here. Nothing had seemed disturbed on the ground floor of the house. The front door had been open, but not damaged. Olivia might have just not locked it, which was common out here. Some people thought they were immune to bad things just because they were on an island. Then there was the city crowd, who were over-the-top cautious.

Maybe it had been random. Someone could have been tracking people coming off the ferries and targeting those they deemed good targets. There had been some cases of that over the past few years, as the island's summer dwellers got richer and flashier and poor people seemed to get poorer. There had been some instances where people had even come over on the ferry with the intent of finding people to rob, thinking the island was where the elite lived. Maybe someone had staked this place out. Seen Tess leave and thought it might be empty. Still, though, how had they found that one room with Olivia in it, out of all these rooms? There had to be ten rooms on the second floor alone. It just wasn't making sense.

I thought of the cat again. I hadn't seen a glimpse of

him this time and kept waiting for him to reappear in some doorway. I thought of Katrina's retelling of the old Ghost Cat lore—that he signified a threshold of no return and shivered.

Then, with a mental head smack, I realized I could just ask Tess if they had a cat.

When Tess reappeared in the hall, she had a duffel bag and a small suitcase I assumed held her and Piper's stuff in one hand and her phone in the other. She clutched it like a lifeline. "Ready?" she asked.

"Yeah, but one thing. What about the cat?"

She frowned. "What cat?"

I felt a chill skip over my skin, making the hair on my arms stand up. "Your cat. Puck? Piper mentioned him when I found her on the beach. I saw him too, but he . . . got away." I didn't want to tell her he'd led me to her mother's body.

"We don't have a cat," Tess said. "Believe me, I hear about it every day. Piper really wants one, but I've been holding out. Maybe it was a stray. The strays always seem to find Piper. Can we go?"

"Yes. Sure. Sorry." I took Piper's bag from her and we headed back downstairs. No cat. At least not one that Tess had ever seen. Was Katrina right after all?

She breathed a sigh of relief when we'd cleared the door. "What a nightmare. Piper is so upset and she doesn't even realize her grandma is . . ." She swallowed.

I felt a pang of sadness for the little girl. I'd been beside myself when I lost my grandmother, and I was in my thirties. "I'm so sorry," I said again. I didn't know her at all, so the words probably rang hollow, but she seemed to appreciate them.

We put the bag in the car and climbed in. "So you're the cat cafe party person," Tess said to me, finally making the connection back to Grandpa's intro from earlier.

"I am."

"We were really looking forward to that party," Tess said softly. "My friends came out and everything. And Piper's dad, of course. My dad was coming. My mom wanted to run it, naturally. She did a lot of due diligence and you were the top contender, hands down."

"My mom likes to run parties too. No wonder they were friends," I said with a smile. "I am curious, though. Since I think we're the only gig on the island," I said, remembering Olivia's comments to me on the phone, "were you guys looking at bringing someone over from the mainland?"

Tess gave me a blank look. "No. There was another woman who had tried to sell us her services. She called us a few times, even came to the door once. She seemed a little disorganized, though, and she didn't have the truck component. It just didn't have the same flavor as yours."

I shot a look at Grandpa. His ears were perked up too. "Do you know her name?"

Tess shook her head wearily. "I don't remember. My brain is so fried." Her phone started to ring and she snatched it up. "Dad. You heard." She turned to the window, blinking back more tears. "Yes, that would be great," she said, the wobble in her voice growing more pronounced. "No, we have a place to stay. An old family friend of Mom's, actually." Another pause. "Thank you. I love you too."

She disconnected then turned to Piper and lifted her headphones up. "Guess what," she said in a forced excited tone. "Grampy is coming to see us! My dad," she said to me and Grandpa. "He was coming out for the party but he's going to try and come earlier."

Piper clapped. "Grampy! When can we see Grammy?" she asked.

"Soon," Tess murmured, letting the headphones drop back over her daughter's ears. "Really soon."

I wanted to press more about this other cat party planner, but it didn't seem the right time. Tess had rested her head against the window and closed her eyes, and I felt weird badgering her.

She was going to be our houseguest for a couple days, I reasoned. Plenty of time to see what other information I could extract from her.

# Chapter 17

When we returned to the house, Grandpa took Tess and Piper upstairs to get them settled, promising he'd be back shortly to debrief.

Which was good, because I had a whole list of things we needed to discuss. For one thing, he'd been about to tell me why Mick wouldn't want our help on this case. For another, I needed to talk to him about Helen Holloway's op-ed and the bed-and-breakfast plans that seemed to be a poorly kept secret. Third, he hadn't told me what the deal was with Neil Caldwell.

I called Lucas, but he was in an appointment so he couldn't pick up. I killed some time by checking in on the cafe. Adele and Harry were used to just running the show at this point, so they'd barely even noticed my absence, but I still apologized and went to say hello to the cats. I found out that Peaches, one of our longest residents, had an adoption application pending and celebrated by giving her some catnip to play with.

When Grandpa finally texted me that he was done, I hurried back into the house and pounced on him.

"Let's go talk in my office," he said. His office was in the basement, and it was the one place in the house where

Tess couldn't stumble upon our conversation accidentally. On the way, he ducked into the kitchen and grabbed a plate of cookies from the counter. "Seems like they need someone to test them out," he said.

I followed him downstairs, through his game room, and into his office. I pulled the door shut behind us, leaving it cracked so we could hear if anyone came down.

He sat behind his desk and pulled the foil off the cookies, taking one out and examining it. With a shrug, he took a bite, then nodded happily. "Butterscotch chip," he said, waving it at me.

I didn't need to be told twice. I grabbed one and devoured it. I hadn't had anything to eat all day after the quiche this morning—had that just been this morning?—unless you counted a doughnut at the station. Well, and one on the way to the station. But how could you count those? I'd found a dead body. I deserved empty calories.

When we'd each eaten two cookies, I grabbed us bottles of water from his mini fridge and sat back down, feeling the sugar take hold. "When we were last interrupted, you were about to tell me why Mick didn't want us helping," I said.

He nodded. "Yes. It has a bit to do with Delia, like you said."

"But that's not all."

"No. It very much has to do with your mother being friends with Olivia."

"When she was sixteen? Why would that matter?"

"Because your mother was at her house when Olivia's body was found," Grandpa said. "And because not many other people knew she was even here, according to all my sources."

I stared at him, feeling a small pit of dread settle in my stomach. "There's a good reason for that," I said.

"Sure. Only verifiable by you. And you're her daughter."

"So what are you saying, Grandpa?" I put my water bottle down, sloshing some out of the top accidentally.

He automatically dropped a napkin from a stack in his top drawer on the spill so it didn't hit his paperwork. "Why do you think Mick showed up so fast today even though he was off?"

"Because he's the experienced detective?"

"He is. And he should have been called in, but Craig could've started the process. No, the chief called him as soon as he caught wind of your nine-one-one call."

"How do you know that?"

"Because Mick told me."

I'd wondered how Mick had gotten out there so fast. And Katrina had said he'd gotten a call directly from the chief. "When did he tell you?"

"After you left his office. Apparently, the chief was already all over his behind about it as soon as he heard the McAllister name. He's going to be keeping a close eye on this one."

I sat back in my chair. I didn't know why I felt hurt by that. It wasn't like Mick had any obligation to me or to us. He had an official job, after all. But still. We'd been through a lot together. I wasn't expecting it.

"But I don't understand," I said. "These people haven't lived here in forever. What's the big deal with them? Becky mentioned some scholarship they fund at the paper, does that have anything to do with it?"

"The McAllisters funded a lot of things on the island, not just the newspapers," Grandpa said. "They wanted their fingerprints all over everything. They were often the largest donors for the causes that mattered. Historical preservation, the arts, the library, the hospital. Ask your dad. I'm sure he'll recognize the name. They funded a whole wing of the hospital in memory of a relative."

This, I hadn't known. "But they aren't still funding things, right?"

"You'd be surprised," Grandpa said. "Delia and her brother Patrick's parents had deep pockets, and they left money to the establishments on this island they cared about. That didn't change when they moved away."

"So Mick is keeping us out because someone's worried about funding? Are they keeping the police department running too?"

"It's not his fault," Grandpa said. "It's the way it is. He has to keep his job, remember."

"And you're fine with this?" I asked.

"Of course not. It doesn't mean we're not going to be involved. I'm just answering your question, Doll."

"So we are going to get involved, then."

"Of course we are," Grandpa said with a small smile. "We just won't be working as collaboratively."

I nodded. "So that means we're not sharing information either."

"Not until it's time."

I asked the one question that had lingered in my mind despite my best efforts to move past it. "Where is our houseguest on your suspect list?"

"Low," Grandpa said.

I felt the same, so I was relieved to know that Grandpa didn't have reservations about her. "I didn't get the vibe either, but wanted to check," I said.

"I understand it looks suspicious, but I just don't see her as the killer," he said. "Especially with her daughter being there alone and everything. Unless she's a complete sociopath, which is always possible, but I don't think she's that good. Mick will focus on her first, even if it's just to unequivocally clear her. I know they're going for any Ring camera footage from the street first."

"Also, Olivia's bed-and-breakfast plans might have gotten around already." I told him about the op-ed penned by Helen Holloway that Becky had been holding. "If Helen knew, others probably did too. Do you think someone could have been mad enough to do something to her over that?"

"Anything's possible, Doll. We've learned that, haven't we?"

"The Randalls knew," I said. "Do you think one of them told someone? Or multiple someones?"

"I can't see Art gossiping about a client like that. Plus, he's pretty old," Grandpa said, a description that made me smile. Some might see it as irony that Grandpa was calling anyone within a decade of his age *old*, but Grandpa was the only one in his mind who never aged.

"The son, then. Cliff? Would he talk? What about their crew? If other people were working out there, what would stop them from talking about it? Or . . ." I didn't like this thought, but it had to be said. "What if someone on the crew did something to her?" You never knew. They'd done our reno and their people had been nothing but professional, but seasonal workers changed every year. You got one bad apple and mayhem could easily ensue.

"The Randalls are solid. But you're right, seasonal people can be a crapshoot," Grandpa agreed.

"Right," I said. "Cliff might be able to tell us if there was any drama that he was aware of as they were making plans."

"He'll be at the top of the list," Grandpa said. "And I'm also very interested in what Helen Holloway can tell us. She'll be a good starting point for this in any event. She was Delia McAllister's best friend."

He said it so casually I almost missed it and had to do a double take. "Wait. What?" I asked.

"Yep. She was the person who reported Delia missing back then. She never let go of it either. When I became chief, she used to come to my office at least once a month to see if there was any chance we'd keep looking into it. She was desperate to find out what had happened to her friend. Helen didn't agree with the family. She really wanted the police to keep going."

"Did she have any helpful leads?"

"She tried. But like I said, the McAllisters had clout. If they didn't want to pursue it, it wouldn't be pursued. I think Helen had a hard time with the idea that her best friend had just up and left and never contacted her again."

"Just like Mom," I said softly.

"Just like Mom," he agreed. "Helen is definitely invested in that family."

"So, say she got Olivia to not turn it into a bed-and-breakfast. Is it just about leaving it alone as is? From a town perspective, what would be her angle?" I asked.

"You know the house is one of the originals on the island. I imagine Helen had grand ideas about perhaps getting it turned over to the town, since it had been empty so long. I'm sure she could envision turning it into some kind of museum," Grandpa said.

"Would they be able to do that? If the family still owns it?" I asked.

Grandpa shrugged. "I'm not sure of the legal technicalities of all that, or even of how Delia had the house set up in her will—or if she even had one. Also, it could depend on if Delia was declared legally dead. I'll see what I can dig up for property records too."

"I can take Helen," I offered. A plan was forming in my mind. "I have the perfect conversation starter too. Do you know about the Ghost Cat?"

He laughed. "Of course I do. It was a fun story your grandmother and I used to tell you when you were little."

"You told me this story? Why don't I remember?" I could not believe that I hadn't recalled a story about a cat.

"Because you didn't want to hear it," Grandpa said with a shrug.

"I didn't? Why?"

He shook his head. "You used to cry about the cat not having a home when we talked about it walking the island. You were absolutely adamant that someone needed to adopt it immediately, so we stopped talking about it."

I smiled. "That tracks. Katrina mentioned it today. She said it was a fortune teller's cat or something?"

"There are a few stories that circulate," he said. "One is that the cat guards the island by walking the shorelines at night, on the lookout for pirates or other dangers coming from the water. When he sees something dangerous, he goes to the town square and cries."

"Ah, the town crier version," I said, amused.

"Why do you ask?"

I tried to sound casual. "I saw a cat at Delia's house. Katrina didn't. She said it must be the Ghost Cat. Piper saw it too. But neither of us could catch it. And Tess said they don't have a cat, and she hadn't seen one around. But Piper says it's her cat."

Grandpa didn't laugh. He regarded me with those eyes that seemed to see right into my brain, that knew even before I did what I was thinking. "Do *you* think it was the Ghost Cat?"

I loved that I didn't need to ask whether he believed or not. I knew he did. We'd had this conversation once or twice since my grandma had passed away. Both of us wanted to believe that she sent us messages and signs from the other side. It usually felt comforting.

Unless we weren't sure of the intent of said spirit.

"I don't know," I admitted. "I know I saw a cat. Whether it was a ghost or not, I couldn't tell you." I tried to keep my tone light, flippant, but I wasn't feeling either of those things. "Are there other stories? About the cat?"

He regarded me for a moment, as if weighing what to say. "That things happen when people see him," he said finally. "Not necessarily good or bad. Some people have said that after they saw the cat, an auspicious event occurred. But . . . I've also heard people say they've seen him right before someone dies."

I felt a little chilled by that one, but I shook it off. They were just stories, after all. Yet I wondered if I had, indeed, come face-to-face with the island Ghost Cat. And if it was there as a harbinger of Olivia's bad luck. Or was I was seeing it for another, more personal reason? "Well, I thought I'd ask Helen about it. I googled it when Katrina told me and found something she'd written on the Ghost Cat. It might be a way to disarm her and get her talking about the McAllisters."

"Good thinking," Grandpa agreed.

"I'll go see her first thing tomorrow," I said. "One more question for now. What's the deal with Neil Caldwell?"

"Ah." Grandpa nodded, a steely look coming into his eyes. "Been around a long time, as you know. Always been a politicker. Knows how to stay in good with the town leaders. His contracts depend on it. The other case I'm working? The one keeping your sister busy?"

I nodded. My youngest sister had recently decided that she wanted to follow in Grandpa Leo's footsteps and be a PI. A few months back, she'd cooked up this idea that she could be useful to Grandpa and also develop her own skills to follow in his footsteps. So, he was giving her hours to put toward her license. "It's related to him?"

"Yes. The fishermen's union is worried that some of the

new work Neil's firm is funded for is going to hurt the ecosystem. The town is divided over it. Some say yes it might, others stand firmly behind the fact that it will help more than hurt. It's become contentious. I'm doing some legwork for the fishermen who are opposing it. Looking into some of the scientific methods, past outcomes in similar climates, permits, that kind of thing."

"That was on the news today," I said, remembering the segment that had been playing to Olivia's empty kitchen. "Is it weird that he showed up outside the house this morning?"

"That was interesting," Grandpa said. "And not entirely coincidental, I'm certain. He knew Delia well. She worked for him back in the day. She'd left his firm a year or so before she disappeared, but there was a connection. His operation was much smaller back then."

"Worked for him?" All these connections were blowing my mind, although I shouldn't really be surprised. I knew what our island was like. Still . . .

Grandpa nodded. "She was a marine biologist. Very into shoreline conservation. Brilliant woman. She also worked on a lot of the curriculum for the school programs."

That, I hadn't expected. "What was their relationship like? Did she leave on bad terms? Was he ever a suspect in her disappearance?"

Grandpa shook his head slowly. "I don't know why she left. Delia never said a bad word about anyone. Also, she'd been separated from the firm for a while before she disappeared, like I said. I looked at him early on. Didn't find anything that would have made us keep the case open."

"Do you think he knew Olivia?" I asked.

He spread his hands, palms up. "Something else we'll have to find out," he said. "And I have just the excuse to be looking into him, so this works out perfectly. Sam and I are meeting in the morning to go over next steps on that case. We'll work this in. Then I'll probably take a run at the Randalls. See what they can tell me. Once you're done with Helen tomorrow, call me. We can meet for lunch and compare notes."

# Chapter 18

It felt good to have a plan for the next day—to feel like we were doing something and not just waiting for this to play out—but this day wasn't over yet. I was shocked to see that it was just after five o'clock when we came up from Grandpa's office. It felt like I'd been awake for a week. But I still had things to do.

I still had some things I wanted to discuss with Tess, but she was in her room and I didn't want to bother her. I figured she wanted to be left alone, and I didn't really blame her. I would be too. On a personal level, I was craving some time with Lucas. And our dogs, Ollie and Walter, who had gone with him to the salon today. Ollie, our pit bull, had been Lucas's dog originally. He'd just come to live with us last year. And Walter was a foster fail—a puppy who kept us all on our toes. He was more like the household's dog, if I was being honest. Val, for one, was obsessed with him. Although it was probably safe to say we all were. He was a little sweetheart and was just the energy everyone needed in the house. Even Ollie. Thinking about him reminded me that I needed to see them. I also needed to check in on my mom and return her car.

After I fed JJ his dinner and put him back in his harness, we left again.

I drove downtown to the grooming salon, making the short but traffic-heavy drive in unbelievable time for a summer evening. I was hoping Lucas wouldn't be too busy to chat for a few minutes.

When I walked in, Marianne, his manager, was in the front of the shop doing paperwork and keeping an eye on our dogs. I could see Lucas out in the grooming area with a pup. The dogs both scrambled out from under the desk and barreled toward me, almost knocking over a display of dog sweaters in the process.

"Hi, guys! I missed you!" I dropped to the floor and let them climb all over me. By the time they were done, they'd licked every inch of my face and Walter had gotten his paws tangled in my hair a couple of times. I looked like I'd just gone through a particularly rough storm, but I was happy.

"Guess they missed you too," Marianne said with a laugh. "How's it going?"

Clearly, she hadn't heard all the drama. "Fine," I lied. "Does he have a minute?" I inclined my head toward Lucas in the window.

"I'm sure he could use the company. He's been back there all day," she said.

"Thanks. Stay here guys," I told the dogs, and headed back to the grooming area.

Lucas glanced up from his grooming table where he had an excited Labradoodle dancing around, tail wagging a mile a minute as he tried to get my attention. Lucas looked concerned. "I was about to send out a search party," he said. "What's going on? Is everything okay?"

I gave him a kiss and went over to pet the dog, who covered my face in kisses. JJ eyed the dog, stuck his tail up like a middle finger, and proceeded to start his usual sniffing tour of the areas where he knew he could find some treat remnants. "I'm fine. But you will not believe this day," I said. "I'm sorry to worry you—things just got a little out of control." Understatement of the year. "What's your name?" I asked the pup.

"Charlie," Lucas answered helpfully when the dog didn't respond. "And he very much dislikes when his face needs a trim."

"Aww, Charlie. I'm sorry," I said sympathetically, rubbing behind his ears. "I feel the same way." He melted against my fingers, giving me his saddest puppy eyes.

Lucas smiled. "Awesome, keep him occupied. So what happened?" he asked.

I launched into the story yet again, keeping it as high level as possible.

He listened, pausing mid-snip of Charlie's beard when I got to the part about the secret room and the body, his eyes getting bigger and bigger as I relayed the whole tale. When I finally finished, he seemed speechless.

"My God. Someone killed her? And hid her in a secret room?" He'd again stopped the scissors mid-snip, and they hung suspended in the air like a stop-motion action shot.

"She was already in the room. She was killed in there, it seemed like."

"Still. That's . . ." He shook his head. "Are you okay?" I could see he wanted to come hug me, but he couldn't let go of Charlie.

I nodded. "My mom, of course, is not. I feel awful for her."

"That must have been so traumatic. For both of you. I mean, you having to find her . . ." He trailed off, shaking his head. "Who are they looking at? Any suspects?" He resumed snipping the fur around Charlie's chin.

"I don't know," I admitted. "It's such a weird story. She

doesn't really have contacts out here anymore, but she did have some things going on, so it's hard to say. Mick is likely going to keep this one close to the vest. Politics, the chief and all that."

"Who are your suspects?" he asked. "Because I know you and your grandfather. Neither of you will be letting this rest. Tell me I'm wrong."

I went over and hugged him around the waist. "You're not wrong. It's personal, so yeah it will be hard to stay away. We have a few thoughts. Oh, and Grandpa invited Olivia's daughter and granddaughter to stay at our place." I figured if I dropped that in casually, he might not bat an eye. I wasn't going to mention her suspicious departure from the house right before this happened.

"That must be so hard for them," he said. "I can't imagine what they're going through."

"I know." We were both silent for a moment. "I have a potentially weird question for you." At his nod to go on I said, "Have you ever heard of the Ghost Cat legend?"

"Of course," he said immediately. "It's one of the first things Marianne told me about when I got here. Said to keep my eye out in case we saw it around here."

Wow. Even Lucas knew this stuff, and he'd been here for five minutes. I was disappointed in myself. "So have you ever seen it?"

"No."

"I guess that's good," I said. "Katrina said he shows up in doorways at turning points in people's lives. Which is creepy because he might've been at the house today. Outside when we got there and then in the doorway to the room where I found . . . the secret room."

Lucas frowned. "You saw it? Get out!"

He sounded way too excited.

"Him. And I'm not sure," I cautioned. "It could just be

a cat who is really good at hiding." But something told me that wasn't the case.

"I don't remember the doorway part," he said. "I heard he was the lighthouse keeper's daughter's cat back in the 1700s. She vanished without a trace one winter night. They speculated she fell off the top of the lighthouse trying to light the way for her own father. The legend is the cat still waits for her, walking the shoreline, crying for her to come home. That's why you hear the meows in the wind sometimes during winter storms." He smiled. "I love living here."

"Maybe there are multiples," I said.

"Maybe."

Marianne stuck her head in the grooming room. "I'm heading out. The dogs are gated behind the desk. Good to see you, Maddie."

"Thanks, Mari," Lucas said. "See you tomorrow."

I waved to her as she headed out, then turned back to Lucas. "I don't know enough about it to know if I saw a real ghost or not," I said. "I was going to go see the Town Historian tomorrow to see if she can shed some light. She wrote a story about it, I guess."

"Cool. What did Leo say?"

"He knew the legend." I left out the part about how he insisted he'd told me and I'd been too upset about the homeless Ghost Cat to pay attention to the rest of it. "But Helen also might be one of the people who was upset about Olivia's return and what it meant for the house, so I need to talk to her about that. This is my way in."

Charlie, still straining to get away from the clippers and get kisses, let out a plaintive howl just as the front door to the shop banged open, startling all three of us. Even JJ paused in his sniffing of the floor for any overlooked crumb and looked up, ears flattened.

The woman who had entered the shop was youngish—younger than me, at least—with short, pink hair and piercings all the way up both ears, in one eyebrow, and in her nose. She wore denim overalls and a tank top that matched her hair. A backpack with a cat's head—a gray-and-white striped cat—sticking out of it was strapped to her back. For a second I thought it might be the cat I'd seen at the McAllisters, thereby eliminating the Ghost Cat idea, but this cat had way more gray than the other cat. My potential Ghost Cat was more white with gray accents.

She scanned the empty storefront and, when she spotted us, grinned and waved enthusiastically like we were old friends, even though I'd never seen her before in my life. "Hi!" she called. "How are you today?"

I glanced at Lucas, a question. He gave a tiny shrug. "Hi there," he called. "I'll be right with you. Mads, can you hold on to Charlie?"

I nodded and stepped over to the table to keep Charlie from trying to jump off and choking himself with the grooming strap. Lucas went into the main room, leaving the door to the grooming room open. I edged as close as I could to the door while still holding Charlie so I could hear.

"What can I do for you?" he asked.

"I wanted to introduce myself. I'm Hazel Hollis." She reached out for his hand.

"Lucas Davenport," he said, shaking hers.

"This is your shop?" she asked.

Lucas nodded. "Sure is."

"Amazing. Then I've got the right guy." She flashed her toothpaste-commercial smile again. "I've got a pet party business. I wanted to stop by all the pet-related businesses and leave my information in case anyone you run into needs a party with some gorgeous cats!"

My mouth dropped open. A pet party business? This

had to be the woman that both Olivia and Tess had mentioned. I leaned in closer to the half-open door to listen without being too obvious about it.

Lucas must've had the same internal reaction, but he kept it professional. "I see," he said, taking the stack of marketing materials she held out. "What kind of party business?"

Hazel laughed. "I know, it's not something that's super common! I train therapy dogs and cats and as part of their socialization I bring them to parties and people get to spend time with them."

"You train cats?" Lucas asked. I stifled a giggle. Anyone who knew anything about cats knew that they were mostly untrainable. Just ask JJ. They might pretend to be trainable, but ultimately they were simply doing what they wanted to do. If they changed their mind at any point, that was thc cnd of it.

Although JJ was currently very interested in the backpack cat. He was circling Hazel, eyes glued to the face poking out of the bag. Hazel hadn't noticed him yet, or if she had, she wasn't fawning over him, which was a bad sign.

"I actually do," she said proudly. "You know, for as much as you can train cats. Anyway, we go all over both islands to do parties."

"I see," Lucas said, studying the brochure. "How big is your team?"

"Oh, we're pretty lean," Hazel said with a big smile. "Just a few of us. We like to keep it simple. Anyway, I'd love to be part of your referral network!"

"Sure thing," Lucas said with a pleasant smile. "I'll make the information available."

"Great!" Hazel beamed. "Thank you! I'll check back in in a week or so!" With a quick glance in my direction, Hazel turned and left the salon, the cat bouncing around a little inside his pack due to her perky walk.

When the door banged shut behind her and Lucas returned, I was bursting. "Now I know what Olivia and Tess meant about me being their top choice. Until today I didn't know there was another choice. Did you?"

"Nope." He tossed the stack of brochures into the trash. "Don't worry. I only refer one pet party business here."

"I don't mind a little competition, but who is she? I've never seen her before. Have you?"

"No. But hey, that's how I started out, remember? Came to town and tried to figure out how to set up shop."

"Yeah, I suppose. But you were kind of an anomaly," I reminded him. Most of the business owners on the island were island lifers, or families of lifers. Lucas was one of the few exceptions to the long-lived, unspoken Daybreak Island rule—outsiders couldn't really hack the lifestyle out here, where your business ran pretty much round the clock from May to September, then you sat back and twiddled your thumbs the rest of the year.

"Here, grab Charlie," I said.

Lucas obliged. "Hey, good luck to her." He picked up the clippers and returned to Charlie's haircut. "I doubt that anything can compare to a mobile cat cafe with coffee."

"Maybe." I went into the front of the store to get a better view of the street, where Hazel was placing the backpack into a car. I pressed my face against the glass for a better look, my spidey senses suddenly tingling.

The car she was getting into was a lime green Hyundai SUV. Just like the one I'd seen careening down Olivia McAllister's street earlier today, going way too fast. The one I'd noticed despite not having any clue about what had happened just up the road.

"What's up?" Lucas asked, noting my distraction.

Dread settled in my stomach as I watched the car pull away from the curb, cutting off two other cars in the process and promoting a prolonged horn honk. "I think

I saw her car today," I said. "Leaving Olivia McAllister's neighborhood."

"You're kidding," he said. "Do you think she lives near there or something?"

"I don't know," I said, still staring out the window at the space the car had occupied. "But I definitely need to find out."

# Chapter 19

I left the grooming salon a few minutes later still thinking about Hazel Hollis. Lucas and I had made plans to meet for dinner after his last appointment around eight. Which meant that I had a couple of hours to get to Turtle Point to check on my mother, then head home to drop off JJ and meet Lucas. He had to bring the dogs home too, so meeting there made the most sense.

I got back in the car, set JJ in the passenger seat, and sat for a minute, drumming my fingers on the steering wheel, thinking. JJ promptly decided he'd use the time to take a quick nap, and within seconds had curled up and fallen asleep.

I wished I could do the same. But a new item had just found its way onto my to-do list: finding out who this Hazel character was and why she'd been in Olivia's neighborhood this morning. I studied the cheap, trifold brochure I'd fished out of Lucas's trash before I left. It was . . . tacky, to say the least. The front cover announced the name of the business as Happy Paws Party Co.! "Where Pets Make Every Party Purr-fect!"

Big cartoon confetti and clip-art balloons covered the

white space over a slightly pixelated stock photo of an orange tabby wearing a paper crown.

An orange tabby.

I was starting to get annoyed. The bottom announced that the company served Daybreak Island as well as Nantucket. I had to laugh at that. I knew the clientele on Nantucket would laugh her right off the island. They had higher standards out there.

The inside of the brochure wasn't much better. The first part invited me to meet Hazel, complete with a selfie in bad lighting with a cat in a bow tie struggling to escape her viselike grip.

*Hi! I'm Hazel Hollis, founder, trainer, and chief fun officer at Happy Paws Party Co. I have a lifelong passion for animals and events, and I've combined them into a magical experience your guests will never forget!*

Chief fun officer? I snorted. Not to mention, the cat looked traumatized. The rest of it listed out the types of parties she did, including something she called "therapy-adjacent." What the actual heck did that mean? I also noticed a line that said "All animals specially trained by Hazel!" but there were no certifications or credentials listed. Also, a disclaimer suggested that "Available animals may vary based on scheduling, temperament, mood, or unforeseen circumstances."

There was a QR code on the back, but the website it took me to looked like someone had started working on it then abandoned it midway through. It was half done and looked in desperate need of a real web designer.

She definitely didn't have a Bones. Our web designer

(and part-time hacker) was phenomenal. He would be mortified if he saw this.

I tossed the flyer next to JJ with a sigh. I didn't want to be snarky and I definitely could withstand competition—especially competition like her—but this bothered me. If it had just been about competitive cat party planning, that would be one thing, but the fact that I could swear it had been Hazel's car on the road near Olivia's today was a whole other story. If she'd been vying for the business, that made sense.

But the timing was interesting.

I wondered where Olivia had heard about Hazel. I certainly hadn't heard of her yet, and I lived here. Although my track record at keeping up with what was going on around me clearly wasn't great. I needed to press Tess for that information. I hadn't pushed it today but tomorrow would be another story.

I pulled away from the curb and headed toward Turtle Point to drop off my mother's car and make sure she was doing okay. She'd had a rough day.

Unfortunately, it hadn't gotten any easier. When I pulled onto my parents' normally quiet street, my heart plummeted at the sight of a TV van—the same one that had showed up outside of Olivia McAllister's—parked right in front of their house.

Which was dark.

I stopped a few houses back and parked at the curb, assessing the situation. I could see Mila, still wearing the same outfit from earlier, standing outside the van scrolling through an iPad. The same cameraman sat in the back of the van with the door wide open, a handheld camera on his lap, seemingly at the ready. There was a tripod on the sidewalk.

I wondered how long they'd been here. And *why* they were here. If they were trying to get more information on what happened, it would make sense to go to me as the one who found the body. But no reporters had called me. The last thing I'd heard was from Becky, who had been angry about the piece Channel Six already aired. Even *her* reporters hadn't asked me for a statement. I checked my phone to be sure, but nothing. Word must not have gotten out about Tess staying with us either, because that would likely drive the media right to our door.

So why were they at my mother's house? Had Mila already figured out the link between Olivia and my mother and hoped to get an emotional reaction piece?

I called my parents' landline. They were probably the only house out here that still had one, but my dad insisted, given his work. No one answered. I tried Mom's cell, but it went to voice mail.

I was driving her car, so where was she?

I called my dad. He picked up almost immediately. "Maddie. How are you doing, hon?"

"I'm fine, but do you know where Mom is? I came by to drop off her car and she doesn't seem to be home."

"She took an Uber here to get *my* car. She said she needed to go out for a drive and clear her head a bit."

"Okay, well, there's a TV crew out in front of your house. Is that why she left?"

"A TV crew? No, she didn't mention that," my dad said. "Why would there be a TV crew there? Because of what happened today?"

"That's my guess."

"Did you call her phone? Do you need me to come home?"

"She's not answering." I shielded my eyes as a car pulled up behind me, headlights shining straight into my rearview mirror. "Dad, let me call you back." I disconnected, eyes focused behind me as someone got out of the car and started over to the passenger side of my car.

I hit the lock button instinctively but then realized it was Lilah Gilmore peering into my window. Jeez, I was jumpier than I'd realized.

Letting out a sigh of relief, I hit the button to roll down the window a crack. "Hey, Lilah," I said.

"Maddie. I think you should come with me," she said.

I sat up straight. "Why? What's wrong? Is it my mom?"

"Nothing's wrong, but your mother is at my house. She said you would probably come by with the car at some point, so I was keeping an eye out."

I almost laughed. Of course she was keeping an eye out. In addition to living on the next street over from my parents, Lilah Gilmore was the real town busybody. If Helen Holloway's niece thought her aunt held that title, she'd clearly never met Lilah. There wasn't a person Lilah didn't know or a story that she couldn't track down around here. Her status also helped—she and her husband were Daybreak royalty and had friends in every high place you could imagine. Lilah was an even better bet than the newspaper when it came to getting information, although I'd never say those words out loud to Becky.

"Is she okay?" I asked.

"She's fine, but she's getting a lot of media requests about Olivia and wanted to lay low for a while. Why don't you drive on over," she suggested, then turned to head back to her car before I could ask anything else.

With a sigh, I refastened my seat belt and pulled away from the curb. When Lilah beckoned, you went. That's just the way it was. But I was actually thinking that a conversation with Lilah Gilmore could be useful. She knew everyone, after all, and she and the McAllisters had likely run in the same circles back in the day.

Maybe she had some insight into who might have wanted Olivia McAllister out of the picture for good.

# Chapter 20

I drove around the corner and took the next right onto Lilah's street. The houses here were much more grandiose than the ones on my parents' street. Lilah's especially. She liked for people to know they were rich.

Lilah could be snobby, but she'd always been nice to me. Although it was most likely because of her relationship with my grandparents and my dad, as well as her position on the hospital board. But we'd had an experience together last fall that had changed things between us. Let's just say that even the most poised and put together of us have secrets. But I thought she respected me now, which might come in handy when it came to information gathering.

I also had a feeling I was one of the only people allowed to bring a cat into her house. "You should feel honored," I told JJ.

He yawned in the passenger seat. It had been a long day for him too.

I pulled into Lilah's driveway behind her car, which she drove right into the garage. When she got out of the car she motioned for me to follow her through the garage into the house. I scooped up JJ and obeyed. Once

I'd stepped over the threshold, the door whirred down silently behind me. I noticed that the other car in the garage was my dad's.

"I'm so glad I caught you," she said. "I just can't believe those television people." She held the door open as I stepped inside. "Vultures," she added.

"Yes, I'm surprised to see them here," I said.

"I'm not. Right this way, dear." We stepped into a small hallway off the kitchen. She led me past the room and into their living room. My mother was perched on the pristine white sofa, a cup of tea untouched in front of her. She brightened when she saw me. "Maddie! I had a feeling you'd be over."

I went over and gave her a hug. "Where've you been?"

She shrugged. "I took a drive. Then when I returned, well, you saw the TV van. So I came here. Lilah's been lovely, hiding me out until they leave." She reached for JJ and I handed him over. She could use the cuddles.

"What about Dad?" I asked.

"He's going to get a ride home. I offered to pick him up, but he's not sure what time he'll be able to leave."

"Would you like tea, Maddie?" Lilah inquired.

"Sure." I checked my watch. "I can't stay that long. I'm meeting Lucas. But I wanted to make sure you were okay."

"I'm fine. You're sweet to worry, though."

I studied her. Something seemed off, although I wasn't sure what. I mean, aside from what had happened today. She might still be kind of in shock, I rationalized. "Why are the TV people there? You think they're looking for reactions about what happened?"

"I'm sure that's it," she said. "I can't imagine why else."

"Do you think they know you two were friends years ago?" I persisted.

She brushed that off. "I hardly think that's a headline, even out here." She wasn't quite meeting my eyes, though.

Lila reappeared with the tea before I could say anything else. I took it and perched on the edge of a wingback chair that looked like it belonged in a museum. Lilah sat opposite me, in a matching chair. As always, she was impeccable in her tailored linen pants and matching top. Her hair looked like it had just been done (it always did) and, despite the cup of tea in front of her, her lipstick was perfect.

"What a terrible day," she said, her gaze moving from me to my mother. "I'm sorry you both had to experience that."

I nodded. "It was very sad. But at least Tess and Piper are okay." I glanced at my mother. "They're staying with us. Did you hear?"

She sat up, surprise flickering over her face. "I didn't. Your grandfather?"

I nodded. "They didn't know where to go, so . . ." I shrugged. "They're with us."

"I'd love to come see her," my mother said.

"Tomorrow?" I suggested.

She nodded.

"That's lovely," Lilah declared. "I can't imagine what they must be feeling."

"Did you know the McAllisters well?" I asked her.

"Of course we did," she said with a small laugh. "Patrick Senior and Elizabeth had family here that went back generations. We knew them as island founding parents, really. Did you know that one of the earlier generations of the family built our first library?"

I had not known that.

"And Patrick Junior and his wife, Marian, were staples of the community," she went on. "On so many boards and fundraising committees. And of course Delia was involved in many of the same causes." The way she said Delia's name suggested she hadn't had the same status as her brother and parents.

"It's unimaginable that something like this could happen to that family, after what they've already been through," Lilah said. "And to happen in her aunt's house like that . . ." She trailed off, shaking her head sadly. "Such a tragedy." She settled back into her chair. "I do wonder how the family will handle things now. Whether they'll come to the island or simply manage it all from away."

"Manage what, exactly?" I asked.

Lilah gave me a look that suggested the answer should have been obvious. "Everything, dear. The house. Delia's estate. Olivia was very much in charge of all of it. Had been for many years."

My mother shifted slightly on the sofa but didn't say anything.

"After Delia disappeared, so much was left unresolved," Lilah said. "There was perhaps about to be some closure to everything, at least from an estate perspective. And now this happens."

My ears perked up at this. "Closure in what way?"

"Oh, some state preservation grants that would've allowed the town to take over the house if certain conditions were met," Lilah said. "I remember hearing about it from Helen. The house is turning three hundred twenty-five years old this year. That had a lot to do with it. Also, the amount of time it's been empty, regardless of ownership."

"Take over the house," I said thoughtfully. "Like the family wouldn't own it anymore?"

"It was in Delia's name. She was never declared legally dead, so it's effectively been in limbo. I'm not sure of the technicalities related to the family's claims to it but suffice it to say this was a big year for that house."

*A big year indeed*, I thought, trying to tamp down my excitement. Looks like Helen and I would have a lot to discuss tomorrow. "So then, who steps in to manage things with her gone?" I asked.

"Well, I wouldn't know for sure, but I assume her brother, Jason, will have to. He lives in Boston, so he's nearby. I don't think their father, Patrick Junior, is in good health," Lilah added. "But from what I understand, Jason was always . . . hovering at the edges of the family. Never quite gone. Never quite welcome either, but still around."

"Why not?" I asked.

Lilah smiled thinly. "That family has always had control issues. Everyone trying to steer, no one willing to let go. It was obvious with every generation." She took a measured sip of her tea. "Olivia, like her aunt Delia, learned early how to manage situations—and people. Jason, on the other hand, was very rebellious. It didn't serve him well. You must remember that well, Sophie, given your proximity to them," she said to my mother.

My mother murmured something that might have been assent.

"Rebellious how?" I asked Lilah.

"Wrong associations. Questionable money. A tendency to embarrass his father," she said crisply. "He was never quite the caliber the McAllisters preferred to present to the world."

Ah. The black sheep. Most families had one. Our family was an exception, thankfully. Even though I'd left the island for a decade to do my own thing, Val had gotten spectacularly divorced from a very high-profile family, and Sam hadn't found her calling yet, our parents never treated any of us like we were less than. I was grateful for that.

But Jason McAllister didn't sound so lucky. I wondered

if he was truly sketchy, or if it was one of those high society things where anything deviating from a certain path was unacceptable?

My mother still had barely said a word.

"Did you know him?" I asked her.

"Jason? Of course," she said without offering additional information.

"Anyway, it's very unsettling, to think someone's running around hitting people over the head in their own home, though." Lilah pursed her lips, shaking her head at the thought of how uncivilized society had become.

Had Mick even confirmed the cause of death? Unlikely, since the official autopsy hadn't been done yet. I presumed the new coroner, Jeanette, had shared the information with her aunt, who had shared it with her friends.

And that was why keeping a secret out here was very difficult.

Now she focused her hawklike gaze on me. "By the way, how is your new venture? I've heard from my friends at the senior center that the day the cafe visits is the most popular day of the month."

That made me happy. I did love our visits to the town hangouts. JJ and I had often gone to visit the senior center and even the hospital a few times, because JJ was kind of like the mayor. And now with the truck, we were able to do even more of that and include more people. "I'm so glad to hear that," I said. "The business is going well, thanks. Who knew I'd be the traveling cat girl?"

"It is an interesting job," Lilah agreed.

I couldn't tell if that was a compliment or not but figured I'd take it as one anyway.

"And Ellen tells me you're doing some programming with the library. She's delighted to have you. There's a party this weekend, yes?"

"Yes, a party for the kids," I said.

"Well, good." Lilah sat back. "I hope that other girl isn't giving you any trouble. I told Ellen not to encourage that behavior."

"Other girl?" I repeated. "What other girl? And what about Ellen?"

"Oh, that Hazel," Lilah said, with a dismissive wave of her hand. "Talk about family problems. That's Ellen's."

*Hazel*. As in Hollis, the chief fun officer? "Lilah, I'm not sure what you're talking about," I said, trying to put the pieces of what she was saying together.

"Forgive me, dear. I'm probably speaking out of turn." She didn't look abashed at this at all. "Ellen's niece Hazel. Her mother—Ellen's sister—sent her out here in hopes Ellen could rehabilitate her. But she's giving the poor woman a run for her money. Got wind of your business model and decided she could do something similar." Lilah sipped her tea. "I don't think it's going well."

Ellen's *niece*? "Are you talking about the girl with the lime green SUV?" I asked, not sure I was understanding her correctly.

"Yes," Lilah said with a grimace. "Putrid color for a vehicle, if you ask me."

"And she's related to Ellen. And Ellen knows about this business she's trying to start?"

"I don't think she condones it. But I don't think she can really do much about it. The girl runs wild. That's why she's here."

"Lilah. Would Hazel have any reason to have encountered Olivia?" I asked.

Lilah thought about this. "I suppose she could have met her or her family if they went to—"

"The library," I finished. I bet that was it. Olivia had mentioned bringing Piper to the story hours at the library.

"Why do you ask?" Lilah sounded intrigued.

"No reason," I said, getting up. "Thank you for the tea.

I have to run. Mom, I still have your car. You want to drop me off?"

It was my way of giving her an out, but she shook her head. "I'm fine, hon. I'll head home in a bit. Keep it for now. I'll use your dad's."

"We have plenty more to catch up on," Lilah added.

And that was my cue to exit.

# Chapter 21

Once JJ and I were back in the car, I started it but didn't drive away yet. I couldn't wrap my head around what Lilah had told me about Ellen being Hazel's aunt. But also, if that was true and she was staying with Ellen, then there had been no reason for her to be on Olivia McAllister's street this morning. Ellen definitely did not live on that side of town.

Unless she was at Olivia's house. And if she was, why? Olivia hadn't hired her. I suppose she could have been going to someone else's house too, but I doubted it. Too coincidental. And what was her deal, anyway? Lilah had sounded a bit mysterious about it, but had hinted at Hazel being a lot, at least according to Hazel's family.

I needed to ask Ellen. But I needed to do that without offending her. Her family stuff wasn't any of my business, and it would look like I was just worried about my own interests if I expressed concern about her niece trying to do cat parties. But if there was any connection between Hazel and Olivia, I needed to figure that out. But I probably needed to sleep on that one.

I left Lilah's and drove down my parents' street to see if the TV crew was still there. It was. Ugh. Since I didn't want another repeat of this morning's conversation, I called Becky in a preemptive strike.

"Got something?" she greeted me.

"I can see your point about Mila Daindridge," I said.

"What'd she do?"

"She's parked in front of my parents' house with her camera guy."

"What?" Becky nearly screeched. "Why?"

I could picture her on the other end of the phone, her blond curls up in a ponytail with a pen tucked into it. "No idea. I'm assuming they found out my mother and Olivia were close back in the day, although that seems weak. There are other connections—like Helen—you'd think they'd be more interested in, if they knew anything."

"Yeah, well, they don't probably know anything," Becky said. "We're looking into the bed-and-breakfast angle right now."

"Also, Olivia's daughter is staying with us. That might be useful to you later."

"Staying with you? Why?"

"Grandpa felt bad for them. She didn't obviously want to go back to the house even once they're finished with it."

"Well, I hope she's not the murderer," Becky said.

That was Becky. No filter. "Why would you think she is? And say it out loud knowing she's staying with us?"

"It's always the family. Unless Olivia's ex got there under the radar and did it. That's always a possibility too. Will she talk to me?"

"I don't know. Probably too soon, but I can poke around," I said. "Have you gotten any updates from the police?"

"Nada."

"Do you actually know anything about the family?"

"Other than one member disappeared forty years ago and another one just got murdered?"

"Yeah. Other than those things."

"Big-time island family, lots of money, lots of clout. Their name still has lawyers swarming. When the news broke today, we immediately got lots of questions from the legal department."

"Did you get any clarity about why they pulled up stakes and took off after Delia disappeared?"

"I didn't," Becky said. "From what I understand though, the family tragedy was too much for them to stick around."

"Even with their family being so entrenched here?"

"Who knows why people react in certain ways after tragedies," Becky said. "They probably didn't want to be around to read the stories and hear the speculation on every anniversary."

"Did you guys still cover it?" I asked.

"We do a story every ten years at this point."

"So why do you think Mila and her people were at my mother's? That's bugging me."

"Your mom was there this morning," Becky pointed out.

"So was I. I found her body, not my mother," I said.

"Still. If they caught wind that her old friend was there, that would be a quote they'd want to pursue. Or it could be they're looking for a reaction from an old friend if they can't get ahold of the actual family. Which we can't."

That made sense. "There's something else I didn't get to mention before. Do you know about the Ghost Cat legend?"

"Of course I do. That's one of the best legends we have out here. I think we did a story about it a couple of Halloweens ago. Why? Did you see it?"

"Can you send me the story?" I asked.

"Oh my God. You totally saw it! I've never met anyone who's seen it."

"I don't know. I may have." I filled her in on that part of the story.

"That's wild. Let me look it up."

I heard her tapping on some keys and muttering to herself. After a minute she exclaimed, "Found it! I'll email it, but here are the highlights. Shows up in doorways, on stair landings, or even curled up on someone's bed the night before something changes or something happens. People have felt it brush against their leg right before they discovered something awful. Can hear it purring . . . Is this for real? Wait, here's a direct quote they got from somewhere. 'The folklore says that if the cat crosses the threshold in front of you, something or someone is about to be lost.'"

The threshold/doorway thing again. That, at least, was consistent with some of the other stuff I'd heard today. "Does the story say it hangs out in specific places?" I asked.

Silence as Becky skimmed the rest. "No," she said. "I always got the sense it covers the entire island. It can show up anywhere."

"I'm going to see Helen tomorrow. I'll ask her."

"Maybe we should do another story on it. Especially if it's connected." I could hear the wheels turning in her head as she planned her editorial calendar for murder follow-ups. "I also want to do a story on these secret rooms. I'm going to have my reporter dig on what other houses might have them, and I want to hear all about this one when you get a chance. Sorry," she added. "I know it's soon. But I have to be thinking ahead on this stuff."

I kind of never wanted to talk about that room again, but I didn't say that. "No worries. I have to run. I'm meeting Lucas for dinner."

"Call me tomorrow," she said.

"I will. But, hey . . ." I hesitated, then impulsively rushed on. "I just wanted to tell you how grateful I am that we're still friends. And that I moved back so I can see you all the time," I told her. "At least, when you're not working. Which, come to think of it isn't that often after all."

I could hear the smile in her voice when she answered. "I'm glad you're back too," she said. "Even though with you home my reporters and I never get a break."

# Chapter 22

*Friday*

The next morning, I woke after a restless sleep to someone knocking on my bedroom door. I'd nearly fallen asleep out at dinner with Lucas, but as soon as we'd gone to bed I couldn't fall asleep at all. When I did, I'd woken up multiple times, with panicked dreams of being locked in a tiny room.

With a bleary-eyed look at the clock telling me it was five a.m., I sprang out of bed, anticipating something else being wrong, the two dogs jumping up with me. Lucas, for once, was still asleep and didn't stir. Same with JJ.

When I flung open my door I saw Piper standing there holding the stuffed version of JJ that we sold in the cafe.

"Piper. Good morning," I said. "Everything okay?"

She nodded. "Can I go play with the cats?" She reached out to touch Walter's nose as he tried to nudge past me to get to Piper in the hall, tail wagging excitedly.

"Um. Where's your mom?" I rubbed my eyes and tried to focus down the hall. The door to Tess's room was shut.

"She's still asleep," Piper said. "I want to go see Grammy, but Mommy said no. So, I thought I could play with the cats."

I knelt down in front of her. I felt sorry for her, knowing she'd never see her grammy again. And I felt sorry for Tess for having to tell her. Piper's long hair was still tangled from sleep, and she wore pajamas with cats on them. She looked sad. "You absolutely can play with them, but here's the thing." I leaned closer. "They're still sleeping."

Her eyes widened. "I thought cats didn't sleep. My cat doesn't."

"Your cat," I said, suddenly fully awake.

"Puck," she said, sounding exasperated in that way only little kids could, where it was cute instead of annoying. "I told you about him yesterday. I want to go back and get him. Mommy said maybe later."

Well. If I was seeing ghosts, at least I knew Piper was too.

"I see," I said. "Well, Puck is a special cat. Our cats are just regular, and they sleep. That way they'll be able to play later. Can we give them a few more minutes?"

Piper thought about this, then hugged the stuffed JJ closer before she shook her head. "No."

"No?" I repeated.

She shook her head. "No. I'll go sleep with them," she declared.

Now I was perplexed. I wasn't quite sure what to do here. I certainly didn't want to cause a temper tantrum at five in the morning that would wake up the rest of the house. Which, I supposed, was how most kids got their way so often.

I sighed inwardly, making a mental note to tell Grandpa exactly how his generosity was keeping me from sleeping. On the flip side, I'd lost a whole day yesterday, and an early start may not be the worst thing in the world. "Fine," I said, with a last, longing glance at my bed, where Lucas still slept with the pillow over his head, JJ's tail resting on top of it. "Let's go."

The dogs had lost interest at this point and went back to bed. I was on my own. I grabbed a sweatshirt, closed the bedroom door behind me, and followed Piper downstairs, hoping that someone may have already been up and started coffee.

My dreams were, sadly, dashed. Sometimes Ethan was up this early, getting some fresh pastries made before the early rush. Usually, he stopped in here to make coffee, but today he either wasn't up or hadn't had time. I set about putting the coffee on to brew, letting Piper have some cereal straight out of the box while I did so. She was quiet, watching me while she munched on some Cheerios.

It was too early even for Adele to be here, and that was saying something. She usually got here around six. So, I figured I'd put Piper to work. Because we all knew the cats wouldn't be sleeping once they saw they could get some attention.

Once the coffee was brewed and I'd poured myself a giant mug, Piper and I made our way through the living room to the French doors leading to the cafe. All was quiet when I opened the doors. Most of the cats, save for the kittens, were smart enough to still be enjoying their slumber and most of them didn't even bother opening both eyes for us. I resisted a childish *I told you so* to Piper, because really, was I going to go toe-to-toe with a four-year-old?

I pointed her toward the kittens. "Why don't you say good morning to them, then you can help me feed everyone breakfast. Does that sound good?"

Piper agreed, seemingly excited at the prospect. She placed her JJ stuffie carefully on the floor next to her, then opened the kitten cage, resulting in an explosion of orange and gray fur. Squealing in delight, she got down on the floor and let them climb all over her.

I was relieved—aside from her quiet determination to

come play with the cats, she didn't seem to be overly demanding. And I could use the distraction for the babies. We had two kittens right now. Their siblings and momma had all been adopted last week. These two wouldn't last long. I was pretty sure Katrina would be showing up with another batch any moment, so I was highly motivated to help get this bunch out the door.

While Piper occupied them, I started cleaning, hoping Adele would be happy that I'd gotten a jump on things. One never knew with Adele. There was always a fifty-fifty chance she'd be annoyed that things hadn't been done to her standards.

While I scooped litter boxes, I let my mind wander over my plans for the day. First stop, Helen. Hopefully that visit would give me clarity on the Ghost Cat, but also on the bed-and-breakfast drama. And a glance at my calendar reminded me that I was supposed to meet with Ellen today about Saturday's party, which was handy since I needed to figure out how to broach the subject of her niece. Or maybe she'd bring it up herself and save me the awkwardness.

"There you are!"

The voice behind me made me jump, sending the litter I'd just swept into my dustpan into the air. I whipped around to find Tess standing there, shaking her head at her daughter. "You know you aren't supposed to go anywhere without telling me!"

"Sorry, Mommy," Piper said, not sounding sorry at all. "I wanted to see the kitties."

Tess looked like she wanted to say more but didn't have the energy. She turned to me. "I'm sorry. I didn't mean to startle you. I just woke up and she was gone, so . . ."

I dropped my dustpan and stood up, brushing litter off my pajama pants. "No worries. I get it." She was probably extra jumpy, given everything. "She wanted to come down here and I figured we'd let you sleep. I was putting her to work." I smiled.

Tess offered back a faint smile of her own, though she still seemed guarded. Her face was drawn and pale. Even her short, chin-length hair looked like it was tired. "Looks like a hard job. Can I help?" She rubbed her arms through her T-shirt. "I can't really sleep anyway."

I shrugged. Why not? I could use the help, and it would give me a chance to talk to her a bit. "Sure," I said. "Want to do food or litter?"

"I can do food," she said.

"Awesome." I showed her where the cans of Fancy Feast were and the list that Adele had made that detailed what and how much each cat should get. Some were quite picky and only liked the gravy kinds; others preferred pâté. A couple of our cats were on diets, so they got less.

Tess seemed to thrive on having something concrete to focus on, and she threw herself into the task. The three of us were quiet for a bit—Tess and I working, Piper playing with cats—until I figured I didn't want to waste this opportunity to have some alone time with her.

"How are you feeling today?" I asked, then wanted to kick myself immediately. Of course the answer would be *not good*.

She shrugged, the movement jerky. "I'm okay. Trying to figure out next steps. My dad is supposed to come and help me. He was coming for Piper's party anyway. He should be here tonight. He travels a lot—he's a photographer—but he tries to be around, especially given my sorry excuse for a life right now," she explained.

I nodded sympathetically. "You mean your divorce?"

"Yeah. It's been rough. Dean hates being away from Piper, but . . ." She lifted her hands in a *What can you do* gesture. "I couldn't stay in the city anymore, and I hate

Florida. I was thinking about moving out here with my mom. I mentioned the bed-and-breakfast?"

When I nodded, she continued. "She's been kind of obsessed with that idea and she's been trying to convince me I should think about doing it with her. Since I work remotely and can live wherever, I was considering it. Piper likes it here." She glanced at her daughter, still intent on the cats. "My mom was really into the idea of us all being out here, where her family is from. And also spending time with Piper. She didn't get to do that the first few years because we were far away."

I heard the hitch in her voice and looked over to see her furiously swiping at a tear with her sleeve.

"I'm sorry," I said. "That must be rough. All of it, I mean." It sounded downright overwhelming: a divorce, a move, all the upheaval even before this tragedy with her mother happened. I wasn't so sure how well I'd be coping, and in that moment I understood why she'd need to go out for a run and leave her daughter and phone behind.

And then, to come home and discover her mother gone in such a violent fashion. Her alibi might have been loose, but whatever she'd been up to yesterday morning, I couldn't see murdering her own mother as being on that list.

"Yeah. Me too." She looked at me, and I could see the pain in her eyes. "Have you ever . . . lost someone like this?"

I thought about how to answer that. I hadn't lost anyone to a violent murder, but I'd been adjacent to a few victims. Still, it wasn't the same as being close to a victim like that. "No," I said. "I can't even imagine what you're feeling right now. And I know the police out here won't stop until they figure it out. It won't bring her back, but maybe it will help."

She nodded, swiping furiously at the tears. "I shouldn't have gone out," she said miserably.

"Do you run every day?" I asked.

She laughed at that. "No. I don't even like running that much. I just needed to try something new to get me out of my head."

"What route do you do?" I asked, hoping I was giving off the vibe that I was a runner too, just comparing routes.

"Just down the street, and through the little park that looks out over the water?" She searched my face for recognition. When I nodded, she went on, encouraged. "Sometimes I sit and feed the ducks in the little pond," she said. "I know I'm supposed to be running, but it's nice to have some time to myself." Then she shook her head, her eyes rapidly filling with tears. "My daughter could have been in danger," she whispered. "I feel awful."

I put a hand on her arm. She tensed but didn't pull away. "You can't think like that," I told her. "If you'd stayed . . . well, you have no idea what could've happened." I moved closer to her so I could speak in a lower voice. "Tess. Do you have any idea who might have wanted to hurt your mother?"

Tess's hands stilled. She didn't look at me, just kept methodically moving the food bowls around in some kind of order that only made sense to her. "I don't," she said. "I don't even know who all she still knew out here. She didn't mention anyone. The only one she ever spends time with is Cliff Randall, talking about renovations. She's been fixated on that."

"Did anyone else know about that?" I asked. "I know she was trying to keep it quiet, but these things have a way of getting around out here. Anyone upset that you knew of?"

"Not that she told me," Tess said. "But I really don't know. I keep thinking maybe it was a home invasion, you know? I would read about those kinds of things all the time near where I used to live. Especially in the rich neighborhoods. But this whole island is rich, isn't it?" She cast a hand in a wide arc. "So even that doesn't really make sense."

It didn't. I agreed with her. But I didn't want to point out the alternative to a stranger being responsible.

"You and your mom both mentioned the other company that wanted to host the cat party," I said. "A woman named Hazel?"

Tess snapped her fingers. "That's it! I couldn't remember. Yeah, she was weird. Very persistent."

"Was she by any chance out at your house yesterday?" I asked.

"Yesterday? Like . . . before everything? No. I mean, we told her no last week. She wouldn't have any reason to be."

*Yet she was*, I thought. "It sounds like your mom was juggling a lot," I said. "The house, the renovations, the future. I'm surprised she was doing all that on her own. Was there anyone else in the family involved at all? I thought she had a brother who lived nearby."

Her head snapped up, blue eyes flinty when they finally met mine. Her jaw was set as she regarded me. "No. Definitely not. My uncle Jason would be the last person she'd want helping her with any of this. I don't even know the last time I saw him. It's . . . been a long time. Anyway, I better give the cats their food. They look like they're getting restless." She nodded at the cats, squeezing past me to do her job.

Tess kept her distance while she finished her chore. That was fine with me. I was clocking the things that had raised more questions than answers: Hazel, Tess's run, and the uncle she clearly didn't want to talk about.

Hazel shouldn't have been out there, but I'd seen her car. So, what had she been doing?

As for Tess, I still didn't think she had anything to do with hurting her mother. My radar for that was definitely not pinging. However, she had told me that for her run she'd gone to the park down the street. That was fine. There was a park down the street. She'd also told me that she stopped to feed the ducks in the pond there.

But I knew there wasn't a pond in that park. Was she simply misremembering, or was she trying to be so convincing that she'd overdone it?

I knew we weren't exactly sharing information with Mick right now, but I needed to pass this along. Just to be safe.

# Chapter 23

Adele showed up at six on the dot and looked mildly put out when I told her we'd already finished the morning chores. That was Adele—very much a do-it-herself-to-make-sure-it's-done-right gal. I wasn't worried about that. What concerned me was how she'd handle having a little kid in the mix for an undefined stretch of time.

Despite years of driving a school bus, Adele wasn't a fan of kids in the cat cafe, and she was especially protective of "her" cats. I pulled her aside and gave her a quick rundown of the previous day and the fact that Piper and Tess were staying with us. She hmphed, muttered that the kid better behave around the cats, and I knew she'd be watching her like a hawk.

When Harry arrived around seven—never as early a bird as Adele—I felt better about leaving everyone together and starting my own day. Except for this morning: Harry had questions. He'd already heard the story, and once a cop, always a cop.

Adele, on the other hand, hadn't asked a single thing. The island drama didn't interest her in the slightest. All she cared about was that the cats weren't affected.

I appreciated her.

I went to wake up Lucas with some coffee, but he was already up and dressed.

"Marianne had a family thing this morning so I have to cover an earlier appointment than I thought," he explained. "I'm going to leave the dogs here today."

"Perfect," I said. "I have a feeling our guests might like to play with them."

I kissed him and went to shower. While I washed my hair, I went over five different approaches on how to ask Ellen about Hazel and then decided I hated every one of them. My phone rang just as I finished throwing my hair up in a ponytail. I grabbed it.

Speaking of Ellen. Shoot, was I late?

"Hi! I'm on my way," I said when I answered. "Leaving right now."

"That's why I'm calling, honey. We're actually outside the cafe. I thought we'd come to you."

"You did?" Ellen had specifically asked to meet at the library so we could talk through the usual logistics—parking, safe access for the kids, anything we'd be doing inside the library.

"Yes! I needed to get out today. Also, I can't resist Ethan's pumpkin mocha muffins and I saw they were on the menu."

I laughed. "Smart woman." Come to think of it, I could use a pumpkin mocha muffin. I hadn't even realized he was making those today. "Why don't I meet you over at the counter, then? We can get muffins and do our planning there."

"That sounds perfect, although it's full." She sounded worried. "We might not get a table."

"Not to worry. I have connections," I said.

I stashed my phone back in my pocket. I had a gut feeling that Ellen didn't want me around the library because she was trying to keep Hazel off my radar. But she wouldn't be able to do that tomorrow—unless she kept Hazel away or canceled the party.

Before I went downstairs, I called Mick. His phone went right to voice mail. Annoyed, I texted him: *Something's off about Tess's run. She told me her route but fudged the details. Thought you should know.*

I hit send and waited a few seconds. No dots appeared. I tried to shake off my annoyance and go about my business.

When I reached the cafe, I brightened when I saw Ellen wasn't alone. She'd brought her beau—one of my favorite people of all time. Leopard Man was in full regalia today, tail included. He usually made sure he was all decked out whenever he came to the cafe. Some people thought he did it to be funny, or to entertain the out-of-town guests, but I think it really was his way of communing with the cats. Leopard Man really, really loved cats. He was a primary reason that we had this place to begin with.

Leopard Man—real name Carl, though we never talked about that—was the island's quirkiest character. He dressed in leopard print from head to toe, every day, hat to boots (and yes, a tail for special occasions) and spoke mainly in Shakespeare verses. For the longest time, going back to when I was a kid until recently, no one knew anything about him, including where he lived. Or even if he had a place to live. People assumed he was crazy, homeless, or a myriad of other things. In reality, he was just a guy with a story. Kind of like all of us.

And now that he was with Ellen, he lived a more mainstream life. Like, in a house instead of the refurbished horse trailer he used to move around the island every few days.

"Hey there," I said, going over to give him a hug.

"Maddie," he said, returning the squeeze. "I count myself in nothing else so happy as in a soul remembering my good friends. Or in this case, visiting them. It's been too long."

"Richard II," I said, snapping my fingers.

"Very good!" he said approvingly.

"And yes, it's been too long. What have you two been up to?"

Leopard Man shrugged. "Ellen has been somewhat occupied lately. Family business," he said.

So I'd heard. "I hope everything's okay."

He tilted his head, suggesting he didn't know if it was okay. "Shall we go in? She spotted a table and went to grab it. I think she felt odd about you kicking someone out."

I laughed. "I wouldn't do that. It would be bad for business." I followed him inside. Ellen had dropped her stuff on a table near the window and waved from the counter, pointing at the muffins.

I saw Sam was working too. She must be getting an early shift in before heading out to help Grandpa wrangle the fishermen. She'd certainly turned into a little go-getter.

"She's bringing you a muffin," Leopard Man told me, translating Ellen's hand signals.

"She's the best. Next to you." I slid into a seat, waving at Ethan behind the counter.

Today's cafe patrons, most of whom were visitors to the island, looked up, then did a double take when they saw Leopard Man. I'd known him since I was a kid, so the garb wasn't even front and center for me anymore, but I could imagine what went through people's minds when they saw a man wearing head-to-toe leopard gear. Bucket hat, shirt, pants, boots, and tail, all in the same leopard pattern. He even had different-sized coats for spring, fall, and winter that matched. The tail was the biggest conversation starter, though.

"Any new kitties?" he asked, tipping his hat to the people openly staring at him.

"Oh, lots," I said. "You know Katrina. She keeps 'em coming. I think you'll like Oscar. He's a little black kitty with a white patch on his back. He's still feeling shy and sits at the top of a cat tree, just watching everything. He came in a couple of days ago."

"Well, I'll be happy to help him feel right at home," Leopard Man said. "I can't wait." He jumped up to help Ellen with all the coffees and food as she started over to us.

"Hi, Maddie! So sorry to change plans on you. I hope it wasn't too much of a nuisance," she said when she reached the table and deposited the goodies and I jumped up to hug her.

"Not at all. I got a muffin out of the deal, so . . ." I sat back down and reached over to grab one of the muffins. It was still warm. "Bless you," I said, taking a bite.

The three of us did the small-talk thing while we ate, then Leopard Man excused himself to go visit with the cats while we talked about the event.

I turned to Ellen. "So, are we ready for tomorrow?"

"I think so," Ellen said. She didn't look as excited as I'd assumed she would be. She'd been talking about this event for months. Since we were talking about doing regular storytelling events, she wanted to make this one a more educational, hands-on day focused on cats. The kids were going to be able to read to the cats in the truck, and they had Katrina coming in to talk to the older children about cat care and rescue before they got to come into the library and visit with the cats.

I studied her face. She looked drawn. Tired. Dark circles under her eyes accentuated that. That usual spark she had was dimmed. "That doesn't sound convincing," I said. "Everything okay?"

"Yes, of course," she said, attempting to brush whatever her concern was away with a wave of her hand. "We should talk about the kids who will be reading to the cats." As she talked, her hands were busy shredding the napkin she held into a million pieces. "And then we—"

"Ellen," I interrupted. "Tell me about Hazel." I hadn't planned to just jump into it like that, but there was no time for games right now.

She stared at me for a moment, a multitude of emotions crossing her face, then to my dismay she started to cry. "I'm so sorry, Maddie," she said through sniffles, pressing a napkin to her eyes. "I just don't know what else to do with her!"

Alarmed at the tears, I reached over and laid a hand on her arm. "You don't need to be sorry, and please don't cry," I said, a little desperate. "I just heard that she was your niece, and I wanted to see what the story was. She came into Lucas's salon yesterday and left her flyers."

At this, Ellen visibly cringed. She looked like she wanted to crawl under the table. "Again, I am so sorry. I'll speak to her again. And at this point, I think I need to send her home. She's my sister's daughter, you see. And she's been getting into some trouble. Her father pressured her mother to send her out here, get her away from her friends and whatever temptations she had. He thought the island being so isolated would be a good thing. So, my sister just"—she waved her hand—"called and told me she was sending her. Didn't even give me a real chance to say no. My own fault. I never was good with boundaries." She sighed.

"Hang on a second," I said. "I don't want to do anything drastic, and it's not about the parties and the business, actually. But I think she had connected with Olivia, right?"

Ellen nodded, still staring at the empty plate in front of her. "Yes. And that's my fault too. I let her come to the library with me to try to keep her out of trouble. And she met Tess and Piper and heard about the birthday, and next thing I knew, she was telling them she could host a cat party for them."

"But they turned her down," I said.

"I don't really know what happened," Ellen said. "She hasn't been telling me much of anything. But I did get wind of this *business*"—she wrinkled her nose at the word—"and told her to please stop. She refused to listen."

I leaned forward and handed her another napkin. "Listen," I said. "You heard, obviously, what happened to Olivia McAllister."

"Of course. It's a terrible tragedy," Ellen said.

"And you may have heard that my mother and I were out there that morning. Scoping out the property for the party she'd hired us to do."

"I hadn't heard that," she said.

"It's not important. What is important is that I believe I saw Hazel's car coming down the street that morning. When we were heading there, before we found Olivia." I paused, letting that sink in. "Do you know what she might have been doing there, if they'd already told her they weren't using her for the party?"

Ellen's eyes were wide now as she processed what I was saying. "I don't," she said. "I can't imagine she would have any business out there. What . . . what are you saying, Maddie?"

"I'm not saying anything," I assured her. "Just that her car . . . stands out."

"I know. It's terrible, isn't it? She insisted on bringing it out with her. Said it was bad enough she had to get shipped away, but she didn't want to be at my mercy for getting around."

Hazel sounded like a delight. I tried to not dwell on that. "I think it's important to see what she was doing there," I said. "Before someone else—like the police—sees her car on a camera and comes to see her. You know?"

Ellen nodded slowly. "I'll have to think about how to broach the subject," she said. "She's not a terribly easy girl to talk to."

I felt sorry for Ellen. I wondered if maybe having Grandpa talk to Hazel might be a better idea. I asked Ellen as much.

"Oh, that might be!" she exclaimed, clearly relieved that she might not have to do it.

"I think he's planning to come with me tomorrow too. Is she going to be at the library for the party?"

"I'm sure she is. She's obsessed with your cafe. Tried to tell me I didn't need to hire anyone besides her for this, can you imagine?" She shook her head.

"She tried to get you to fire me?" This girl had gumption, that was for sure.

"Don't ever worry, Maddie. Wasn't happening." Ellen spied Leopard Man coming back in the door and started to get up. "I don't want to worry him," she said to me. "He knows it's been difficult." She waved at him, pasting on a smile. She turned to me. "I'll see you tomorrow, honey. And again, I am so very sorry about this."

With a quick kiss on my cheek, she hurried out.

I watched her go, not envious of her position. Families were something, even when you had the best ones.

When you didn't . . .

It made me think of Delia McAllister, and what Lilah had said about her family. Controlling. Everyone wanting to be in charge. I wondered if that had been difficult for a brilliant scientist who may have felt trapped here. Maybe there was something to the rumor that Delia had up and left, just to get away from them.

It was a long shot, maybe, but preferable to being murdered.

# Chapter 24

After my talk with Ellen, I got JJ into his harness and ready to hit the road. I figured bringing him might break the ice with Helen Holloway. JJ always made it easier to start a conversation. As I was getting JJ loaded into the car, Grandpa came out of the house.

"You heading to Helen's?" he asked.

"I am."

"There's some drama up the street. Caldwell." He didn't need to say more. He got in his truck and motioned for me to follow him.

But we didn't get far. As we drove down our street, the traffic came to a dead stop right in front of our friend Damian's restaurant, The Lobstah Shack. Nothing moving in either direction.

We pulled over to the side of the road and parked. "What is going on?" I asked Grandpa when he got out of the truck.

"Caldwell's team is doing some demos to show the townspeople what the project is all about. The fishermen are showing up to protest." He pointed to the green space across from the restaurant. I could see a crowd of people and a big easy-up tent thing. And a big commotion in the street.

I grabbed JJ and we hiked the rest of the way. There was a crowd of fishermen standing in the middle of the road, refusing to let traffic by. A makeshift podium had been set up under the tent. A man stood at the podium, speaking to a crowd that had gathered in front of him. I could see other tables set up with some giant coolers, some emitting a foggy substance into the air. There was a police car with flashing lights pulling in just as we walked up.

The crowd at Damian's was watching too—people sitting outside at the picnic tables, as well as people inside pressed up against the windows watching. The unlucky patrol officer who'd just arrived was trying to talk to the guy who appeared to be the head of the group, but he didn't look like he was getting anywhere. The honks of car horns were turning into a cacophony, coupled with shouts from car windows.

Grandpa headed toward the fishermen.

As I watched, Damian came up next to me. "Better than the movies," he said.

I laughed. "At least there's popcorn at the movies." I nodded to the restaurant. "Looks like people are passing the time by eating," I said.

He nodded. "It's good, but also I may run out of fried clams before dinnertime."

"Well, that's a good problem to have," I said. "And hey, I'm sure you can get more in a pinch. We do live on the ocean."

Fresh-fish jokes were a dime a dozen out here, but he always took them in stride. "Yeah, I have my clam baskets and my rubber boots out back," he returned without missing a beat.

I had to giggle at the image of Damian out in fisherman's gear, scooping up clams from the water behind the restaurant.

"Seriously, do you want something? I don't have popcorn, but I do have fries. And I can tell JJ wants something too." He reached over to scratch behind JJ's ears. JJ was squirming happily at the sight of his friend and food source.

"I do, but I can't," I said. "As soon as this gets moving, I have to go, sadly." I hated missing out on a chance to eat here, but I was happy he was doing so well. He'd turned a takeout shack into something that could be considered gourmet out here, while still retaining the original feel of the place. All of that was great, but what had really endeared me to him was his relationship with Becky. They had become a thing last year, and I don't recall her ever seeming so happy. His continued success out here meant he'd want to stay, which was always a gamble with a transplant. In Damian's case, he was from the Midwest, and some would say they didn't have the constitution to take up residence on an island in the middle of the Atlantic, never mind figure out how to run such a location-specific business at the same time. Yet he'd defied all logic and odds, was killing it, and had found love too.

JJ sniffed happily at Damian's hands, while Damian scratched behind his ears. "I didn't bring anything with me," he told him. "Maybe on your way home your mom will stop."

"I will," I said absently, hoping I remembered. "This is wild." I motioned toward the melee.

"It really is. I should probably know what's going on, but I don't." Despite his partner's line of work, Damian barely read the paper. It seemed to work for them.

"Something about eelgrass restoration," I said, hoping I sounded like I knew what I was talking about.

Damian shrugged. "Okay. Cool."

More police cars were pulling up now. I saw Grandpa talking to one of the fishermen, gesturing around as he did. I couldn't tell if he was trying to get them to move, or what.

"Where are you off to, if you ever get out of here?" Damian asked.

"I'm actually off to hear about the island Ghost Cat," I said.

"The one that hangs around the ferry docks?"

Of course he'd already heard about the Ghost Cat. One version, at least. I really was behind. "I'm not sure," I said. "I've heard a lot of stories about this cat. Maybe we have more than one."

I was only kidding, but Damian's eyebrows lifted. "Ooh, I hadn't thought of that," he said excitedly. "I heard a shipwrecked sailor washed ashore with only his cat. The sailor didn't survive, but the cat did. It became a fixture on the island. When the cat eventually died, locals swore its spirit stayed to protect the community. What have you heard?"

"How much time do you have? There's the one about the lighthouse keeper's daughter's cat, the one about thresholds, the fortune teller's cat." I shrugged. "Maybe there's one for each of his nine lives?"

He laughed out loud at that. "Could be. I just love the idea of a sailor's Ghost Cat roaming the island looking for him. It's such a New England–y take on the ghost widow in the lighthouse."

"Oh, we have those too," I started to say, but before I could continue a siren cut through the chatter around us. More flashing blue lights strobed over the crowd. Two more police cars had pulled up and now a cop with a bullhorn was ordering the fishermen to get off the street. This looked like a full-on protest.

I watched with interest as this new scene unfolded. And then, Neil Caldwell climbed the steps to the stage, nudging the younger speaker out of the way. He wore an official-looking white lab coat, and the same plaid hat he'd been wearing when he showed up at Olivia's house yesterday. He looked relaxed and in charge, despite the drama unfolding in front of him.

The fishermen had raised their voices to be heard over the bullhorn now. "These coves need to be clear for fishing!" one yelled.

Others joined in the catcalling:

"You're trying to destroy our livelihood!"

"You're shutting us out in the middle of the season!"

The crowd of people turned to stare at the fishermen. Some people had already, predictably, whipped out their phones and were recording, no doubt hoping for some kind of altercation to post to their TikTok feeds. In the sea of faces, I saw one I recognized. Two, actually. Piper sat on her father's shoulders. They stood on the outskirts of the crowd. He held on to her legs, draped around his shoulders, and she hugged his neck. In his hand he held her JJ stuffie. He must have come by to take her out for the day and give Tess a break.

Caldwell lifted a hand, his expression calm, practiced. He had that polished, evening-news voice, the one that made it sound like he was explaining something simple to a reasonable audience.

"This project is about cleaner water," he said. "Community science. Education."

He smiled, warm and reassuring. "We respect the fishing community. Completely. But we also have a responsibility to make sure these waters stay healthy. You can't fish what isn't there."

A few people murmured approval.

"That's rich," one of the fishermen shot back. "You collect just enough data to lock us out, then call it conservation."

"And that eelgrass you're so proud of?" another added. "You drag sensors through it all summer, then blame us when it dies."

That got a reaction. A louder murmur rolled through the crowd.

"Save the eelgrass!" someone yelled. It sounded like a kid who wouldn't know eelgrass from an actual eel, but such was life in the days of the quest for viral social media videos.

Caldwell didn't miss a beat. "We already have a monitoring site operating just down the street," he said, gesturing vaguely in the direction of our house and the cove beyond it. "The data coming out of that site has been invaluable. This work is giving us real insight—and it's incredible for the schools. We're training the next generation of marine biologists."

Education again. Definitely a talking point for them. But instead of calming things down, it seemed to pour gasoline on the fire. Half the crowd started chanting again about saving eelgrass. The fishermen answered back, shouting about clean water, closed beds, lost income.

The cops had had enough. So had the traffic. Drivers on both sides of the blocked road doubled down on the honking and shouting. One of the cops joined forces with Grandpa, and finally they got what appeared to be the head guy to cave and the group started to move off the road, at least enough that cars could get by. Luckily, no one in the fishermen crew decided it was worth getting into a physical altercation with the police about.

As phones lowered and attention drifted, the formal presentation quietly wrapped up. Volunteers began directing people toward the demo tables flanking the tent, as if nothing unusual had happened.

Caldwell and his team looked unfazed. Smiling. Professional. Already resetting.

"Well, that was interesting," I said to Damian.

"Yeah, wild," he said. "Maybe they'll be hungry and come on in. I better get back." He squeezed my shoulder and headed back across the street.

I stayed where I was for a moment, watching the fishermen disperse in tight, unhappy knots, the shellfish group slipping seamlessly back into their educational talking points.

Grandpa appeared next to me.

"That was intense," I said.

He inclined his head in agreement, still watching Caldwell.

"What's up?" I asked. "Were you trying to get the fishermen to stop protesting?"

"I was trying to make sure they didn't hurt their own cause," Grandpa said. "I know how this guy works."

"What do you mean?"

Grandpa shifted his weight, hands still in his pockets. "Caldwell doesn't need to win an argument," he said. "He just needs to look reasonable while other people lose their tempers."

I glanced back at the tent. Caldwell was laughing now, one hand on a cooler lid, talking to a small cluster of people like they were old friends.

"He lets them yell," Grandpa continued. "Lets it get messy. Lets the optics do the work for him. By tomorrow morning, the story won't be about closed coves or bad data. It'll be about fishermen blocking traffic."

"That seems . . . calculated," I said.

"It is," Grandpa replied. "And it works."

I thought about the way Caldwell had stepped in—calm, polished, unbothered—like this was exactly how the afternoon had been meant to go.

"You sound like you've seen this before," I said.

Grandpa exhaled slowly. "I have."

"With him?"

"Yes," he said. "Not like this, exactly. But the pattern's familiar."

I waited.

"When Delia disappeared," he said. "I did talk with him."

"I was curious about that," I said. "Why did you talk to him, if she wasn't working there at the time?"

"Small island," he said with a smile. "People usually can't get that far away from each other. It made sense to widen the net beyond her current day-to-day. Especially since she went from a science job to a library job."

"Library?"

Grandpa nodded. "At the time of her disappearance she'd been running the library."

"You're kidding. That seems like a career change."

"It does. And I wondered why."

"And?"

"And Caldwell was cooperative," Grandpa said. "Prepared. Had timelines, project summaries, explanations ready. Everything neat. Professional. She was a great scientist. She left because she'd just wanted a change of pace, he told me. No bad blood, everything was fine."

"And that was that," I said.

"That was that," he agreed. "Since I had nothing to suggest otherwise and we were being told to drop it, there was nothing else to do. That's the thing about someone like Caldwell—he doesn't lie. He just narrows the field until the questions he doesn't want asked fall away."

I looked back at the tent, at the charts and displays and the volunteers resetting like this had all gone according to plan. "And now?"

Grandpa's mouth flattened. "Now I'm watching him

do the same thing again. Different issue. Same playbook."

I felt a little chill at his words. "So, what are you saying?"

Caldwell glanced up then, his gaze sweeping the crowd, over us, before moving on.

Grandpa watched him for a moment longer, then put his arm around my shoulder. "Come on," he said. "We've both got people to see."

As we turned away, I had the uneasy sense that if Caldwell had any answers we needed, he'd been practicing how to keep them just out of reach for a very long time.

# Chapter 25

Grandpa and I agreed to touch base when I was done with Helen and he was done with Art Randall, and we went our separate ways.

Once we got past the cluster of cars around the ferries, traffic opened up. I was almost to the center of town, where the historical society building lived a few doors down from the town hall, when I wondered if I should've called ahead. Did eightysomething-year-olds work regular hours? I had no idea. But we were here now.

Turns out, I didn't need to have worried about Helen working reduced hours. When I approached the door to the small brick building, I saw it was propped open with a doorstop, allowing the sun and ocean breeze to pour into the space. Which desperately needed it, I thought, as I stuck my head inside the dark room, rapping on the open door with my knuckles.

"Hello?" I called. "Ms. Holloway?"

A head topped with hair white as a cotton ball popped up over a stack of books on the desk in the back. I could just see her eyes, accented by oversized cat's-eye-shaped glasses. They reminded me of an alligator's, peering out of the swamp while the rest of its body stayed below the surface.

"Helen, dearie. Can I help you?" she asked pleasantly. Then she noticed JJ in my arms. "Oh! It's JJ!" She popped out from behind the desk and almost ran over to me, reaching for him. "My favorite cat. Hello, handsome," she crooned, almost snatching him out of my arms.

I had to laugh. I wouldn't have bet on Helen recognizing me, but I shouldn't have been surprised about JJ. When he was around, even people I knew pretty well would be so enthralled with him they barely remembered me. I was constantly overshadowed by my own cat.

As it should be, of course.

Now that I was face-to-face with Helen Holloway again, I realized she looked exactly as I remembered her—except I had never registered how tiny she was. I'd be surprised if she was five feet tall. She masked this with her giant Doc Marten combat boots that she wore under a pair of jeans rolled up at the ankles. They probably added a couple of inches to her height. Coupled with her sparkly red top, she looked like she'd be right at home at a protest that had started in the seventies and never ended.

"You know JJ?" I asked.

"Of course I know JJ," she scoffed. "Who on this island doesn't? He visits the senior center with Leo once a week." She pulled her glasses down, letting them fall to her chest where they dangled with a long gold chain. "And you're Leo's granddaughter."

"Yes. Well, one of them. Maddie," I said, holding out my hand.

"I know," she said impatiently. "The prodigal daughter." She looked me over—a bit critically, I thought—then sniffed. "Are you back for good?"

I felt a little defensive at having to answer that but swallowed it down. I needed information from this woman, and if she wanted to give me a hard time for moving away for a while, so be it. "Yes," I said. "Happy to be back."

That seemed to placate her. She smiled, a little more warmly, then said, "Wonderful. I should stop by your cafe some time. Do you have blueberry muffins?"

"Um. Yes, I believe we do," I said, even though I had no idea if that was something Ethan made regularly. I liked the more chocolaty-flavored pastries myself.

"Good," she said. "I don't trust cafes that don't have tried-and-true staples like a good blueberry muffin. People try to get too fancy nowadays with all this new mocha-ginger-chai nonsense."

While that sounded like a terrible combination to me regardless, I didn't argue. But I had to smile thinking of the pumpkin mocha muffin I'd enjoyed with Ellen a few hours earlier.

"Well, yes, you should stop by," I said. "We're open every day."

"Excellent. I'll do that. So, what can I do for you, Maddie James?" She looked at me expectantly.

"I have a historical question for you," I said.

"Well, you're in the right place, then. Come, sit." She turned and led me past the desk she'd been working at to a small corner of the room with two armchairs that looked like they'd come over with the Pilgrims themselves. When I sat tentatively in one of them, a cloud of dust rose up and made my nose itch.

"I wanted to talk to you about the Ghost Cat legend," I said, when she'd settled into her own chair.

A smile lit up her face. I wondered how often people actually still sought her out for information. It had to be lonely sometimes, holding so much history so close to your heart when most people were more concerned with newer, showier things. Like mocha-ginger-chai muffins.

"Our Ghost Cat!" She actually clapped in delight. "Of course, lovey. Stay right here." She sprang up from the chair with more energy than I could usually muster by this point in the day, handed JJ back to me, and scurried over to the big desk.

"I just love talking about this," she said with a glance over her shoulder. "It's one of our most favorite legends, you know. Well, what am I talking about. Of course you know that. You're the cat girl!" She chuckled at the ridiculousness of me not knowing the legend.

I felt my face redden a little bit. "Yeah, about that," I said, hoping I could fake my knowledge based on what I'd learned in the past twenty-four hours. "I know there's a lot of different stories out there, and I'm curious about which one is actually true."

Helen straightened and turned to me with a horrified look on her face. I actually got nervous and looked over my shoulder to see if someone was behind me. "What?" I asked, alarmed.

"There is only one. True. Ghost. Cat. Legend," she said, slamming the large ring she wore on her index finger down against the desk. "And for anyone to say anything else is blasphemous!"

I sat very still in my chair, wondering if it was safe to move. She certainly took her legends seriously. "Right. Sorry," I said. "Didn't mean to offend. That's why I came to you. To make sure I had the right story." I gave her my most earnest smile.

She still regarded me with a bit of suspicion but went back to looking for whatever she was trying to dig out of that pile of dusty books. Not finding what she was looking for there, she straightened, jamming her hands onto her bony hips, and thought, tapping the toe of her oversized boot on the ground. Then she moved to the back of the room to an overstuffed bookshelf that looked like it had no rhyme or reason to it. She scanned a couple of the shelves, then with a triumphant "Aha!" pulled out a thin book and brought it over, waving it above her head. "My analysis of the Ghost Cat was published in this." She handed me the book.

I took it, glancing at the title: *Four-Legged Ghosts of New England—Legends of Paranormal Animal Activity*. This had to be the excerpt I'd found online, but I hadn't realized there was a whole book about ghostly animals. I glanced up at Helen, who waited expectantly for my enthusiasm. "Wow," I said. "I didn't know there were . . . that many ghost animals."

She scoffed at that. "You think human spirits are the only ones walking around?" She clucked her tongue, clearly disappointed in me.

I hadn't actually given much thought to any spirits walking around, human or animal, but I saw her point. "Are there others on the island?"

"Oh, yes, m'dear," she said. "Plenty of ghostly animals, including at least one whose being itself is a legend. That's a water creature. I didn't write that one," she added with a wrinkle of her nose, as if she wished she had.

"A water creature? You mean like the Loch Ness Monster?"

"No," she scoffed. "That's not real."

Well, of course not. How silly of me.

"Our water creature is real. We just don't know exactly what it's called. But we know it's real. Well, some of us do," she amended. "Others are very closed-minded."

I needed to get the conversation back on track. "I'll have to definitely check out the book," I said. "But for today I'm really curious about the cat, specifically. How did you come to . . . research this?"

"How could I not? I'm the historian," she reminded me. "And Puck is part of the history of our island."

"Puck?" I felt a chill race up my spine, like someone's cold fingers had touched my bare skin.

"That's his name. Puckett, but Puck for short."

Piper had called the cat she said was hers Puck too. Was it coincidence? I doubted that very much. They say kids are very in tune with the spirit world. Had Piper heard the legend? Maybe remembered the name and assigned it to the first cat she saw?

Or was the answer more complicated than that?

And now it clicked for me, what I hadn't connected when I first read the story. The midwife. Temperance Puckett. I just hadn't put the two pieces together.

"The story's right in there. Take a look," she said, nodding at the book she'd handed me.

I glanced down at the book, which seemed to be covered in a thin layer of dust. I brushed at it as I opened the book, sneezing as the particles went straight up my nose. So did JJ. He shook his head as if to clear it, then commenced sniffing around.

"Page forty-seven," she said impatiently, jabbing her index finger toward the book.

Jeez. She was bossy for a little old lady. I flipped to the page titled "Puckett, the Promise-Breaker's Cat." The story was about five pages long, but I recognized the handy summary page. It was what I'd found online when I'd first looked it up yesterday.

*Among the many tales handed down through Daybreak Island's history, none endures quite like the story of* ***Puckett****—Puck for short—the white and gray cat who appears when the truth is about to rise to the surface after too long underneath.*

*The earliest accounts date to the early 1700s and the life of* ***Temperance Puckett****, a midwife who served the island when it was little more than a* *scatter of cottages and salt-stained docks. Her small cat followed her everywhere, slipping into homes ahead of her as though announcing her arrival. Islanders called him Puckett's Shadow.*

I skimmed through the section that covered Temperance's run-in with the lying trader, his untimely death, and the ways the cat made himself known, then slowed down to read the conclusion.

*Though stories differ, they agree on one point: Puckett appears when people lie—especially lies that alter another person's fate.*

*Some believe his presence is a warning. Others say he keeps a record of broken promises, half-truths, and outright lies. Some say when he appears, it means the truth is about to come out.*

*The truth is all of these things at once.*

*And the consequences? Well, Puck is not responsible for those. Because death, after all, is simple. But the causes and effects are much more far-reaching.*

I kept my eyes on the page for a moment after I finished reading, even though I could feel Helen's eyes on me, eagerly awaiting my reaction. I wanted to know more—what other instances were attributed to sightings of Puck. My mind raced through the experience I'd had yesterday: the first sighting out by the driveway, the uncanny ability of the cat to turn up in front of me multiple times when I'd never seen it slip by me. Cats were stealth of course, but still.

If this was Puck, and not just some neighborhood stray—since Tess had confirmed they did not have a cat—what was he trying to tell us? Someone was dead, obviously. But what else? How did we know who was lying?

"Well?" Helen finally demanded, clearly unable to wait any longer for my reaction.

"Very enlightening," I said, looking up at her. "I heard a lot of other versions. Might there be multiple cat spirits like this?"

"No," she said adamantly. "None like Puckett. I mean, of course there are other animal spirits, like we just talked about. But *the* island Ghost Cat that delivers us messages? Only him. This"—she jabbed again at the book—"this was the result of data, old writings that were found and salvaged, and companion accounts. I do a lot of research for my work."

I nodded emphatically. "I can tell," I assured her, flipping through the pages behind the summary. I was looking for a picture of Puck, but there wasn't one in this book. I asked Helen.

"Yes, isn't it shameful? They cut all the illustrations and photos out of this book to save printing costs. But I have a drawing in the version I wrote for the local tourism bureau. They have it at the little booth downtown and at the chamber office. I must have a copy somewhere." She returned to her desk to rummage around in search of it.

While she looked, I skimmed the full story, my eyes seeking out words that might give me what I was looking for—although I wasn't sure what that was, exactly.

"I didn't do the drawing myself," Helen said, still talking as she went through stacks of books and papers, although I wasn't sure it was to me. "We got that commissioned by a local artist, but it was based on the research we'd done. Aha!" Her triumphant shout startled me, and I almost dropped the book in my hand.

She came toward me waving a laminated sheet of paper. I could see print on both sides. As I took it from her, my eyes were drawn to the top of the front side. Next to the title, which was the same as the story in the book, was a full-color sketch of a white and gray cat. Medium-haired, with piercing blue eyes.

There was no mistaking it.

The cat in the drawing was the exact cat I'd seen multiple times at Olivia McAllister's house.

# Chapter 26

"What's wrong, dearie?" Helen asked. "You look like you've seen a ghost." With that, she laughed and slapped her own knee, startling JJ, who jumped off my lap—after digging his claws into my bare leg.

She stopped laughing abruptly. "Really, what?"

"This is real?" I asked.

She looked offended. "Of course it's real."

"I think I saw this cat," I said slowly.

A gleam came into her eyes. She pulled her chair so close to mine our knees almost touched when she sat down. "You did? Where? When?"

"At the McAllister house yesterday." I said it deliberately, watching closely for her reaction.

She was good, but I was better at looking for tells. Grandpa Leo's granddaughter and all that. The shock that passed over her face was fast but clear as day before she got control back. "You were out at . . . Delia's house?"

I nodded. "I found her niece's body. You heard about Olivia?" I watched her face closely.

Helen nodded slowly. "I did. Incredibly tragic."

"It was," I said. I pointed at the picture of Puck. "This cat led me to the secret room where her body was."

Helen sat back in her chair, gripping the arms so tightly I could see the skin on her fingers turn a translucent white.

"Helen," I said, waving at her.

Slowly, her focus returned to me. "In a secret room," she said softly.

I nodded. "Hidden behind a bookshelf. The door handle was a book."

"I always thought there were secret rooms in there, but never knew for sure," she murmured.

That surprised me. "You didn't?" I asked.

"No. It was rumored to have them, but Delia never found any of them. Or at least, she never told me if she did."

"You and Delia were friends back in the day," I said.

"We were," she said, her gaze focused just past my shoulder. "Besties, as you kids would say today." She looked sad. "I've missed her every day since the last time I saw her at the market, buying her usual Ritz crackers and peanut butter." Helen shook her head. "All she ate. No idea how she sustained herself on that diet."

"I'm sorry," I said. "Did you stay in touch with her family?"

Helen shook her head. "They didn't really want any reminders," she said, her tone disdainful. "Especially when they thought she just took off to do something as ghastly as live her own life."

"Do you think that's what happened?"

Now Helen's eyes narrowed. "Why do you ask?"

"I'm curious. Given what happened yesterday."

Helen seemed to think that was fair. "No," she said. "I don't."

"What do you think happened?"

"Well, I have my theories, but we don't know, do we? Because no one cared enough to find out," she said.

I thought of Grandpa as a new detective, bound by

politics and pressure he likely hadn't agreed with. "Probably not everyone," I said. "What are your theories?"

She shook her head. "Theories don't matter if no one wants to do the work to prove or disprove them," she said.

She wasn't wrong. "Were you in touch with Olivia? Did you know she had returned?" I asked.

"No. I haven't seen anyone from the family since they left abruptly. Why do you ask?"

"I heard a rumor that Olivia wanted to turn the house into a bed-and-breakfast," I said. "Had you heard that?"

This time, she couldn't quite mask the surprise that I would know this. "I have no idea what you're talking about," Helen said, a little too quickly. "How would I hear that anyway? I just told you I haven't seen her."

I wasn't quite sure how to play this. I didn't want Becky to come under fire for anything, and since the op-ed hadn't been published—plus it didn't specifically say anything about plans for that particular house—I couldn't really mention it. I opted for a more logical tact. "I know you work closely with the town, and since it's a historical property, I figured you'd have heard something—"

"Well, I didn't. But that's not the important thing." She waved the words away. "The important thing is the cat." Now Helen's gaze was intense on mine. "Are you sure you saw him?"

Was she purposely trying to change the subject, or was she that fixated on the cat? Obviously she was lying about the bed-and-breakfast. But why? The question now was how much did she know—and how much had she cared?

She waited for an answer from me about the cat. "I'm sure I saw *a* cat," I said. "I saw it a few times, inside and outside. I . . . I thought it was their cat. It didn't look like a ghost." The words sounded ridiculous even as they left my mouth. Would I know a ghost if I saw one? If it wasn't all shimmery and see-through?

And yet . . . that drawing.

"But you're not sure it was him?" She jabbed a finger with a long red nail at the photo.

"Well no, I'm not sure. I mean, how would I be sure I saw a Ghost Cat? I've never seen one before. But it looked very much like this cat." I thought about how Katrina hadn't seen the cat, even though I'd tried to point it out multiple times. "Does this cat only show itself . . . to certain people? And is that bad?" I didn't love being the only one who could see a ghost, if indeed this cat was a ghost. Because what if it was some kind of bad omen that only I could see? Had the cat been trying to lead me to the body in the house? Or was it trying to warn me about something related to the McAllisters' story overall, like the mystery of Delia? Suddenly I felt cold in this dark, dusty room surrounded by stories of the past.

"Like I wrote in the story. It's not about people. The people who are open to seeing him will see him. No, it's about situations. Lies. Secrets. Especially ones that have remained hidden for far too long." The look on her face was faraway now, and I got the distinct impression she wasn't simply talking to me anymore, but that she was lost somewhere in the past. Thinking about Delia? Or some other secret?

Either way, I'd gotten what I came for: information about the Ghost Cat, and a sense of whether she knew about the bed-and-breakfast. And my overwhelming sense was that she wasn't telling me the truth. I shifted in my chair and reached down to pick up JJ. "This has been very helpful," I said.

She snapped back to the present, then held up the finger with the giant ring. "I have some of the original journal entries by the author who first documented Puck's history here. They've been preserved. Would you like to see?"

Without waiting for an answer, she jumped up again

and went through a doorway behind her desk. JJ watched her go. I wasn't sure if I should get up, so I stayed where I was. It seemed to be the right choice, because she returned a few minutes later with a big book that looked almost like a photo album.

She put it on the table in front of me, then, standing over my shoulder, carefully flipped to a page that was encased in a plastic covering. "This is Clementine Bannon's journal entry after she first saw Puck," she said.

I wondered if I was supposed to know who Clementine Bannon was. Given the reaction to me asking about the cat, I didn't dare inquire. I peered closer at the paper. The ink was so faded it was barely legible, the handwriting flowery and expressive. I saw a sketch of a cat face in the margin and peered more closely. The ink was darker, like the artist had gone over it with multiple strokes. The face was the same as the one on the flyer Helen had handed me, minus the coloring. "It's hard to read," I said.

"Of course it is! It's old. It's gone through multiple reconstructions, since the pages were so deteriorated." She nodded at the book I still held. "That excerpt tells about one of the first sightings, and Clementine was the one who found evidence of Temperance. You know she was one of the earliest researchers of island history," she said, her tone indicating she didn't really think I would know.

I nodded noncommittally.

She traced a hand almost lovingly over the page. "So much history." Then she looked at me, her eyes gleaming with something I couldn't quite put a finger on. "Temperance Puckett lived out on the land near where the McAllister home is."

I stared at her, my heart doing a weird little skip thing in my chest. "She did?"

"Yes. The rumor is that Puck has an even more special connection to that part of town."

I wondered what, exactly, that meant. Did he hang out there more? Was he more in tune with bad or good things happening there? I really did want to know. "Fascinating. I'd love to read the whole story." I held up *Four-Legged Ghosts of New England—Legends of Paranormal Animal Activity*. "May I borrow this?"

She nodded. "You may. On one condition."

I frowned. "Condition?"

"Yes."

Next thing I knew, she had whipped her cell phone out and come to stand behind my chair. She was so short she barely had to stoop for us both to be in the frame. JJ, sensing a photo op, jumped back on my lap.

"Setting the record straight about Puck, our island's most famous Ghost Cat," she said in a news reporter's voice. "I'm here with Maddie James, the island's prodigal daughter . . ."

Then I realized her phone was recording. I tried to move out of the frame, but she clamped a hand on my arm. "Maddie is one of the owners of JJ's House of Purrs. And JJ's here too!" She moved the camera to capture JJ. Ever the professional poser, he stared directly at the camera, tail high. I swore he was preening.

"And I got to explain to Maddie the real story about Puck," Helen went on. "Which was extra meaningful because Maddie experienced a sighting!" She feigned a look of shock and awe for the camera. "Our Puck will see to it that the truth comes out about the island's latest murder. The heiress to the historical McAllister property was killed in . . . That. Very. House. He's already on the case." With one last close-up of our faces, she hit stop and turned to me. "You could've interjected, you know."

"What even was that?" I asked, mortified.

"My TikTok update for today," she said with a shrug. "I'll do a follow-up later about Puck helping solve the crime. Do you have any commentary you want to add?"

"Why would you do that?" I cringed, thinking about who would see it. At least Mick Ellory probably wouldn't. He didn't seem like a big TikTok guy to me.

"I have to make sure I'm counteracting the nonsense from the younger generation, who thinks Puck is a big joke and make up other stories about him." She frowned at me, disapproving. "You don't follow me on TikTok?"

"I . . . don't get on there much," I admitted.

"Well, you better start," she said. "It's the new future of media. And my videos go viral all the time. I'm one of the most popular historian accounts across the country." She puffed out her chest, clearly proud of this accomplishment.

I could not get the vision of Helen in this dusty room, wearing sparkly clothes, surrounded by old books making TikTok videos that were going viral, out of my head. It was kind of funny, for one. And it made me feel like a slacker, for another. I had a plethora of content at my disposal to do the same thing with our cats, and I had taken a completely hands-off approach and handed the job over to one of our volunteers. Who was absolutely doing a good job, but she had limited hours and wasn't around the cats all the time like I was.

Helen was making me rethink my strategy.

"Well, thanks for coming by, dearie. I hadn't done a video yet today, so this was perfect! Make sure you bring that book back in the condition it's in today!" With a wave, she scurried back to her desk, dismissing me.

*In the condition it was in today? Covered in dust?* Shaking my head, I got up and slunk out the door, sneezing a few more times before I got back out into the fresh air.

# Chapter 27

I was glad to get back outside in the sun after my conversation with Helen. I felt slightly off-kilter, like I'd had a drink on an empty stomach. Of course, I hadn't. But I had to admit I'd gotten a little spooked by her story and the picture of the cat.

And I certainly hadn't intended to end up on TikTok. Not like that, anyway.

"I can't believe she did that," I said to JJ as we got back in the car and I got him settled in the front seat next to me.

He squeaked, but I couldn't tell if it was an agreement or an admonishment.

I glanced at the book in my hand, hesitating before putting it in the back seat. I thought about sitting here and reading the story right now but figured I'd do it tonight when I could focus. I wasn't sure what I thought of it all yet, although I appreciated the sentiment of a cat trying to be the voice of truth, regardless of where it led.

I looked at JJ again. I knew he'd seen the cat too. He'd alerted me to it, when it appeared behind me in the doorway to the study where Olivia's body lay in the secret room. I wasn't imagining it. It was moments like this that I wished he could talk.

Instead, I pulled out my phone and opened TikTok. I had to sign in again—it had been that long since I used it. When I got to my account, I shook my head. I had three followers and one video I'd made last year of walking on the beach with JJ. It had gotten over fifty thousand views—proof that cat content was gold.

I searched for Helen's account and laughed out loud at her handle: @HipHistorianHelen. Then I saw she had nearly half a million followers. I had to zoom in on the page to make sure. Yep, it was true.

She'd already posted the video she'd just created. The thumbnail featured the two of us, her face in a wide-eyed, hamming-it-up expression next to my deer-in-the-headlights stare. The caption read: *#DaybreakIsland #GhostCat #Puckett is back on the case with a murder investigation! Follow this page for updates.*

I hit the search icon and did a search for "Puckett." Immediately a thread came up: *#PuckettCheck.* I clicked on one of the videos. A kid who looked like he was barely a teenager was very adamantly saying that he had evidence that Puckett was a collective of white felines, past and present, preparing people for the reality of aliens landing on the island soon. That one had a quarter of a million views, which told me everything I needed to know about TikTok.

Another video was of three giggling girls, doing the whole teen drama thing about seeing Puckett at the cemetery last Halloween. "He's, like, scouring the graves for secrets," one of them declared. One showed a kid saying that Puckett was the original snitch and was trapped in limbo because nothing was worse than being a snitch. Other videos said that Puck showed up in doorbell camera footage, or only in mirrors, or when people were cheating, and on and on.

When I'd had enough of that thread, I did a more general "Daybreak Island Ghost Cat" search and found a bunch of Helen's videos. Then, halfway down that same search, a video caught my eye. The title was intriguing: *Daybreak Island #GhostCatHunting*. But the thumbnail was the clincher: Mermaid Cottage.

When I clicked on the video, it swept the front of the McAllister house, with a man's voice-over telling me that this was the first known sighting of Puckett the famous Daybreak Island Ghost Cat and that he was spending the day on a private ghost hunting tour. At the very end of the clip, the video rested on a woman standing by the gate smiling, but she quickly turned away from the camera when she realized it was recording.

I paused the video and zoomed in. That woman was Tess. No doubt in my mind. Wearing the same running clothes she'd turned up in at the police station yesterday.

I looked at when the video was posted and saw that it had gone up last Saturday. Did that mean it was recorded then, or earlier? Regardless, it put the McAllisters in town last weekend. Did that mean anything? And who was the guy filming this video? His profile was no help. The handle was @GhostIslander985 and seemed to focus on properties and ghostly stories on both islands. But the guy didn't seem to like the camera, because none of the videos showed his face.

I wondered if Tess would tell me if I mentioned it. Given how guarded she was, it seemed unlikely.

I started the car. I was still driving my mom's car—it was nice having a vehicle I could count on actually starting up when I needed it to. I had to check in on her, but first, I needed to regroup with Grandpa and fill him in on the morning's adventures.

I called to make sure he was home before heading that way.

"Doll. I was just about to call you. Where are you?"

"Just leaving the historical society. You?"

"I found Art at the senior center and talked to him. He's pretty out of the loop as far as being hands on, but he said Cliff's been close to the McAllister work. I'm going to head to the office now. Want to join me?"

"You bet," I said.

He recited the address. "Meet me there in ten."

I made it in fifteen. I had to stop and drop JJ off at Lucas's salon. I surveyed the cheerful three-story, mint green house as Grandpa got out of his truck and walked over to meet me.

"This the right place?" I asked.

"It is," he said. "The office is in the basement. This is Art's house."

"And Art's been taking care of Delia's house this whole time?"

"He took care of it before Delia. Patrick McAllister Senior hired him as a landscaper back when they bought the house. Art was just starting out. He was with them for years, and then after . . . everything, the family asked him to take care of the house indefinitely. His son has been working with him, doing the physical labor for the past twenty years or so. Art is still involved, but Cliff is handling mostly everything. He broadened the business to doing renovations when he jumped in full time and says it's been going well."

We crossed the street and walked through a little iron gate onto the walkway. Now I could see a sign that read Randall's Renovations pointed away from the front door to a smaller path that led around the side of the house and to a separate door. The inside door was open, and I could see a man sitting at a computer through the screen.

Grandpa knocked once, then opened the door.

The man stood up, a welcoming smile automatically spreading across his face. "Chief Mancini! How the heck are you?" He went over and clapped Grandpa on the back, pulling him into a hug. "Been a while!"

"Hey, Cliff. Good to see you too," Grandpa said, returning the back clap. "You remember my granddaughter Maddie," he said, waving toward me when he stepped back.

"Hi, Maddie," Cliff said, shooting me a quick smile. He was handsome in a rugged I-spend-a-lot-of-time-outdoors way—brown hair highlighted by the sun, calloused hands, and uneven skin tones that suggested he often forgot sunscreen on key areas. "How's the cat business going?"

I smiled. "It's booming, actually. Let us know if you ever want to have a cat party."

Cliff nodded. "I heard you'd expanded. Congratulations on that. The cat party business seems to be a thing now, huh?" he said, turning to Grandpa with a grin.

"Sure is," Grandpa agreed. "Listen, I wanted to ask you about the McAllister property."

Cliff's smile faded faster than cloud cover rolling in over the island sun. "I . . . I heard what happened out there. My God. On our own island," he said. "Is that what this is about?"

"You were working out there?" Grandpa asked.

Cliff hesitated. "My father has been overseeing the care of that house for—well, too long to even count," he said finally. Which was, I thought, a nonanswer.

Grandpa did too, by his reaction. He just waited expectantly for more, eyes fixed on Cliff. I hid a smile. People still could not be on the receiving end of Grandpa Leo's interrogation face and not cave, even though his years as police chief were solidly in the rearview mirror. Cliff Randall was no exception.

"I was in conversation with the owner about possible next steps for the property," he said finally. "But no, I wasn't actually working out there . . . yet. I mean, we were still planning."

"The owner being . . ." Grandpa prompted.

"Olivia McAllister," he said.

Grandpa nodded. "I see. What was she hoping to do with the property?"

Cliff didn't reply right away. He looked at me, then around the room as if hoping to find some sort of answer materialize in the air. When it didn't, he turned back to Grandpa. "Mind telling me why you're asking?" His tone was friendly, but he was clearly guarded about something. "I mean, it's probably not happening now anyway, right? Now that she's"—he swallowed—"dead."

# Chapter 28

The word hung in the small office over us. Grandpa waited for Cliff to say more.

Cliff shifted from one foot to another, clearly uncomfortable. "Look, it can't matter now. She didn't really want to broadcast it anyway."

"Why don't we sit," Grandpa suggested, motioning to the waiting area that was in the front half of the small, two-room office.

If Cliff was offended at being invited to sit in his own space, he didn't show it. He sank down in one of the armchairs, seemingly still rattled.

Grandpa settled into the other while I perched on the edge of the small sofa.

"I'm here in the capacity of my investigative firm," Grandpa said. "Talking to a few people who knew the family and had been familiar with their return. We know she wanted to turn it into a bed-and-breakfast."

Cliff sighed at that. "Guess you really can't keep anything a secret out here."

"Not usually," Grandpa agreed. "Do you know why she wanted to keep it secret?"

"Ah, jeez. How much time you got?" Cliff asked dryly.

When Grandpa didn't respond, he said, "The family, for one thing. She didn't want word getting around. They're weird about that house."

"Which family members in particular?" Grandpa asked.

"Her dad and brother, mainly," Cliff said. "But that didn't work. Her brother was all over her by her second trip out here. It's like he had the place bugged or something." He shook his head in disdain. "Loser, that one."

I tried to keep the surprise off my face. Her brother had been out here? No one else had mentioned that. And Tess had seemed downright determined to convince me that they were not in contact with her uncle.

"So he knew about her plans," Grandpa said.

"Well, yeah. He showed up one weekend. They had it out. Liv was mad."

Liv. I clocked the nickname. Pretty familiar for a contractor just thinking about plans for a property. I glanced at Grandpa to see if he'd picked up on that too. Of course he had. I could see the glint in his eyes that he always got when some piece clicked into place. "Why was she mad? What happened?"

"Guess he wanted her to sell the place. Something about a statute of limitations being up and they could get rid of it. Make some money. He's kind of a deadbeat. At least from what she said."

"When did he come out to see her?"

Cliff thought. "Probably a month, six weeks ago?"

"You seen him since?" Grandpa asked.

"Nope."

"She mention him since?"

"Not a word."

"So why else did she want to keep it secret?" I asked.

Cliff glanced at me, as if surprised to remember I was still there. Then he looked at Grandpa, as if to see if he should answer. At Grandpa's nod, he turned back to me. "That nosy historian," he said reluctantly.

"Helen Holloway?"

"Yeah. She was like a dog with a bone about that house. Showed up at the door so many times, Liv started pretending she wasn't home. It was so obvious she wanted it for her own sake. Well, the town's," he amended. "Liv couldn't even figure out how she found out about her intent. She hadn't filed for anything yet. There was nothing public. She was using her ex's name when she came out here. But man, that house . . ." He shook his head again. "You ask me, the thing is cursed anyway. Especially after this." He rubbed his hands up and down his arms as if suddenly cold. "'But that was part of the charm,' she said. The mystery of her aunt, the secret rooms, the history, the Ghost Cat. She wanted to capitalize on the legend stuff and open by the fall."

"The fall? That seems ambitious," Grandpa said.

Cliff spread his hands wide. "She had the bones. That's a giant house with a lot of rooms already. And doing it in stages like she wanted would've made it easier. Being ready for the season was more important to Liv."

"She knew about the Ghost Cat?" I asked.

Cliff looked at me like I was crazy. I was getting used to it. "Course she did. She lived here, remember? She's known about it since she was a kid. Told me she even saw it once or twice back then. Who knows if it was true. I never saw it, myself. I did wonder a few times if she was making it up for her granddaughter. But either way, it would be a draw along with the rooms. People love that kind of thing—especially the ones who aren't from the East Coast. Stay at the B&B on the ocean with the Ghost Cat and secret rooms? I mean, that's too easy."

"You seem to have known a lot about her," Grandpa

said, his tone matter-of-fact. "I don't remember people calling her Liv. Had that changed, or was that a special nickname?"

Cliff's gaze went to his lap. I could see the flush rising up his neck. That, I hadn't seen coming. Olivia had a fling with the contractor? Kind of clichéd, if you asked me.

"You were seeing her," Grandpa said. A statement, not a question.

Cliff's smile was forced. "Guilty," he said, holding up his hands in mock surrender. I could see the tan lines on his ring finger accentuating what was no longer there. "My divorce is almost final," he said defensively. "No law about moving on, is there?"

"Course not," Grandpa said. "How long were you seeing her?"

"Four, five months. When she started coming back regularly. Look, are you . . . doing anything with this information? I don't want it getting back to my father. I don't want to hear about his policies about not getting involved with clients."

"So, you kept *this* on the down-low too. Along with the B&B plans," Grandpa said. I noticed he didn't answer Cliff's question.

"Had no choice, really," he said. "Liv preferred that too."

"Did her daughter know?" I asked.

"I don't think so. I mean, she didn't say she told her. Maybe she knew and didn't say anything," Cliff said.

"Lots of secrets," Grandpa observed.

Silence. We all sat there looking at each other. The only sound was the occasional dinging of what I assumed was Cliff's email server receiving mail.

"When was the last time you actually saw her?" Grandpa asked.

Cliff's face fell. "Tuesday. We were having some challenges. With the planning. She was upset with me. And then I had another job in Duck Cove for the next few days. Long hours. I figured I'd let things cool off anyway, and we'd catch up over the weekend. But I . . . never got a chance."

"So you had a fight," Grandpa said.

Cliff's eyes narrowed. "Like I said, a disagreement."

"And you didn't see her Thursday morning."

"No," Cliff said, his voice cool now. "And if you're asking if I killed her, that's a no too."

The two watched each other for a moment.

"My condolences on your loss," Grandpa said. "It was a terrible thing. Anything else you can tell us? Anyone else have a problem with Olivia that she'd mentioned?"

Cliff almost smiled at that. "Liv had a problem with lots of people," he said. "Honestly, she could be difficult. She micromanaged everyone's lives: her kid, her grandkid, her ex, even her daughter's ex. Our company and the work we did," he added. "Why do you think my dad made me take over the account?"

Grandpa thanked him and stood. Cliff followed us out, holding the door as we left. I could feel his eyes on my back until we were around the side of the house.

Once we were back on the sidewalk, Grandpa glanced at me.

"That wasn't the whole story," he said.

"No," I agreed.

We didn't know what parts were missing yet. Only that Olivia McAllister had been quietly setting things in motion, and people—like her own brother and Helen—were mad about it. And Cliff Randall had been closer to it than maybe anyone. And it sounded like he too had experienced the difficult side of Olivia.

For all the talking to people we'd done today, I felt like we knew less than we had even just this morning—except that more people than I'd imagined had a problem with Olivia McAllister.

# Chapter 29

"Debrief over lunch?" Grandpa asked.

"Definitely," I said. "I'm especially curious about why Helen denied seeing Olivia to me."

"So am I," Grandpa agreed.

We started across the street to our cars. I saw Mick first, standing beside my mom's car looking like he was waiting for us.

"Uh-oh," I said, nudging Grandpa, trying and probably failing to be discreet.

"Don't mention what we were doing," Grandpa said quietly as we approached.

Mick regarded us somberly. His eyes were hidden by sunglasses, but he was not smiling. "Time to grab a bite to eat?" he asked.

I let Grandpa take the lead on that one. He thought for a moment, then nodded. "Where to?"

"I heard that new Mexican place in Duck Cove is delicious," Mick said.

Fifteen minutes later, we were sitting in a booth in the back of the restaurant. It was quiet, since it was between lunch and dinner. It was also not lost on me that instead of going to one of the gazillion restaurants literally around the corner from the Randalls', we'd left town.

"What's up?" Grandpa asked once we'd ordered water and Cokes.

Mick took his time responding. When he did, he looked at me. "How come you didn't call me right away to tell me the Ghost Cat has the answer to Olivia's murder?" he asked, deadpan.

I cringed inwardly. That stupid TikTok video had already circulated to the police department? "You didn't tell me you were on TikTok," I responded lightly.

"I'm not. Katrina is. She showed me."

"Traitor," I muttered. "Also, I didn't know you believe in ghosts."

"I don't," Mick said. "Neither does my chief."

I frowned, not following. "Okay. So?"

Mick rubbed the bridge of his nose. He looked exhausted. I wondered if he'd slept at all since yesterday. He certainly hadn't shaved—his five-o'clock shadow looked more like noon-the-next-day shadow. "I do have some good news."

"You do? What?" I asked eagerly.

"Your houseguest didn't kill her mother. Also, that was kind of you to take them in," he said, although the look he shot Grandpa told me I wasn't imagining the hint of sarcasm in his tone.

"That's good. Did you talk to her again? What did you find out?"

"After you sent me that text—thank you by the way—I went back through the footage from the Ring cameras we'd collected. She did indeed leave when she said she did. Although her run was short-lived. She got picked up in a Ford Explorer halfway down the street."

"By whom?" Grandpa asked.

Mick pulled out his notebook. "A guy named Mark

O'Brien. He's a local. Lives in the harbor, works at the school. And has a hobby as a paranormal investigator, according to his social media accounts."

I sat up a little straighter. "That's the guy who shot the video I saw. At the McAllister house. Tess was in it. He was narrating so I couldn't see his face."

Mick nodded. "That's him."

"So she did lie," Grandpa said thoughtfully.

"She sure did. But not so she could kill her mother. Apparently so she could meet her, what, boyfriend? Fling?"

I thought of Dean and wondered if he was why she'd been keeping whoever this guy was on the down-low. Dean certainly seemed like he wouldn't be opposed to giving their marriage another chance. Clearly Tess didn't feel the same way.

"I don't care why. I just care that she did," Mick said. "I don't love when I have to waste time. I'm going to bring them both in just to scare them, but she's officially off my list."

Grandpa nodded carefully. "So who's still on it?"

Mick's eyes held Grandpa's. "I don't know how to say this any other way, so I'm just saying it. The chief is putting pressure on me to narrow the investigation."

"You have real suspects! Great," I said, but Grandpa laid a hand on my arm. I recognized it as a warning to be quiet.

"Narrow it to whom?" he asked.

"To Sophie," Mick said, meeting his gaze without flinching. "And unfortunately, there are . . . opinions that Maddie's story about finding the room because of a Ghost Cat plays into the theory that she covered up what her mother did."

I actually felt lightheaded as I processed his words. Speechless, I looked from him to Grandpa and back. "You can't be serious," I said finally.

"I'm dead serious. Because really, who's going to believe a ghostly cat—not even a real cat—led you to a dead body that was well hidden? Put yourself in our shoes for a minute," he said.

"But—"

"Be quiet, Madalyn," Grandpa said. I could tell without even looking at him that he was furious. I could feel the anger emanating off him like a forcefield. "Do we need a lawyer?" he asked Mick.

The waiter appeared with a tray of drinks and took his time setting them down with a flourish, along with a bowl of chips and salsa. "Are you ready to order?" he asked.

"No," we all said in unison, not even looking at him.

His smile faded and he backed away, muttering something about giving us more time.

Once he'd retreated, Mick said, "You might."

"Thanks for the heads-up," Grandpa said. "Let's go, Maddie."

"Leo. Sit," Mick said as he started to rise.

Grandpa ignored him, prompting me to get up so he could get out of the booth. I hesitated.

"Look. You think I don't know it's BS? Why do you think I'm risking my job here talking to you?" Mick said in a low voice, his tone urgent.

Grandpa paused. I could see him weighing his options. I put a hand on his arm. "Let's hear him out."

"Five minutes," Grandpa said, sitting back down. "And if you think it's BS, the only thing I want to know is what you're doing about it."

I knew that tone, and I knew you didn't want to be on the receiving end of it. I'd only heard it a couple of times in my life, and only when something was impacting his family. I tried to bring a rational tone to the table. "Why would the chief think that?" I asked Mick.

"Because of the history between your mother and Olivia."

"Mick. Isn't that a little obvious that he's just holding a grudge? They were friends as teenagers. I don't see—"

"There's a little more to it than that," Mick said, holding up his hand to stop me.

"Like what?" I demanded.

He didn't respond. "Look. I know the chief has his issues." He looked at Grandpa. "I also know that he ultimately wants to do the right thing. And thirdly, I know that this case is wildly political. He got a call from Patrick McAllister before I could even talk to the guy."

"What did he want?" Grandpa asked.

"He wanted to make sure this wasn't going to 'dredge up what happened with his sister.' That's a direct quote."

Grandpa's laugh was harsh. "So, they're trying to make it about a teenaged friendship gone wrong? And say what, that my daughter has carried a grudge for forty plus years because her friend moved away? That's the most ridiculous thing I've ever heard." He was getting amped again.

"No. The chief was curious about that phone call but the only thing it made him do was exactly that—go back and look at the file on Delia McAllister. What he could find, anyway. There wasn't much, as you probably know, Leo. No, it was a different conversation that got his attention."

"With whom?" Grandpa asked, his voice still dangerously quiet.

"Neil Caldwell." Mick said, eyes fixed on Grandpa.

"What about him?" Grandpa asked.

"He came in late yesterday. Insisted on speaking to the chief, but the chief called me in after he heard what Caldwell had to say. Wanted me to hear it firsthand."

"And what did he say, exactly?"

"He said that he hoped this would put Delia's case to rest also."

Now I was confused. "How?"

Mick finally looked at me. "Because he thinks Olivia and your mother had something to do with it."

A stunned silence settled over the table again as Grandpa and I processed this.

Grandpa looked positively murderous. He half stood, slamming both hands down on the table. "Caldwell. I should have known. And the chief bought into his crap? I'll go over there and tell the two of them—"

"Leo. Listen to me. You can't go off like a bomb here. We both need to tread carefully," Mick said. "It's not just me who's on the line here. If this gets sideways, they'll say you threw the investigation on Delia to protect your kid. It would call your whole career into question. You want that?"

I watched the reality of that settle over Grandpa's face. I knew him well enough to know that he'd do anything for his family, even if it meant a stain on his own career. I also knew that it would kill him.

I turned back to Mick. "Why is he claiming that?"

"Caldwell said he'd seen the girls there at Delia's that last day Delia was seen, and she and Olivia were having a terrible argument."

"That's not true," Grandpa said. "Helen was the last to see her. At the market. The family stated multiple times they hadn't seen her that day. It never changed."

"I read that, yes," Mick said.

"Well, who's to say it's not true? Unless Caldwell was looking for a way to explain away why *he'd* been there," Grandpa said. "If he was afraid someone saw him, perhaps. Why *was* he there, did he say?"

"He said he'd been there because of the beach access. Delia let him use the property to get to the cove, going back to when she worked with him. He said the family had wanted to keep it as quiet as possible—the potential that Olivia could've done it—so they shut everything down. Claimed he wanted to see one of the island's most notorious stories put to rest and said Sophie could help with that."

I was afraid to even look at Grandpa. "How's that?" I asked.

"He said the guilt must've been eating at her all these years." I could hear the disdain in Mick's voice even as he relayed the story, and took comfort in it. "That when she found out Olivia was back, she confronted her to come clean. And when Olivia wouldn't, she killed her. He also pointed out the secret room—and how there weren't many people who knew about it."

I thought about that. "Then how did *he* know about it?"

Mick pointed his index finger at me. "Bingo. I asked as much. He said Delia had shared the features of the house with those in her inner circle."

But she hadn't. Helen Holloway hadn't even been sure—unless she'd lied about that too. I didn't offer that up, though.

"And your chief's response to this?" Grandpa asked.

"He told me to bring her in and talk to her. I wanted you to know."

"So, Caldwell gives him some wild story and he just goes with it to say he closed two cases?" Grandpa shook his head and made a move to get up again.

"I don't think he bought in. He's playing it close to the vest, but I think that's why he wanted me to hear the story. You know the politics. The McAllisters still hold half the town hostage with their money. They donate to council races. The mayor has been around forever, so he's going to be sensitive to it. At least that's what the chief says. And Caldwell is influential in his own way. More than half the town bigwigs are eating out of his hand with this restoration project. He's been here forever, knows everyone. You know how it is. The chief has to play it the right way."

I hoped that was true and he wasn't just trying to get back at Grandpa for some perceived grudge. "You think he tipped off the media too? They were at my mom's last night," I told Mick.

Mick grimaced. "I wouldn't doubt it. But that would explain the calls I keep getting from Mila Daindridge."

"And they were working on that other story together. Her and Caldwell," I said as that piece clicked into place. "That's why Becky had no idea about this. Mila has access and used it to her advantage."

"So, you're bringing her in to question her," Grandpa said to Mick.

"Yeah. I stalled a bit, but I'll have to do that sooner or later."

My phone buzzed in my pocket. I pulled it out under the table. It was my mother. I silenced it and slid it back into my pocket. "You know, there are people who wanted that house pretty badly," I said. "Town people. Like Helen Holloway."

Mick frowned at me. "The eightysomething-year-old historian?"

"Yes." I told him what we'd learned about the bed-and-breakfast, Helen's attempts to contact Olivia and her denial of ever seeing her, and what Cliff Randall had told us about Olivia's brother. Grandpa didn't stop me. "It seems to me you might have a few other people with bigger motives than my mom."

"Including Caldwell," Grandpa said.

We both looked at him. "Caldwell? Why would he kill Olivia?" I asked.

"Well, I told you I talked to him about Delia back then," Grandpa said.

"And you said there was nothing that suggested he did anything."

"Right. There wasn't. That doesn't mean he didn't. It just meant that I never got very far," Grandpa said.

I sat back and let that sink in.

"You suspected him?" Mick asked.

"I had questions for everyone in her circle," Grandpa said.

"I'm wondering if others did too, then," Mick said. "And ultimately if that was what prompted Olivia's return to the island."

"You mean, you think she came back to solve her aunt's case?" I asked.

Mick shrugged. "Maybe. Maybe she thought she found evidence. Or maybe she *did* find evidence. You know what they say about letting sleeping dogs lie."

# Chapter 30

Mick left the restaurant first. None of us had eaten anything. The waiter had been too scared to come back to our table, so Grandpa had thrown a twenty to cover the three sodas we'd ordered. After giving Mick a few minutes head start, we left too.

"Are you okay?" I asked Grandpa.

"I might kill him," Grandpa admitted.

"Who?"

Grandpa thought about that. "Caldwell first. Then the chief."

"Because that wouldn't be bad for your reputation at all," I said. I was feeling a little shaky myself. I was a suspect in covering up a murder? Was this even real? I had to remind myself that I trusted Mick. He, like Grandpa, was the real deal. And he didn't believe it for a second. I had to take comfort in that.

My phone buzzed again. My mother was still calling. Had the chief sent someone else to bring her in, causing a panic? She never called me this many times in a row if I didn't pick up. Or maybe she just needed her car. "Mom's calling."

"Answer it. But don't tell her anything yet."

"Hey, Mom," I said as we got back into the car. We'd left Grandpa's truck parked near Randall's place. "Everything okay?"

I expected her to still be in shock, or maybe depressed. What I wasn't expecting was her hushed, urgent tone and the request she had. "I need you to come to Shady's Tavern. Right now."

I glanced at Grandpa. "Why are you at a biker bar, Mom?"

"I followed Jason McAllister here."

"Why is she following Olivia's brother?" I asked Grandpa as we sped over to the beach where Shady's was located. "And did anyone know he was here?" Mick hadn't mentioned that. And it wasn't like we could call and ask him. We'd all agreed to keep any interaction with Mick completely off the books, to protect both him and Grandpa, as well as the integrity of the investigation.

"No idea," Grandpa said. I could see how tightly his jaw was clenched and hoped this whole drama wasn't going to take a toll on his health.

When we pulled up near the bar, he told me to go in. "Jason may recognize me. I don't want to draw attention. Text me when you know what's going on."

"Okay." I hopped out of the car and hurried to the door. When I pushed it open and entered the dark room, it took my eyes a few moments to adjust. When they did, I immediately spotted my mom at a corner table, trying—and failing—to look inconspicuous. For one thing, she never dressed inconspicuously. Like, ever. Her bright yellow maxi dress stood out against the black leather backdrop of the other patrons. She had jammed a wide-brimmed hat over her unruly curls, and she wore sunglasses. Inside a room that was several degrees darker than the outside. Also, my sister Sam was with her. Also wearing sunglasses reminiscent of Jackie O.

These two needed some spy lessons if that was the look they were going for.

I sighed and made my way over to them. "Do I even want to know what you're doing?"

"Hi!" Sam said. She leaned closer and whispered, "We're investigating."

My mother slid her glasses down. "It's about time! He's over there!" She jabbed a finger toward the bar. I followed it, not sure who I was looking at, but when I scanned the bar, I saw a familiar face. Adam, my nurse, now EMT and friend, was here. I wasn't really surprised. If Damian's was my Cheers, this was his.

"Jason?" I asked.

She let out a very exaggerated sigh. "Yes, Jason. Don't you listen to me at all?" she whispered.

"How did you know he was here? And why are you following him?" I thought of what Cliff Randall had said about Jason gunning for his sister's house.

"I've been following him since last night. Let me tell you the whole story before you comment," she said.

I slid into a seat where I could watch the door and the bar and motioned for my mother to go on.

"I went back to Delia's house last night."

I gaped at her. "You did? When? I thought you stayed at Lilah's?"

"No, I was just waiting for you to leave," she said. "You can be nosy. Anyway, I was going to sneak into the secret room. I wanted to see it again."

"Mom! Do you know how bad that could look?" I had visions of the cops staking out the house, waiting for their killer to return to the scene of the crime—then finding my mom sneaking around. "Were the police there?"

"No," she said. "They'd left the crime scene tape up but took the detail away." She paused. "But when I pulled up, there was already a car there. Parked a little ways away. Someone was still in it, so I waited. And eventually, Jason got out and walked up the street. Went around the back of the house."

"How did you know it was him?" I asked.

"I've known him since I was a kid, Maddie. I recognized him right away."

"After all this time? I thought you hadn't seen him since you were sixteen."

Now, her gaze slid away. "I looked on social media."

"You can find anyone there," Sam chimed in. "By the way, congrats!"

"On what?" I asked.

"You're a TikTok star!" Sam said. "I saw you on Helen's channel. Her follow-up video was great."

I grimaced. "You and the rest of the island, apparently. Show me."

She pulled out her phone, swiped around for a minute, then turned it for me to see.

I stared at the image of my face frozen in some kind of twisted consternation at whatever Helen was saying. Someone had recut the photo into a video playing on a loop with spooky music and captioned it *Cat cafe owner gets the bleep scared out of her by island Ghost Cat after murder! Is she next?*

"Oh for the love of God," I muttered.

"I mean, I hope you're not next. Wait, there's another one." Sam swiped again. This was a still image of me and Helen with a more serious title overlayed: *Ghost Cat holds the secrets to brutal murder.* "They're both going viral," she said matter-of-factly. "It should definitely bring in more cafe business."

At my glare, Sam shrugged. "She's always on, and her videos are good! She's got a lot of followers."

"Super," I said, turning back to my mother. "Please tell me you didn't try to confront him. Did he see you?"

"No. He went in. I waited for a bit to see if he would leave, but he didn't come out. And I didn't want him to get suspicious if he saw a car parked outside."

"What do you think he was doing there?" I asked. "Mom, do you know anything about this guy? Do you think he's dangerous?"

"You mean do I think he killed his sister?"

I shrugged. "Yeah. I guess that's what I mean."

"I can't imagine that, Maddie. I mean, what would be the reason? But I have no idea what he was doing there," she said. "Maybe he just wanted to see the place for himself. I can't imagine what he must be feeling."

"Okay, let me ask you this," I said. "If you don't think he's suspicious at all, why are you following him? Why didn't you just go talk to him?"

Now she looked uncomfortable. "I haven't seen him in a long time," she said. "I'm not really sure why, honestly. I didn't know how he'd react, I guess."

I looked around the bar. "Where is he?"

She pointed again to the corner of the bar where Adam sat. "Right there, in the white T-shirt. Talking to the man with the tattoos."

That gave me pause. Because the man with the tattoos was Adam DeSantis. She was pointing at the guy sitting next to him. Why was Adam talking to Jason McAllister? Did he know who he was? Did he know *him*? Or was this a chance encounter?

Only one way to find out. I stood up. "I'll be right back."

"Maddie—" she began, but I ignored her.

I headed over to them, tapping Adam on the shoulder as I came up behind him. "Hey!" I exclaimed, feigning surprise. "I thought that was you!"

"Maddie!" He gave me a hug. "What are you doing here?"

"My mom and I were in the neighborhood and thought we'd pop in," I said, realizing it would sound weird to Adam. It wasn't the sort of place my mom and I hung out regularly. But I trusted him to not say that in front of Jason.

But he didn't seem to think too much about it. "Excellent," he said, raising his nonalcoholic beer. Adam didn't drink, which made it funnier that he hung out here. But he had a ton of friends who did. He'd been riding motorcycles his whole life.

I glanced at the man my mother said was Jason McAllister, who looked uncomfortable since I'd walked up, swirling brown liquid around in his glass. He was tall, broad-shouldered, with dark hair that curled just enough to look intentional, even when it probably wasn't. His face had strong bones and the kind of mouth that suggested he smiled easily when he wanted to. If I'd passed him on the street without context, I might've seen him as someone who'd aged well. Someone who used to turn heads and still could, under the right lighting.

But here, I could see faint lines around his eyes that hadn't come from laughter, and stubble along his jaw that gave him a perpetually unfinished look. He looked tired. And a little drunk.

"Hi. Maddie James," I said, offering a hand. I took a gamble that he wouldn't connect the name to my mother. Unless he'd been following her life, he'd have no reason to.

"Jason," he said, reluctantly taking it. His was damp. He took his hand back and drained the glass, then stood. "You'll call me later, then?" he said to Adam. "For sure?"

Adam nodded. "Thanks for coming by."

Jason threw a bill on the bar and walked away, weaving slightly as he did. I assumed that wasn't his first drink. He didn't even glance in my mother's direction as he passed their table.

"Friend of yours?" I asked Adam.

"Not really. He's looking for a buyer for his restaurant. I heard about him through a friend and set up a meeting."

"He wants you to buy his restaurant?"

"Well, he wants someone to buy it, and I'm interested." Adam shrugged. "Why?"

"You know the woman who . . . died at that big house on Cliff Walk Lane yesterday?" At his blank nod I added, "That guy is her brother."

# Chapter 31

Twenty minutes later my mother, Adam, Sam, Grandpa, and I traded Shady's for Bean. My other Cheers.

We huddled at a table near the window, watching island tourists wander around with their cameras and no cares in the world—at least no cares like figuring out who killed Olivia McAllister in a secret room of a house belonging to her decades-missing aunt before someone innocent took the fall for it.

"What were you two up to?" my mother asked Grandpa and me.

Grandpa waved her off. "Nothing. Let's focus on this. It was reckless, going to that house, Sophie," he said.

She gave him a look I'd never seen her give him before. "I was careful, Dad."

Adam was still spiraling about the whole thing. "I can't believe that's her brother. He didn't say anything!" He fiddled with the lid of his coffee cup. He hadn't taken a sip yet, and we'd been sitting here for half an hour. "I mean, wouldn't you say something if that was your sister? Better yet, wouldn't you cancel the meeting?"

My thinking exactly. What was so important about a business transaction that your murdered sister wouldn't take priority over it? I really wanted to know if Mick had spoken with him. I pulled my phone out and texted Katrina.

*Can you talk?*

*Was just about to call you. Yes, call me.*

"I'll be back in a second," I told them, and hurried over to the hall leading to the bathrooms.

Katrina answered before the first ring had finished. "What kind of people are you hiring over there? I know you're busy, but seriously?" she demanded.

I winced and lowered the volume so my eardrum didn't shatter. "Hi to you too. What are you talking about?"

"That girl you hired. Who came in and asked me for ten cats that she could take around to sign-up parties! I don't even have ten cats here, thanks to you, but what was she thinking?"

I was thoroughly confused now. "Katrina. Slow down. Who are you talking about? I haven't hired anyone." Did she mean a volunteer? But none of my volunteers would ever do that. And none of them, save Clarissa the college student, could accurately be described as a *girl*.

"I don't even remember her name because she annoyed me. And I didn't have time to call you on the spot. I told her to leave and I'd discuss it with you. She tried to talk me out of that but then hightailed it out of there when I pulled out my taser."

"You pulled out your *taser*? Katrina!"

"Well, what do you expect? She was getting pretty demanding. I can't just have random people coming in asking me for cats to put on display! They aren't toys."

"What did she look like?" I interrupted her next rant.

"Typical Gen Zer. Pink hair, enough piercings to let her brain cells leak out, barely wearing any clothes."

Pink hair. I closed my eyes. Hazel Hollis. Seriously, this

girl was becoming the bane of my existence. And she certainly did not work for me.

Was she impersonating someone from my business to get her hands on cats?

I so did not need this today.

"If she comes back, I need you to get her name. But she doesn't work for me. I think she's someone who's trying to start a cat party business here on the island. Apparently very unethically." I didn't mention Ellen.

"Wait. You're kidding." Katrina sounded stunned. "Well, jeez. If that's true, I'm sorry for yelling at you. I should have tasered her."

"No, you shouldn't have. Just let me know if she comes back. In the meantime, I have something more important I need your help with."

"What?"

"Can you call Mick and ask him if he spoke with Jason McAllister? Don't text him."

A pause. Then she said, "Why aren't you calling him yourself? Something's up with this case, isn't it."

"I can't really explain now. Can you just do that for me? Ask if he knew he was on the island, then call me back and tell me? Again, no texts."

"Sure, yes, I'll do it now."

"Thank you." I disconnected and went back to the table, where the debrief and discussion about Jason McAllister was still in full swing.

My mother was on her phone, looking up the restaurant that Adam said Jason McAllister owned. "The Ledger Room," she said, turning her phone to show me pictures. "It sounds upscale but looks like, well, the place we just left." She shot Adam an apologetic look. "No offense."

He waved her off. "None taken. I don't eat there."

"Is his restaurant nice? Have you been?" I asked Adam.

"Not yet. That was going to be the next step, once I'd met him, if I was interested."

"How did you find him again?" Grandpa asked Adam.

"I got word through a buddy who knew I was looking to potentially buy in Boston," he said.

Adam was certainly full of surprises. "Not only did I not know you were an EMT, but I had no idea you were a restauranteur," I said.

He smiled at that. "I'm not. But Marco and I were looking for a new venture to do together and thought that might be cool. We'd have people who knew what they were doing running it, of course. But we wanted something in the Seaport, since that's such an up-and-coming district in the city. Figured it would be the perfect place. This place's location is good. The rest of it . . ." He held his hand out and wavered it from side to side indicating it was so-so. "We can fix it though. We've got the cash flow."

Well, yes. Marco was a movie star, so that was no surprise.

"What did he tell you about why he was selling?" Grandpa asked.

"Nothing, really. Just that he was getting out of the business, running a restaurant isn't all it's cracked up to be, that kind of thing. I didn't question it. Got the sense he just wants out and I didn't poke at it too much."

"He leave a number?"

Adam nodded and pulled out his phone. I recorded the number he recited into my notes app.

"Has this meeting been set up for a while?" I asked.

"No. We'd connected about a month ago and he was a little vague on timing. We were supposed to connect again in August. But then he called me yesterday with a fire under his butt. Sorry," he said to my mother.

She shook her head as if to say, *I've heard worse.*

"Yesterday," I said slowly.

Adam nodded. "Like, I got the message after my EMT shift."

"The shift where you were called to his sister's house because she'd been murdered," I said.

He nodded, looking rattled by this reality. "Yeah," he said. "That shift. He said his timeline had changed and he was looking to sell as soon as possible, and could we meet because he was out here on the island. So I said yes."

"He was out here on the island the day his sister was murdered," I said slowly. "But no one seems to know it." I thought of Mila Daindridge's dogged determination to find this story—and possibly pin it on my mother. If she'd caught wind, surely Mila would've pursued him for an on-air comment.

"He had to be keeping it pretty low-key," Adam said. "I'm sure he didn't want the publicity, with what you all have told me about the family."

I looked at my phone, willing it to ring so I could get that answer.

"He say where he was staying?" Grandpa asked.

"The Seashore Motel."

Definitely not an upscale choice. Sounded like he needed money.

"What was the conversation like?" I asked. "I feel bad that I interrupted it now."

Adam waved that off. "We were done. You did me a favor actually. He was pressing me to give him at least a verbal commitment, which I wasn't about to do until I saw the place."

Yep, he needed money.

"He say anything else?" Grandpa asked.

Adam thought. "He mentioned liquidating other assets," he said. "Other property. Mentioned property out here."

Grandpa and I exchanged a look. "Details?" Grandpa asked.

"Just that he had another meeting today with the town. That they might be buying some family property because it was, in his words, *historic and worth a crap-ton of money*. Sorry again, Sophie."

Again, she waved him off.

"Did he mention anyone specifically?" I asked.

"He did." Adam tapped his temple as if trying to jostle it loose. "In passing. He got a text, so I think he was using that to see if it would impress me or something. Like he was some big property owner who was in demand. Helen!" He snapped his fingers as it came back to him. "He said something like, *This is Helen, so I gotta go deal with the other property*. Then he tried to say he had another potential buyer for the restaurant also calling him, and did I want to grab it before it got snapped up."

Helen. I didn't know any other Helen associated with "the town" aside from Helen Holloway, and he'd mentioned specifically a *historic property*. Holy moly. Helen and Jason McAllister? I looked at Grandpa. "Any other Helens in a town position like that?"

"Nope," he confirmed. "Looks like she may have been closer to the family than anyone thought after Delia."

"The Town Historian," I explained to Adam, who looked lost. "She apparently had her eye on the house for the town to take over. And Olivia had different ideas. She was planning to turn that house into a bed-and-breakfast, according to her daughter, who was likely going to work with her. I heard from a different source that her brother was involved in it. But when I tried to bring it up to the daughter, she acted like I'd suggested Freddy Krueger was on the team. And said they weren't close."

"Maybe they were fighting over the house," Adam said grimly. "Maybe he was pressuring her to sell . . . and things got ugly."

"Maybe," Grandpa said. "But then why was he talking to Helen?"

"She might've been playing him." Sam spoke up, but kept her eyes on her phone, where she'd been focused for the past few minutes.

# Chapter 32

We all looked at my sister. She handed the phone to me. It was open to an article from the local paper, dated May 2.

**State Grant Could Fund New Chapter for Historic Island Property**

The Massachusetts Historical Commission, in partnership with the Massachusetts Cultural Council, has announced a new round of Commonwealth Heritage Preservation Grants, offering matching funds to restore historically significant properties across the state.

Among the properties believed to be eligible is the long-vacant Mermaid Cottage on Daybreak Island, a eighteenth-century residence with documented cultural and architectural significance tied to the island's early families.

The grant program provides funding for structural stabilization, roof repair, and restoration of historic features, as well as adaptive reuse projects that make properties available for public benefit, including heritage tourism, archival use, and small cultural centers.

Sources familiar with the process say qualifying properties could receive six-figure matching grants, depending on scope and preservation plans. The grant also provides direct matching funds to property owners, significantly increasing the value of historically significant homes that qualify for restoration.

Eligibility requires clear proof of ownership and an approved preservation plan, meaning any application would need cooperation from the current homeowner or legal heirs.

Local historian Helen Holloway has publicly advocated for the preservation of Mermaid Cottage, citing its importance to the island's cultural record. "We're at risk of losing pieces of our history simply because no one is willing to take responsibility for them," she said.

Applications are due in June, and grants will be funded by October 1.

"Nice, Sam," my mother said approvingly, reading over my shoulder.

"Thanks, Mom." Sam beamed, clearly proud of her investigative abilities.

I showed the article to Grandpa, who scanned it, then nodded. "Explain what you mean about playing him," he said to Sam.

"Well, she could have told him that he would be getting a lot more money if he helped her get the grant. It just says 'six figures,' right? So she could have totally played it up, put it near the million-dollar mark. And if he's as desperate for money as he sounds"—she shrugged—"he'd be willing to believe it, is my guess."

Grandpa nodded approvingly. "Very good."

"Now we just need to find out if she filed the application, right?" she asked him.

"Exactly right," he said, glancing at his watch. "It's almost four. Sam, think you can make it to the town clerk's before they close and check?"

"On it," Sam said. She stood, then looked around. "I don't have a car. I came with Mom."

"I took Dad's car," she said. "Since Maddie needs a better car."

"I'll take you," Adam said. "As long as you don't mind a motorcycle ride."

Sam brightened. "Mind? Are you kidding?"

They left, Adam promising to get in touch if Jason reached out again. Grandpa told Sam we'd pick her up in a bit. I could tell he wanted her out of the mix for the next part of this conversation.

"Soph," he said, once it was just the three of us. "We need to talk to you. We just left Mick, who had to sneak out to see us."

"Sneak out? Why?"

"There's some political nonsense going on. I don't want you to worry," he said. "We'll get it handled, but here's the story." He gave her a toned-down version of what Mick had told us. At first, she looked like she didn't quite believe it. But as he went on, I could see the implications quietly sinking in.

While he talked, my phone buzzed. Katrina. I answered, pushing my chair away so I was removed from their conversation. "Hey."

"I have Mick here," she said, and passed the phone off.

"I called the brother yesterday," Mick said without preamble. "Didn't get a call back until late in the afternoon. Sounded shocked, but I couldn't get a real read on him. Offered to come out today and do what he could to help."

"Today, huh?"

"Yes. Why?"

"Help how?"

"Talk to us, try to fill in some blanks about his sister. He did say they weren't close but that he'd do what he could. And then said something about being available to get things wrapped up with the house, which seemed preliminary, but I figured I'd get more out of him when we talked."

"So did he come talk to you?"

"No. He hasn't followed up and I haven't had a chance to call him back yet, with everything else going on. You have something to tell me?"

I gave him a scrubbed-down version of the truth about seeing Adam and Jason at the bar together and Adam's story about the restaurant, about Jason being on the island the day his sister had been killed and his meeting with Helen.

"That's good information," Mick said. "Convenient that you happened to be hanging out at a biker bar this afternoon."

I let that go.

"Hold on," Mick said.

I could tell he put me on mute, because the line went dead silent. A minute later, he returned. "You got a cell for McAllister? The number he gave me is mysteriously out of service."

"I do." I gave him the number Adam had given me.

"Thanks. Later you can tell me how you really ended up meeting McAllister." And he was gone.

I pulled my chair back over to my mom and Grandpa Leo.

"We have to nip this in the bud, Sophie," Grandpa was saying. "The chief is hearing that you and Olivia were the last ones to see Delia, when we all know that wasn't true, and he's using that as some reason to think you've been hiding something all this time. I can also get Helen to talk to him," he said, almost to himself. "Why didn't I think of that before? She was the last one to see Delia. She reminded me of that for years, every time she came to my office to see if we were looking into it. I want you to make a statement through the lawyer I'm calling, and that's all we're—"

"I can't do that, Dad," my mother said firmly.

"Why on earth not?" he demanded.

"Because it is true," she said, meeting his gaze head-on. "Olivia and I were there that last day Aunt Delia was seen, when she came back from the store. And they had a massive fight."

# Chapter 33

Neither Grandpa nor I had any idea what to say to that. When he finally found his voice again, he said, "Why did you never tell me this, Sophie?"

"Because I was sixteen," she replied. "And I was sneaking around with Jason after you told me not to see him."

"Jason?" I piped up, unable to help myself. "As in Olivia's brother?"

She nodded. "We were dating."

Oh, boy. I wanted to shrink in my seat as I imagined my then-sixteen-year-old mother defying her strong-willed, police officer father. But Jason McAllister? The kid who'd always been trouble, according to Lilah Gilmore? I wanted to ask, but didn't dare.

She was still focused on Grandpa. "When I finally realized people were wondering if Olivia killed her own aunt, I really didn't think I could tell you."

I froze. That was the same story Mick said Caldwell had brought to his chief. Grandpa and I had dismissed it as the fiction of someone hiding something and trying to divert attention. But he'd been telling the truth?

Grandpa held up a hand to me, still not taking his eyes

off my mother. "Start at the beginning," he said tersely. "And do not leave one thing out."

"Fine. Coffee first?" she asked.

Grandpa started to say no, but I cut him off. "I'd love some," I said, partly to ease the tension and partly because, well, I always wanted coffee.

"I'll get it." She got up and went to the counter. Grandpa didn't say a word while she was gone, and I didn't know what to say. But at least he had time to catch his breath.

When she sat back down, she looked steadier. "Where should I start?" she mused, then turned to me. "Maddie, you know Olivia and I were like sisters. We'd been friends since we met at four years old in dance class."

That, I hadn't heard. I knew my mother loved to dabble in different things, but I hadn't known she'd been a dancer. A true onion, this woman. So many layers to uncover.

"We were inseparable from that first day. But Olivia had always been . . . very strong-willed. Looking back, I can see it was a bit of a dysfunctional relationship as we got older. She loved—needed, actually—to be in charge. She operated that way with her family and her friends. It was one of the reasons she clashed with her brother. But I was the person closest to her, and I got the brunt of this. Especially when we were teenagers. But it just became second nature to me to let her run the show and go along with it."

This was surprising to me. My mom was a force. I couldn't imagine her being subservient to anyone. She certainly spoke her mind and stood up for what she believed in, not with a wrecking ball but with a smile and the ability to make you think you'd changed your mind all on your own.

"I had never spent much time with Jason, but one day I was outside waiting for her to stop being mad at me about something stupid and he came home. We started talking, and he asked me why I let her treat me like that. It was a hard question for me, but I realized he was kind of right. She could be a bully. I didn't do anything about it at that point, but it opened my eyes. And, I started to spend some time with him." She looked at Grandpa. "You found out and were upset."

"Darn right I was. He was bad news. Still is, apparently."

She smiled a little. "Yes, Dad, but every teenaged girl needs to spend some time with a bad boy in their life. Anyway, he wasn't doing anything bad that I could see. He just wasn't falling in line with the family expectations. Refused to go to college, wanted to go to cooking school, not so much a new story. But I figured it wouldn't be hard to keep it from you. Sorry," she added. "I did think it would be harder to keep from Olivia, though, and I was intent on that. Because she would've been furious."

"Why?" I asked.

"Because it would've meant the dynamic in our relationship would change."

Made sense. I nodded. "Go on. Where does Delia come into this?"

"I told you that she was super close to Delia. Not so much her own mother—they butted heads like crazy. But Delia and Olivia were a lot alike. Delia was a very strong woman. It mostly worked . . . until it didn't."

"Meaning?"

"Olivia had been at odds with her parents—specifically her mom—for a while. She'd been spending more time at her aunt's. Weekends. Long stretches in the summer. Olivia started leaving clothes there. That year, our junior year, she decided she wanted to move in with Delia permanently."

"Move in?" I asked, glancing at Grandpa. He still had barely said a word as he digested this story.

"Yes. She was adamant that she couldn't live at home any longer."

"Wow," I said. That must've been so hard, as a teenager, to be so at odds with your own family. I'd been really lucky in that department. Aside from a little too much closeness and some meddling here and there, I had no complaints. They had my back and I had theirs. I couldn't imagine any other way. But a lot of other people weren't as lucky. "Was it her mother, or her, or both?"

My mom hesitated. "Who knows what really happens behind closed doors," she said finally. "Like I said, Olivia could be overbearing, especially when she wasn't getting what she wanted. But it was typical teenage stuff. She was young. She felt things intensely. Her mother was pretty normal. She didn't seem overly strict or anything. Olivia did pretty much what she wanted. Her mom was, however, very conscious of the family name and the optics of it. So was Delia.

"Delia knew what it would look like to the rest of the family if she let her live there. Olivia's parents would see it as rejection. Her brother would've been upset. Jason always loved that house, and he also knew that Delia favored Olivia and she'd probably be the one to get it.

"I also believe that Delia didn't want to raise a teenager. She'd chosen not to have kids of her own, and I'm sure she figured Olivia would be a handful. Honestly, we kind of were. I remember us treating that house like it was already ours. That's how we found the secret room."

"You found it on your own?" I asked.

She nodded. "We were probably eleven or twelve. That was the one time I remember Delia getting upset with us. We were in her office where we weren't supposed to be and we were playing with the books. Olivia found the mechanism to open the door, and we couldn't resist. We had to check it out."

"What was in it?"

"It was just a small office. A desk, books, the usual office things, as far as I can remember."

I pictured the room I'd seen so briefly. It sounded similar to what it had been back then. "Why did she get mad at you?" I asked.

"She said it was dangerous. For one, she didn't want us to get stuck in there. I'm not sure if the mechanism to get out was hidden like the way in? In any case, she gave us a good talking-to. Remember, Dad? I told you about it because I thought she was going to call you and I'd be in trouble."

"I remember," he said.

"Was it true? That it was dangerous?" I asked.

"They were ages old, remember. The doors could get stuck, the air quality could've been poor. Could be as simple as mold growing in there. Who knows?" She shrugged. "The point is, she probably didn't want to have to structure her house and her life around a child even more than she already did by being generous with her space."

"So she said no to Olivia," I confirmed.

"She said not yet," my mother corrected. "She told Olivia she couldn't live there full time. That she needed to finish school at home and figure out what she was doing for college and all that first, because she would probably move away anyway. That running away from family problems doesn't solve them."

I pictured Olivia—sixteen, stubborn, convinced she'd finally found a place where she fit—and felt a pang of sympathy. "When was this?" I asked.

"The week Delia disappeared," my mother said. "So yes, the timing was terrible. When Delia said no, Olivia got very upset. They fought about it for two days. And then that final day . . . we went back to her house."

I waited, transfixed.

"I didn't know we were going there. Olivia just decided she needed to give it one more run. But then Delia told her that she'd told her parents about the ask, which was probably going to cause more problems for Olivia. That didn't go over well. I had to go outside they were shouting at each other so loudly. I was stuck there. It was very uncomfortable. But also, I remember being a little afraid of how angry Olivia was."

"Did you see Delia again after the fight?" I asked.

My mom shook her head slowly. "Olivia finally came out. She was upset and crying. Just got into the car, so I got in too. She dropped me off and we never talked about it again."

Grandpa reached over and laid a hand on hers. "Why didn't you tell me, Sophie?" There was a sadness in his voice.

She reached over and covered his hand with her other hand. "I'm so sorry, Dad. I really didn't know what to do. And when I started hearing that Delia was missing, that just took over. And then they left. I never put any of it together until I was much older." She looked at me. "And one more thing I didn't tell you." She took a deep breath. "I saw the Ghost Cat that last day, at Delia's house. The one we saw yesterday."

That threw me. My mother hadn't mentioned the cat yesterday at all. Then again, I hadn't either. "You saw a cat yesterday too? Where?"

"In the driveway when we first drove in, and then later in the yard. Right before I left."

"Are you sure it wasn't just a similar-looking cat—"

She held up a hand to let me know it wasn't up for discussion. "I know what I saw, Maddie. And I know the stories. It was the cat. The same cat," she added.

Grandpa was back to saying nothing. I couldn't get a read on what he was thinking here.

"Okay," I said finally, trying to make sense of this whole thing. "So, the Ghost Cat came to warn you that something was about to happen, and then Delia vanished? Are you seriously thinking she killed her aunt? How would she have gotten rid of the body so no one found it?" That seemed awfully elaborate for a sixteen-year-old. I thought of Becky and myself at that age. Could either of us have orchestrated someone's actual disappearance in such a way that they were never discovered? I highly doubted it. Most adults, even the ones who plan to do bad things, got caught eventually. Also, we didn't have deviant minds, so there was that.

"I'm not saying anything like that," my mom said. "I know my best friend. Even though she could be a lot, she wasn't a bad person. I know that in my bones. But I know her family sometimes worried about how . . . intense she got when she was set on something. And when the rumors started, well, her grandparents would never want to be associated with any kind of scandal. And maybe they thought it would save Olivia from any scrutiny if they all left and cut ties, which was why I presume Olivia was forbidden to contact even me."

"So, you think they were just reacting to perceived optics and taking the easy way out?" It seemed like a lot to go through for something that wasn't true. Unless . . . A really dark thought crossed my mind. What if the family had evidence Olivia did something and covered it up to protect her? Then used their "grief" to leave town, and their status to kibosh the investigation?

Had my mother grown up with a murderer?

"Maybe. Whatever the reason, I never spoke to my best friend again. And I've felt guilty about it ever since."

"You? Why?"

"Because I could've reached out when we got older. No one was keeping us from each other as adults."

"So why didn't you?" I asked.

"I've thought a lot about this over the years. Honestly? I think I just got so consumed by the rumors that I was afraid I'd find out something I didn't want to know. And then I felt terrible for even entertaining any of it."

"What about Jason? What did he say?"

"He withdrew also, when Delia vanished. It was like the whole family went into some kind of lockdown. I only saw him once or twice after that, and it was never the same. And then they were gone." She turned to Grandpa. "And I think I need to tell Lieutenant Ellory this story. It's time. There's no family really left to protect aside from Jason, and I don't think he's going to care."

"That's all well and good, but don't talk to them until I get a lawyer involved," Grandpa said. "Just in case."

# Chapter 34

After my mother promised she wasn't going to go rogue and get ahead of Grandpa's plans, we went our separate ways. Grandpa asked me to pick up Sam—we'd nearly forgotten about my poor sister at the town hall—and then gone straight home to take care of the lawyer without another word. My mother's story had thrown him, I could tell. I felt bad for both of them and wished fervently that Olivia McAllister had taken a page out of the rest of her family's book and stayed far away from our island.

This felt like the longest week ever.

Sam, on the other hand, still had a lot of energy. She waited out front of the town hall, nearly bouncing up and down with excitement when I drove up.

"She did apply for the grant," she said excitedly, jumping in the car almost before it stopped. "And she got it. Well, the town got it."

I'd almost forgotten about the errand she'd been on. I had to reorient my brain around it. "I thought the recipients weren't being announced until October?"

"Officially. But Helen pulled strings, and she was always going to get it. It's, like, her last hurrah."

"How did you find this out?"

"Hello? I just left the town clerk's," she said, clearly exasperated at my inability to keep up. "Where do you think I found out? I've made friends with Aggie Hennessy, the assistant clerk. She loves Grandpa. I think she has a crush on him. Anyway, whenever I tell her something's for him, she trips over herself to give me what I need."

Ah, small towns. They were great when you knew who to go to for information. "Nice," I said.

"That's not all I found out. Aggie was thrilled to talk about the McAllister house. Proximity to the news and all that, I guess. Anyway, she made a comment about how this house was, like, the most popular piece of property on the island this summer. Apparently there was some permit drama."

My hands tightened on the steering wheel. "What do you mean?"

"Olivia had been in the process of filing for a permit to start working on the house. The contractor of record was Randall Renovations. But Olivia was trying to use her name to get the town to have the permit on file but not make it public record until she was officially ready to start work. Said she didn't want to deal with nosy people, or something like that. The planning board didn't agree, according to Aggie. Because that's not how they roll, and also because there are specific steps they need to take when it's a historic property. Apparently—and this is Aggie's perspective—Olivia tried to use her family's name to circumvent that. She and the planning board director had a disagreement about it in his office. But apparently the mayor told him to let it go."

"So, what happened?"

Sam shrugged. "He let it go. It sat on his desk, I guess. Then on Wednesday . . ." She paused for dramatic effect.

"Sam. Not the time," I said through gritted teeth.

"Right. Apparently on Wednesday, Olivia McAllister

called the clerk's office and told them she wanted to change contractors and asked how to do it. They told her she'd have to request a new permit. She wasn't pleased with that answer, according to them, but this time she didn't go to the mayor, she just caved. Told them fine, go ahead and cancel it for now. They never heard back, and obviously we know why."

"Because she wanted to change contractors? Meaning . . ."

"Sounded like she fired the Randall firm," Sam said.

I thought about that. "If that's true, she didn't just fire the firm. She fired her boyfriend."

"Boyfriend?" Sam's eyes widened.

"Yeah. She was seeing Cliff Randall. We just found out," I said. "Although it seems he left the detail that they'd parted ways out of his story." Because if she'd fired him, it surely meant their relationship was over. Didn't it?

Sam sat back, clearly proud. "So, good info?"

"Really good info," I assured her.

Now it was just a matter of getting Mick to pay attention to it. Because between Cliff Randall—who may have had multiple motives, if this information held—and the alliance between Helen Holloway and Jason McAllister, not to mention their individual reasons for wanting to gain control of the house, any reasonable person would see that any of these three had more of a motive than my mother did to want Olivia out of the picture.

Not to mention Neil Caldwell and whatever he was trying to hide. His actions suggested that there was something about Delia McAllister specifically that he didn't want coming out.

Sam chattered on a bit about Helen and Jason McAllister and what our next moves would be until we pulled into our driveway. She immediately headed to the basement where Grandpa had already locked himself away to give him the news.

I was about to follow to discuss how Grandpa wanted to alert Mick to this information, but Adele saw me through the French doors and called me in to the cafe. I knew she wouldn't take no for an answer, so I detoured that way.

But I didn't expect to see her with such a big smile on her face.

"About time you got here," she said.

"Sorry. Busy day. Is everything okay?"

"It's great. Did you meet Tess's friends yet?"

"Tess's friends? Uh, no," I said.

"Well, come on, then," she said impatiently, pulling me into the room. "They're going to probably adopt Elroy. And hopefully George, but I'm still working on that," she added in a stage whisper.

I followed her into the cafe, where Tess McAllister stood with two women. A redhead in baggy jeans and a tank top, her hair pulled into short pigtails, held Elroy, one of the two kittens we had left, snug against her chin. The other, a brown-skinned woman in a cream-colored sundress and dark curls pulled into a tight bun, leaned over her shoulder, smiling as she cooed at the kitten.

Tess stood nearby, seemingly in the conversation, but she looked like her mind was a million miles away. Dean was there too, standing slightly away from the group watching his daughter play with some of the other cats and looking a little awkward. When he saw me, he lifted a hand in a self-conscious wave. I waved back as I walked up to them.

"Hi," I said to the new people. "Maddie James. One of the owners. I see you've found a friend."

"I love him," the redhead confessed, giving me her free hand to shake. "I'm Carrie. This is Shea."

The other woman waved at me. "Hi. Nice to meet you."

"I'm trying to convince them to take George too. He's hiding." Adele motioned toward the kitten cage. George and Elroy were the last two of our Jetsons litter. We'd adopted Judy, Rosie, and Spacely already. George was the more timid kitten, and he sat in there on his favorite bed just watching.

"I love George," Shea admitted. "I'm still trying to make him love me."

"Give him a few," I said. "He'll come around."

"Perfect. We have all the time in the world. Well, at least another week." She grinned. "We came over to convince Tess to still have Piper's party, since we're all here. But we were thinking about a cat anyway, and this place is amazing."

Piper's party. I'd almost forgotten about it. I couldn't imagine how Tess would be able to focus on that, but also couldn't imagine disappointing the poor kid. I looked to where Piper was sprawled on a beanbag chair at the other end of the cafe, with three cats draped over her like blankets. She looked positively euphoric.

"I can't have a party after my mother's been murdered," Tess said miserably, tuning in to our conversation. "That would be . . . wrong. Wouldn't it?" She looked to her friends for direction.

Carrie shook her head vehemently and started to reply, but Dean took a tentative step closer and stepped in. "Tess. I know it's a horrible time. But this is for Piper. She's been waiting for this for months," he said. "I think we should do it."

Tess turned on him with a frown. "It's not that easy."

"It is, though," he said patiently. "We don't have to make it a big thing and announce it around the island. Your mother would want you to make sure Piper enjoyed her birthday. Right?" he said, turning to Carrie and Shea.

"Amen," Carrie said approvingly.

"Agree a hundred percent," Shea said. "I don't think you have a choice, girl. It's not an I'm-glad-my-mom's-dead party. It's for your kid."

I liked this woman. And she was right. Still, it wasn't my place to say, so I stayed shut.

"Isn't your dad coming all the way here too?" Dean asked.

"He's getting here tonight," Tess said reluctantly. "He was coming out for the original party."

"Maybe we can do it here?" Dean looked at me expectantly.

"Um," I said. "I guess we'd have to—"

"We definitely can, as long as it's not on the weekend," Adele said, fixing me with a stare. Now I knew I must've fallen into a parallel universe. Adele, championing a kid party in the cafe? Where was I? "We close early on Mondays. We could do it then?"

All eyes turned to Tess. She looked trapped for a minute. I got the sense this was a woman who was not used to making decisions. "We could keep it low-key," I assured her. "Just a small thing. Dean's right, it doesn't have to be advertised."

She sighed, giving in. "Fine. Sure. You're right. It would make Piper happy, and she doesn't deserve to have her birthday messed up."

Carrie and Shea cheered. Dean looked relieved. "I'll go tell her," he said.

"I'm coming," Tess said, hurrying after him. "You don't get all the glory."

"I'll get the paperwork on Elroy going," Adele said to Carrie. "In both your names?"

"Please," Carrie chirped. She followed Adele to the desk, leaving me and Shea.

"Want to give it another go with George?" I asked.

"Yes, please."

I grabbed some treats I knew he liked and we went over to sit in front of the kitten cage. I gave her George's favorite feather toy, and she dangled it through the cage to warm him up.

"I'm so happy they're going to have the party," she said, watching as Piper jumped up and started shrieking in delight as the cats scattered. "The aftermath of this is going to be tough for her. And for Tess."

"It's awful," I said.

"Yeah." Shea was quiet for a minute, then she said, "But ultimately, I think it's giving Tess another chance. I know that sounds weird. And maybe bad. But I don't mean it that way. She never wanted to live out here anyway."

# Chapter 35

This was news to me. "What do you mean, she didn't want to be out here? I thought she was moving here to work with her mom."

Shea rolled her eyes. "All her mother's idea. At first, she asked her to come out to help her get some things squared away with her aunt's old house. Spend some weekends together, give Piper a chance to experience island life like she did as a kid, blah blah. So, Tess goes along with it. Then Olivia got this bright idea to turn their property into a bed-and-breakfast and basically told Tess she needed to help her run it. Even though Tess has a job that she loves. But that was Olivia. Kept her thumb on her, and Tess could never figure out how to get out from under it. I mean, not to speak ill of the dead or anything." Shea glanced up at the ceiling as if issuing an apology to the sky. "Then she met this guy and seemed to feel better about all of it for the past month or so. But that could just be circumstance, you know?" She held her breath as George inched closer to the cage door, curious, but still didn't exit.

A guy. The ghost hunter Mick had tracked down, I assumed. But I wanted to hear it from someone who knew the story. I sat back on my heels. "What guy?"

"She met some guy out here she's been seeing. I don't know if it's just a rebellious thing or what. But it seemed to make the idea more palatable."

I thought about my mother's story from earlier, about how controlling Olivia was. If that was the case, it made sense her daughter might be a victim of it too.

"Especially after the divorce," Shea said, nodding toward Tess and Dean. "It was like she wanted to control everything Tess did from here on out. She didn't like Dean in the first place," she confided. "But then again, she didn't like much of any decision Tess made if she wasn't involved in it."

"So, she's seeing someone here and didn't want anyone to know," I said. That tracked with what Mick had discovered, about Tess hopping into someone's truck when she was supposed to be out for a run. My gaze drifted to our houseguest, standing stiffly next to her ex-husband, clearly uncomfortable.

Shea brought a finger to her lips, glancing in her friend's direction to make sure she was still occupied. "Still is, but don't say anything in front of Dean. I think he still thinks he can win her back," she said with a smile. "Yeah, she didn't want her mother to know about the guy. She would, like, pretend to go out running or something to meet up with him. Crazy, right?" she said at the look on my face. "Tess always hated running. Like any sane person. But I think that was the only reason she started to entertain the idea of moving out here, even just for a while. She planned to keep her job though and maybe help her mother out at night or whatever. We thought it was nuts, but who are we to judge? She's been through a lot and we were just trying to be supportive."

I handed her some treats from my bag. Shea put the treats in her palm and held it out to George. He crept over and took one, watching her while he ate it. Then he started purring and nuzzled her hand with his face.

Shea looked overjoyed. "That's a good boy," she said softly. "Come here!" She scooped him up. He didn't protest. Instead, he started purring louder. She turned to look at Carrie and Adele, who were watching, and flashed a thumbs-up. "He doesn't hate me!" she called in a stage whisper.

"Yes!" Adele said, fist shooting into the air. "Paperwork's ready."

"Maddie?" Dean approached, shoving his hands in the pockets of his jeans. He looked nervous. "Can I talk to you for a second?" He inclined his head toward the far side of the room to show me he wanted to do so in private.

I rose and followed him over to the French doors leading into the house.

"So, since we're having the party Monday, I'm going to be out here a bit longer than planned," he said. "I only have a room through tomorrow night. The hotel is booked after that, and I couldn't find anything else open that didn't have a three-night minimum."

"Yeah, that happens during the summer," I said.

"I wondered . . ." He glanced over his shoulder at Tess, whose head was bent over her daughter's as they talked softly. "Do you guys have another empty guest room? Tess mentioned that you might. I hate to impose, but not sure what to do. If not, don't worry," he said hastily. "I can always go stay on the mainland I guess and come back and forth. The ferry makes me kind of seasick, but it's fine. I'll do it happily for Piper."

He was putting me on the spot. I wasn't sure how Tess would feel about it. Since she was already here, did that make her a priority? Maybe, but I didn't really know how else to answer. "No, don't be silly," I said, hoping Grandpa would be okay with it. "We definitely have the room. It's fine." Perhaps that would be our next income stream: cat bed-and-breakfast. Since now Olivia's bed-and-breakfast wouldn't be coming to fruition.

"Really? You're a lifesaver," he said, clasping his hands together in a gesture of thanks. "Thank you so much." Then he surprised me by leaning over and giving me a hug. "I appreciate you," he said. "We'll all be out of your hair on Monday night after the party. Promise."

"No problem." I patted his back awkwardly.

"I'll tell Tess and get my things." He gave me a salute, then hurried away.

"What was that about?" Shea asked with interest when I returned to her and George.

"Dean needs a place to stay for a couple of nights," I said.

Her eyes widened. "And he's staying here? Poor guy. He really thinks proximity fixes things." She grimaced a little. "Tess will be less than thrilled. But don't worry, she hates conflict. Anyway, at least Piper will be happy."

"How about you guys? Are you good on a place to stay?"

"We are. We booked an extra week from the jump. This is our summer vacation!" She grinned. "This place is cool. I mean, murder aside," she added quickly, the smile falling away.

"Right, of course. Also, the cats can stay here until you head home, then," I said.

"Thank you!" She snuggled back up with George.

I watched Carrie and Adele bent over the paperwork up front. Dean had rejoined Tess and Piper. The cafe settled back into its usual rhythm—happy voices, a cat purring somewhere behind me, Piper's chattering. Dean leaned into Tess and spoke. I couldn't see her face as she received the news, but I was acutely aware of Shea's take on the situation.

I had the uneasy sense that I'd just invited one more complication into our home.

# Chapter 36

*Saturday*

Saturday morning thankfully brought more good weather for the library event. The party itself had come together nicely. Lucas was working it with me. And my mom would be within my sight all day and not running around following Jason McAllister. All that was positive.

My main issue today, though, was handling the Hazel Hollis problem. I'd gotten so distracted by Mick, my mother, and her story yesterday that I'd forgotten about Katrina's call and the claim that Hazel was impersonating one of my staff. This girl needed to be reined in, and fast. Not to mention figuring out why she'd been in the vicinity of Olivia's house on Thursday. I could assume: clearly, she hadn't wanted to take no for an answer about the party. Tess said she'd been hounding them about hiring her. For whatever reason, Olivia hadn't. Had she gone there in person to try to get her to reconsider?

Also, would failing to book a party be something worth murdering someone over? I didn't know Hazel, so I couldn't speak to her state of mind.

Really, I wanted Grandpa to help with how to approach her. Only problem was, he was not in a great place.

Between yesterday afternoon in the cafe and this morning, he'd gotten the best lawyer he knew, a guy named Chip Meyers, to help my mother if needed. Chip was semiretired living out in a Boston suburb, but Grandpa had convinced him to come out to the island today. I wasn't sure about trusting my mom's future to a guy named Chip, but Grandpa seemed confident.

I knew how worried he was about us and this forced narrative that somehow my mom had something to do with this. But as worrisome as the conversation with Mick had been, I was holding tight to the fact that there were several other people who could be seen as the real threat to Olivia.

Mick just needed some clarity—and a little breathing room to investigate outside of the chief's mandates. At least, that's what I was telling myself.

When I got downstairs, our kitchen was absolute mayhem. I couldn't remember the last time our house had been this full. Grandpa's secret dream that he'd confessed only once to me was that he'd always wanted to have a bed-and-breakfast. Maybe not a full-time one, but he definitely enjoyed hosting people. This week, he'd gotten his wish—even though the circumstances were not ideal.

Piper seemed to be enjoying herself immensely, between Walter and Ollie and all the cats. Despite the cloud hanging over this whole situation, she was succeeding in brightening things just a bit. Any kid that loved animals this much was okay by me. When I got to the kitchen, she was on the floor under the table, squealing in delight as Walter licked her to death and Ollie sat on top of her, which couldn't have been comfortable since he probably weighed more than she did. She seemed to love it, though.

She seemed equally as happy to have both her parents in the same house, even though Tess and Dean were having a standoff about whether or not she could have a Pop-

Tart for breakfast when I walked in (he was for, she was against). Ethan swooped in and saved the day, offering an early batch of his homemade banana bread as an alternative. I was happy to taste test it first and show her how good it was.

Grandpa was already gone. I wasn't sure which lead he was following up on first, although when we talked briefly last night, he'd been most interested in Cliff Randall, especially considering Sam's discovery that Olivia had apparently fired him. He'd had the means, the motive, and the access. He knew about the secret room. He could've been keeping an eye on the house to see if Tess went out. If she'd been "running" on a schedule, perhaps he'd anticipated this and waited for her to go, then snuck up on Olivia and got his revenge. He had potential as our guy.

The Helen and Jason McAllister angle was also interesting. I wished I had time before the party to go back to see Helen. I wasn't sure an eightysomething-year-old woman would be able to bludgeon someone like that, but who knew? If she was motivated enough, it was certainly possible, especially with the giant boots she wore to make herself taller. Or she could have simply put the idea in Jason's head that Olivia's death would benefit them both. He certainly sounded desperate, although would he be desperate enough to harm his own sister for financial gain? I didn't know the guy, so it was hard to say.

My mom, for her part, seemed to be holding up well. She'd arrived at the house bright and early, dressed in her JJ's House of Purrs T-shirt and a pair of jeans, curls wrapped in a scarf, smiling like nothing was wrong. "This is going to be fun," she assured me. "Give me a job. But first"—she glanced into the kitchen, where Tess sat at the kitchen table, still looking like she was somewhat in shock—"I'd like to talk to Tess."

I'd figured as much. "I'll be in the cafe," I said. "Take your time."

I got some coffee, then went to get all the cat carriers ready for the cats we were putting in the truck. Lucas joined me a few minutes later. "Want me to go make sure the truck is set up?" he asked.

"That would be great." I gave him a kiss, then wrapped my arms around him for an extra-long hug. "Have I told you how grateful I am for you?" I asked.

He grinned and kissed the top of my head. "Not yet today."

"Well, I am." I gave him one more squeeze and then stepped back. He headed out to do his thing while I gathered the supplies I would need. Unsurprisingly, Piper followed me, dragging her dad behind her. The cafe was her favorite place to be, and she was curious about all the activity.

"Are you taking the kitties somewhere?" she asked, after watching me set up carriers.

"I am," I said. "They're going to the library to play with some kids."

Her eyes lit up. "Can we come too?"

"I don't see why not, but you'll have to ask your parents." I glanced at Dean.

"Is it a private party?" he asked.

"No. We had the kids who wanted to read to the cats register, because that will be a certain period of time, but there's some unstructured time where the kids can go visit the cats," I said.

"Then I'm sure we can stop by later," he told Piper, smiling at her enthusiastic squeal. "But first we have to go take a bath and get ready. Maybe Walter will want to help?" he suggested.

This pleased her too, and she made a beeline back toward the house to go hunt down the dogs. They passed

Val, who was walking in as they left. She gave them a nod as she made her way over to me. "When do you think Grandpa's going to start charging people?" she said under her breath. "With the number of strangers staying here, he could at least be making money off of it."

"Who knows," I said. "He does like to start businesses. Come talk to me over here." I led her to the swag cabinet. I hadn't had much time to catch up with her the past couple of days and wondered what she'd heard about the drama going on.

"Is Mom okay?" She sounded worried.

"I think so. She's just figuring out how to deal with all of it." I pulled a batch of the JJ stuffies out of the cabinet. We were giving them to the little kids who read to the cats. "Have you talked to her?"

"No, and no one's really telling me what's going on. But she's in there with that woman who's staying here, and they're both crying, for one. And Grandpa is doing his silent thing, which he only does when he's really concerned about something. And given what I've heard, I'm putting my own story together." She tapped the side of her head. She'd recently cut her auburn hair into a sleek, chin-length style that really suited her. Whether it was that or her recent marriage, she positively glowed.

I didn't really have time to go into the whole story, nor was I sure Grandpa wanted me to right now. "It's just been a tough week," I said. "Losing her friend and all that."

"Yeah. I feel bad for her. Do you think it would help if I agreed to do the official wedding?"

I stared up at her in surprise. "Really?" Val and Ethan had eloped a few months ago, leaving my mother with an almost-completely-planned wedding that she wasn't sure what to do with. They'd been struggling with the stress of everything and chosen to go off on their own and just get married. My mother had struggled to be supportive, but I knew she'd been disappointed.

"Yes, really. I mean, she was a good sport about the elopement. And if that will make her feel better . . ."

"I think she'd love it," I said.

"Okay. I'll tell her." She turned to go, then turned back to me. "It doesn't feel as oppressive since we're already married. Maybe it can actually be fun." She waved and headed back into the house.

I packed up all my stuff and went outside to put it in the truck just as Grandpa pulled into the driveway. When he got out of the truck, he didn't look happy. I immediately went on alert.

I detoured over to him. "What's wrong?"

Grandpa blew out a breath. "Cliff Randall's not our guy."

I felt the blow of that almost like a gut punch. Not that I wanted our former contractor to be guilty of murder, but with my mother in the crosshairs, that seemed like the lesser problem. "What? How do you know?"

"I just left him. He didn't deny the breakup, or the fact that she'd pulled the job. Didn't deny being angry either." He shook his head. "But his alibi holds up. He was on a job Thursday across the island. Crew of three. Permits. Time-stamped photos. Sam already checked it all out."

"You two work fast," I said. "So . . . that's it?"

"For him, yeah." He sounded frustrated.

I understood. I was too, not so much because I wanted Cliff to be a killer, but because I wanted my mother left alone. I glanced at the truck. The party clock was already ticking. "What now?" I asked. "Have you talked to Mick?"

"Not yet. I'm holding that at bay as long as possible." He checked his watch. "I'm going to see Helen. I need to find out what she was up to with Jason."

I guess I was handling Hazel on my own. "Okay," I said. "Be careful."

He gave me a kiss on the cheek then got back in his truck and drove away.

As I went inside to get the cat carriers and start loading them into the truck, I caught movement around the side of the house. White and gray, gone almost as soon as I registered it.

I stopped, heart giving an unnecessary thump.

"No," I muttered to myself, shaking it off. I didn't have time to wonder if my eyes were playing tricks on me or go back down the rabbit hole I'd been living in for the past few days.

I went up the steps and back inside. I had a party to get to.

# Chapter 37

When Lucas, my mom, JJ, and I arrived at the library, a gaggle of kids and their parents were already there, clustered in a group outside waiting for us. They cheered when we pulled up. One of the librarians got everyone's attention and started putting them in a line. I saw Katrina's animal control truck pull into the parking lot right behind us. She would be heading inside to talk to the older kids.

I parked without accidentally running anyone over or hitting any cars—I'd gotten much better at driving this thing around—then turned to Lucas. "I'll go check in with Ellen."

He nodded. "I'll check on your mom and then bring the food in." My mother and JJ had ridden in the back with the cats on the way over.

I headed toward the library steps, scanning the parking lot for the lime green SUV. I didn't see it. On the one hand, I was relieved. On the other, I knew it was only putting off the inevitable. Aside from the obvious, infuriating question about what Hazel thought she was doing pretending to work for me to get her hands on some cats, there was the whole other question about why she'd been near Olivia's that morning.

The way this week was going, anything seemed possible. Or was I just grasping for something to give Mick to get my mother off the hook?

"Maddie! You made it." Ellen held the door open, motioning me inside. "Everyone's so excited. Many of the kids were early!"

"I saw that," I said. "We're excited too."

Ellen looked a bit more like herself today, I noticed. I hesitated to ask her about Hazel just yet, and she didn't mention her.

"I'm going to have Kelsey, one of our children's librarians, come out with the books," Ellen explained. "She's collecting them now. We'll have two kids at a time in the truck, as we discussed, and the rest of them can be in here rotating through the activities."

She led me to an area in the middle of the big, circular room where cushioned window seats curved along the walls, dotted with pillows and small reading lamps. Sunlight streamed in from every direction, and low bookcases and rugs divided the floor into inviting nooks clearly designed for lingering. They'd set up stations in here for the kids: coloring books, puzzles, and a cat-themed scavenger hunt.

"Katrina will be upstairs in the smaller room for the talk with the older kids," she finished.

"It looks amazing. Lucas will be in with the snacks any minute."

"Perfect. The snack table is over here." She pointed toward a separate area in the hall, far away from the books. "Sticky hands and all that," she said with a smile.

"I hear you."

The front door opened and Katrina walked in, followed

by Lucas. Their hands were full of bags of snacks and some healthy treats Ethan had made for the occasion—oatmeal applesauce muffins and little bags of homemade granola, all neatly labeled. He was a gem.

"Welcome, you two." Ellen went over to greet them and showed them where to put the food. The library was full today. We had a beautiful library on the island, and tourists even made time in their beach days to come check it out. We were definitely going to have a good turnout of kids.

I made sure they were good with the food, then headed back outside to the truck. When I got there, I heard voices from inside. Curious, I pulled the door open and found my mother, trapped in a one-way conversation with none other than Hazel Hollis—the shock of pink hair and the cat peeking out of the backpack gave it away, even though I couldn't see her face yet. My mother looked apprehensive as she listened to the barrage of words coming at her. I couldn't believe the audacity of this person.

"Can I help you?" I interrupted, cutting Hazel off mid-sentence.

My mother looked relieved. "Maddie," she said. "I just met Hazel. She's interested in joining forces with us." She gave me a raised eyebrow that said, *Not sure what's going on here.*

Hazel turned slowly to face me, and I could see the wheels turning in her head as she calculated how to play the situation. I saw a flash of recognition—she must have finally put together that I was the person she'd seen at Lucas's place the other day. "Hello!" she exclaimed. "I've been *literally* dying to meet you!"

I nodded. "You saw me at the grooming salon," I pointed out. "But I imagine it would help to actually know the person you're pretending to work for to get your hands on cats."

At this, she at least had the grace to blush. "About that," she said. "I didn't mean any harm. I really just wanted to see how you did it. I love your business model—"

"Save it," I interrupted. "That was not cool. And you almost got yourself tasered. In fact, Katrina's here today and there's no promising that she won't taser you anyway, just as a matter of principle."

"Hey," she protested. "I think that's illegal!"

I held up a hand. "Stop. I think you and I need to have a chat. Alone." I glanced at my mother, who looked like she didn't know whether to laugh or be alarmed. "Can you give us a few?"

"Of course." She gracefully slipped past us, then paused with her hand on the door. "No tasering in front of the children," she warned me, then left, closing the door behind her.

# Chapter 38

Hazel and I stared at each other for a moment. She was trying for *defiant*, but I could tell she was a little unnerved about what was coming.

Good.

I stayed in front of the door, effectively blocking any exit she might try to make. I wasn't big into threatening people, but she had it coming.

The cats were on alert too—most of them were watching our interaction from their cubbies as if it were a particularly interesting bird video.

"So," I said, as if we were sitting down for coffee. "You want to start a pet party business."

She lifted her chin. "I already did," she informed me, tone haughty.

"Impressive," I said. "You've been here, what, a few weeks?"

"A month."

I nodded. "Where'd you get the idea?"

At this, her eyes dropped to the floor. "My aunt told me about your business and how she was hiring you for parties and events here. I thought it might be a cool idea.

Look, just because this is a small island doesn't mean you can monopolize a market," she informed me.

"Of course it doesn't. I'm just curious why you're pretending to work for me to get cats if you have your own business," I said.

She flushed again. "I have a cat. Bessie." She jammed a thumb toward her backpack. "I rescued her when she was a stray kitten."

Okay, she got points for that. "But you need more than one," I pointed out. "And what's the deal with saying you have trained therapy dogs and cats?"

"Oh, you've been to my website?" she asked brightly.

I gave her a look.

She shut up.

I let the silence linger, thinking about how Grandpa would handle this. I decided to keep her on her toes. "How did you connect with the McAllisters?" I asked, changing tack.

Hazel's eyes widened to deer-in-headlights size as she took a step away from me, as if anticipating an attack. "I don't know them. I swear. I met the kid here and she wanted a party, so I tried to sell myself. That's all."

*Interesting reaction*, I thought. "And they said no."

That defiant chin raise again. "They were on the fence."

"So you went to their house on Thursday morning to convince them. The morning someone killed Olivia McAllister." I didn't know how much she knew about what had happened, but I needed to find out what she was doing there.

She had the grace to look scared when I said that. "I didn't have anything to do with that. Do I need to, like, plead the fifth or whatever?" She took another step away from me. "Can I please leave?"

"You don't need to plead the fifth. This isn't court. And

no, you can't leave until we're done here." Now I took a step toward her. "Were you at their house—yes or no?"

Hazel's eyes flicked around the truck as if searching for an exit that she hadn't noticed before. Finding none, she crossed her arms over her chest. "You can't keep me here. That's, like, kidnapping."

I bit back a sigh. I would guess Hazel wasn't more than eighteen or nineteen years old. Clearly, she was having some challenges in her life. And even though she was currently making *my* life challenging, I forced myself to find some empathy for her. "Look. I'm not trying to blame you for anything. But I know I saw your car that morning. It's probably the only car like it on the island. And I need to know if you saw anyone around their house. This is important, Hazel. That was my mom's best friend when she was about your age. And she's really devastated about what happened to her. If there's anything you can do to help, I wish you would."

She seemed to consider this. Then she cocked her head. "What's in it for me?"

Now I was wishing for Katrina's taser. I'd just used my last bit of patience to try to appeal to her, and she was breaking my chops. "How about I won't turn you in to the cops," I said. "They're actively looking for anyone in the area that morning, and they're going to turn over every rock until they find them. And I'll try to convince Katrina not to press charges for trying to steal cats. How's that?" I held up my phone. "I have the lieutenant on speed dial. We're friends. My grandfather is the former chief of police. I can make a call right now. Your choice."

That seemed to wake her up. She dropped the attitude and her defensive posture. "I didn't do anything," she protested, her voice starting to wobble. "I swear. I went there to do a demo with Bessie. I do have her trained and she can do really fun things. I just wanted a chance to show them."

"So what happened? Did you talk to anyone?"

"No. I didn't get a chance. I saw the kid's mother leave, which was fine because I knew the other lady was the one I needed to convince. The grandmother. She was, like, high maintenance. I mean, sorry she's dead and everything. But she was. Anyway, I was on my way to the door, but then I saw a dude waiting on the doorstep."

"Waiting? Like, for someone to come to the door?" I asked.

She nodded. "He was ringing the bell and then trying to look in the window and stuff. It looked like the door was kind of open, but he wasn't going in."

"Hang on," I said. "What did he look like?" Was it possible she'd seen the actual killer? Was she going to describe Jason McAllister? I realized I was holding my breath.

"He was an old dude," she said.

I blinked. I wasn't expecting that. "Old?"

"Yeah. White beard, little plaid hat."

Old dude with a plaid hat. My money was on Neil Caldwell. He'd been wearing that orange-and-black plaid hat when he showed up outside of the house an hour or so later too. "Did he see you pull up?"

She shook her head. "I'd parked my car on the street and cut through the yard. When I saw him, I kind of stopped. Wasn't sure who he was or whatever. Then he kind of looked around, like maybe he was looking to see if anyone was watching. I think he might've been about to go inside. But then he saw me."

I waited. "Then what?" I asked when she didn't say anything else.

"He started walking toward me. I don't know, I just felt weird about it. So I turned around and booked it back to my car." She stared at me, face pleading. "I swear, that's all. I didn't even really see anything. Please don't tell my aunt. She'll throw me off the island and make me go home and I . . . I kind of like it here." Hazel's eyes filled with tears. "I want to stay."

# Chapter 39

This had taken an unexpected turn. I hadn't been expecting tears. And I definitely hadn't been expecting Neil Caldwell.

I was trying to process what Hazel had told me. Neil Caldwell had been at Olivia's house the morning she was killed. Not later, not with a TV crew in tow—but earlier. Way earlier, before the so-called relocated shoot. I should have seen this coming. I'd wondered what his deal was. He'd seemed very invested in Olivia and her family.

But even though his presence was highly suspect, the timing was off. By the time Hazel had panicked and sped away—and by the time my mom and I arrived—Olivia had already been inside that house, probably dead. Hazel was certain she hadn't seen Caldwell hadn't come out of the house. He'd been on the porch.

Waiting.

"Hazel. You did the right thing, telling me," I said. "No one's going to throw you off the island." I had no idea if that was true—I guess it depended on how much Ellen could put up with—but I didn't have time to be Hazel's therapist right now. "Are you sure you didn't see that man coming out of the house?"

Hazel shook her head. "Positive. He was just waiting."

Waiting. For what? Waiting for Olivia to answer the door? Or waiting because he already knew she wouldn't and was trying to look innocent for any cameras in the area?

"Will you be willing to tell the police this if they ask? It might be helpful for a timeline of the events," I said. At her hesitation, I added, "You'll get props for being cooperative."

Before she could commit, someone banged on the door. Urgently. I cracked it open and peered out. Lucas. "I'll be right out," I started to say, but he cut me off.

"Mick's here," he said, and the look on his face told me I should get out there now.

"Stay here," I said to Hazel, and went outside.

Mick was just getting out of his unmarked when I rushed over to intercept him. He had another cop with him—thankfully, not Craig, which would have been awkward if they had to take my mother into custody. "Hey," I said. "What's going on?"

"Is your mother here?" he asked.

"She is, but she's busy. Why?"

He gave me a look. The kind that meant he wasn't in the mood for games. "Don't make this harder than it needs to be, Maddie. I need to speak with her. I told you I would."

"Then speak to her later. At home," I said, heat creeping into my voice. "What are you thinking, showing up here and pulling her aside like she's a suspect?"

"I'm not doing that," he said evenly. "And I need you to trust me when I say that."

"That's hard to do when you're standing here with another officer."

He exhaled. "We need to tighten the timeline. That's all."

"By taking my mother in like a criminal?"

"By *talking* to her," he corrected. "I talked to you already, right? I never got to get her independent statement. That's all I'm doing."

"Then why does it feel like more? And why now?"

He didn't answer.

I leaned in close, trying to keep my composure and hold my voice down. We were already attracting attention from the already big crowd gathering for the day's events. "What about the other people we discussed? I gave you facts that her own brother lied about being on the island already when she was killed—and pretty strong evidence that he was trying to take the house out from under her. Not to mention, there's something there with Neil Caldwell. I know it. I have someone right here who saw him on Olivia's doorstep that morning—"

"Your mother was there that morning too."

"So was I," I said through gritted teeth. "You already know this."

"Did you know your mother tried to connect with Olivia the evening prior to her death?"

That stopped me in my tracks. "What?"

"Exactly."

My mind spun at that. It must've meant that my mom hadn't wanted to wait for me to be ready to go over there the next morning. She'd wanted to talk to her old friend immediately.

Understandable. But then why hadn't she mentioned it? And had they connected?

"Just give me some room here, Maddie," Mick said. "Please."

"Did you even question Jason?" I asked.

"I am on it," he said. "Please trust me."

"Then why are you here?"

"Because right now," he said carefully, "the chief has been very clear. We keep the family out of this unless or until we can't."

I stared at him. "Meaning?"

He held my gaze. Didn't answer.

Behind us, my mother stepped out of the building, Ellen in tow. They were laughing. Ellen had a bag of cookies in her hand. My mother had a stack of plates and cups.

Ready for the party.

"I don't like this," I said quietly.

"I know," Mick replied. "But if Jason's lying, I need to have my facts about everything else so nailed down there isn't even a hint of a question about it. Look, we'll talk to her here if she wants. Or she can follow us to the station. No one's getting arrested. Okay?" He rested a hand on my shoulder briefly, then headed toward my mother.

And in that moment, any lingering questions about where to focus disappeared.

If Jason was willing to let my mother sit in that chair to buy himself time, then I wasn't waiting for the police to catch up.

I pulled out my phone and made two calls—one to Grandpa to let him know we needed his lawyer here ASAP, and the other to Adam to tell him he was about to buy a restaurant.

It was time to go find Olivia's brother.

# Chapter 40

I left Lucas and Ellen in charge of the party and, praying I wasn't making a mistake, told Hazel I'd pay her a hundred bucks—and convince Katrina not to press charges for attempted cat theft—if she helped out under her aunt's watchful eye. She agreed without hesitation. JJ would be supervising, of course, since he couldn't exactly ride off with me on Adam's motorcycle.

Adam dropped everything when I called him with my plan. I went to him because he was the one person I was confident Jason McAllister would actually take a meeting with. Jason had already told Adam he'd be sticking around until he heard back about the restaurant sale, and I wanted to reach him before he changed his mind. Adam texted to say he was ready to move things forward—but only if they met today.

That was my way in.

I didn't think Jason would talk to me if I just showed up unannounced. And if I was wrong about him—if he really was capable of killing his own sister—I wanted backup. Especially backup the size of Adam.

The Seashore Motel was on the outskirts of Daybreak Harbor, close enough to town to pretend it belonged there, far enough away that it wouldn't offend anyone. When we pulled up on Adam's bike, it was as bleak as I remembered it. One of those hotels only Jack Reacher and certain types of unsavory individuals might stay at.

"Nice place," Adam said with a grimace as we got off his bike and secured our helmets to the hook under the seat.

"No wonder he's so eager to talk to you," I said. "If these are the types of accommodations he needs to stay at."

Adam scanned the room numbers, then pointed to the second-floor end unit. "That one. Number twenty-two."

I followed him up the stairs and stood to the side while he knocked on the door. It took longer to answer than I expected, especially for someone who needed money and thought his payday had arrived. When he finally answered, it appeared we'd woken him up. He squinted against the daylight like it irritated him, then reached out to shake Adam's hand. "Hey, man," he said. "Come on in."

The button-down shirt he wore with a pair of faded jeans was wrinkled and half-untucked, the collar stretched like it had spent the night twisted in his hands. His feet were bare.

"Hey, Jason." Adam nodded, then motioned me inside. "I brought someone with me."

I stepped into view. "Hi. Maddie James. We met at Shady's."

Jason didn't look impressed by this. "Okay. Come in," he repeated, obviously uncomfortable in the sunlight. "She your business partner or something?" he asked Adam as we stepped past him into the small, stale room.

"No," I said. "I'm Sophie Mancini's daughter."

That sobered him up. His head snapped back to me, taking in my face differently now that he knew who I was. We stared at each other until he broke eye contact.

I closed the door behind me. "My mother is talking to

the police right now," I said. I hoped it sounded like she was giving them information versus being interrogated by them.

"Okay," he said in a tone that suggested he didn't know why I was telling him this.

"About your sister," I said, louder now. "Remember her? Someone murdered her?"

He flinched, just a little, then pulled out the chair at the desk and sank into it. "Sit," he murmured, waving his hand.

Adam and I took in the unmade bed and the uncomfortable-looking chair in the corner and both declined.

"Look," I said. "I know you and Helen Holloway were trying to get the house away from Olivia's control to sell it and get what you thought would be a windfall." I hoped that was right. It was what I'd managed to piece together from the information we had. His silence now made me think it was. "What I don't know is how you decided killing her would be the easiest way to do it."

His eyes widened now and he jumped out of his chair. Adam stepped forward, just a smidge, to let him know he should keep his distance. Jason looked at him, then sat again. "You think I killed my own sister?"

I shrugged. "You lied about not being on the island before she died, when you clearly were." I motioned to Adam. "Meeting with him, for one. You think that's a secret?"

Jason slunk down in his chair, eyes dropping to the floor.

"And your relationship with Helen," I continued. "Which is especially damning. You wanted something your sister had. Helen did too. And it seemed like she didn't want to share. What am I supposed to think? What are the police supposed to think?"

But he was shaking his head vehemently. "No way.

You're not putting this on me. For years of my life, I had to deal with the nuclear fallout of Olivia's every whim. You want to know why I was out here? Aside from trying to offload my restaurant to him?" He jabbed a finger in my direction. "Because my sister called me. She wanted to talk. In person."

"Why?"

He lifted his shoulders, palms up. "No idea. She bailed on me. Never showed."

I gave him my best skeptical face. "That's convenient. You weren't out here to meet with Helen?"

Jason dropped his gaze again. "I was doing that too. I told Helen that Olivia had called me. I was kind of hoping she was ready to play ball."

"So why did you lie to the police about not being out here?" I asked.

"Knee-jerk reaction," he said with a shrug. "When I heard what happened, I got freaked out. Figured it would look bad for me. My sister and I, we never really got along. I knew it was going to get complicated. Look, I know it's stupid. But at the same time they couldn't check my ferry ticket because I got a lift from a friend with a small plane. So no one actually knew I was here except for you"—he turned to Adam—"and Helen. And Olivia."

"So, was Helen just working through you? Or was she in contact with Olivia too?"

"Of course she was in contact with her," he said with disdain. "Helen knew the second Olivia set foot on this island months ago. She's probably been badgering her ever since about the house. She's wanted her hands on that thing for a million years. Wants it to be a museum or probably some shrine to my aunt." He rolled his eyes. "Meanwhile, it's just a house and it can make us some cash. I never understood why this family could never shake this place off. No matter how long we'd been gone from here it's like some cursed magnet, pulling us back." He was almost talking to himself now, hands fisted in his hair.

"Jason," I said. "Are you telling me you never saw your sister at all?"

"Yes. Because I did not." He enunciated each word carefully, to make sure I understood.

"Not even the morning she died?" I persisted. "Didn't you try to get in touch again? Weren't you curious why she didn't show?"

"No. I figured she was just playing her usual games with me. And then Helen told me she was dropping it."

"Dropping what?"

"The house," Jason said. "Helen was giving up on getting the house."

"Why? That doesn't sound very on brand," I said, using Adele's new phrase. "Does this have something to do with the grant she was supposed to get?"

Jason's eyes locked on me again. "How do you know about that?"

I didn't answer.

He muttered something under his breath. "Yeah, it was about the grant. But apparently the condition was that she needed full cooperation from the official heir and for them to willingly sign over any future claim to the house. Olivia was never going to do that."

"Olivia told her that?" I asked. "Or did Helen just tell you that so she didn't have to deal with you anymore? Maybe she'd decided she didn't want to pay you off."

He chuckled at that. "I wouldn't put it past her, but no. She and Olivia connected that night. The night I was supposed to see her."

"The night before she died."

"Right."

"Helen told me she hadn't spoken to Olivia at all. That she didn't even know she was back."

"Well, it's obviously a lie," Jason said.

"How do I know *you're* not lying?"

He shrugged. "You don't. But I'm not. Bottom line, Olivia nipped it in the bud. Went to Helen, told her she wasn't giving up our aunt's house. Basically, Helen was cornered."

"And she told you this during a meeting that conveniently happened when someone else decided to kill Olivia."

"You can be skeptical all you want, but it's easily provable," Jason said. "Check the cameras at the historical society. Helen records everything going on at that building." He spread his hands wide. "I didn't kill my sister. Helen didn't either. Not that either of us probably didn't want to at some point. But we were nowhere near her house Thursday morning."

"Who did kill her, then?" I pressed.

Jason leaned back, the cheap desk chair creaking under his weight. "You don't get it, do you," he said. "But you're still playing amateur detective. Man, I can see the family resemblance," he muttered, more to himself than me. "Look, Olivia was a pretty polarizing figure. In life, in her own family, everywhere she went, basically. She had a talent for getting involved in everything, even when it was none of her business."

I waited, but he didn't go on. "That still doesn't tell me who else wanted her gone."

"Why do you care so much? Why aren't you letting the cops deal with it?" he shot back.

"Because they won't," I said, stepping closer to his chair so I was now towering over him. "Because your family saw to it decades ago that any real investigation isn't going to go anywhere if they don't like where it's going."

"Well, then you can see where she got it from," he said

sarcastically. He stood now, whether to intimidate or just to make his point, I couldn't tell. But I stood my ground.

"My sister treated the world like it was a play and she was the director," he said. "She decided who belonged in each scene and who needed to be written out. She pushed and cornered and bullied people into decisions they weren't ready to make, and she didn't care if they agreed, as long as they complied. She went after the ones who felt trapped. The ones who couldn't—or wouldn't—just walk away. And she told herself she was helping so she could sleep at night. So you're asking who wanted her gone?" He shook his head slowly. "You should be asking who she backed so far into a corner they ran out of room."

Then he turned to Adam. "So, are you going to make me an offer on my restaurant, or what?"

I realized just how pathetic Jason McAllister was—mid-sixties, still looking for his proverbial ship to come in.

"Sorry, dude," Adam said. "That's not happening."

# Chapter 41

*Sunday*

"I don't want to do this event today," I confessed to Lucas.

It was a small private party we were hosting at the cafe itself—no truck, thank goodness—to celebrate an engagement. It was an out-of-town couple who had booked this six months ago, and I wouldn't have the heart to cancel it.

He squeezed my hand. "I don't blame you. There's a lot going on."

It was nearly eight a.m. and we were still in bed. But neither of us had been asleep for a while. We'd been discussing Saturday's events—Hazel, Mick, my mother, Jason and everything he'd told me, and Tess.

Mick had been busy. According to Grandpa, before he crashed our party at the library to corner my mother, he'd pulled Tess and her boyfriend into his interrogation room to do as he'd promised—scare the bejeezus out of them for lying to him. Once he'd made his point, he'd officially cleared them as suspects, but they would likely remember the experience for a long time to come.

With Tess crossed off his list, Mick moved on to the harder part. He'd satisfied his chief's requirements in questioning my mother—or rather, he got enough proof that they had absolutely no reason to look at her further.

She'd admitted—first to him and then later to me when I'd gone over to talk to her—that she'd tried to reach Olivia the night before she died, after learning she was back on the island. But she'd been unsuccessful, and she'd told no one about the attempt. When I asked why (1) she'd called her in the first place when we were going over there the next day, and (2) why she hadn't mentioned it, she'd simply said she couldn't stand not knowing why Olivia had left and never called. As for why she hadn't mentioned it, she'd told me that Olivia coming back had dredged up what she'd never quite made peace with—the fact that, despite herself, she'd wondered if Olivia had hurt Delia and that's why the family had vanished so cleanly.

For my mom, calling Olivia wasn't about answers so much as it was about finally hearing her voice again, after years of knowing she'd let the worst assumptions stand. And once Olivia was dead, admitting the call felt like admitting that failure out loud.

Since her activities the morning Olivia died were well-documented, from leaving her house to coming to ours to the two of us going to Olivia's together after she was already dead, Mick was confident telling the chief they had to move on. There was no way they could try to change that story.

That didn't make where we were today any better or easier. It was strange how quickly something could become officially over without feeling finished at all.

"I don't blame your mother," Lucas said now. "She must be dealing with so many emotions about this. I mean, of course she would've tried to call her. I would've done the same."

"I agree. I just wish she'd told us." I threw the covers off and swung my legs over the side of the bed, feeling like I had chains attached to my ankles. I hated unfinished business.

Dean had told me they were all leaving tomorrow after the party—him, Tess, and Piper—and I assumed that meant leaving the island, not just our house. I hadn't confirmed with Tess, but I didn't imagine she'd be fighting to stay, especially after what Shea had told me. But it felt like when she left, the whole thing would get put on a shelf. Just like Delia.

Would we be talking about Olivia McAllister in forty years like we talked about her aunt today? I hoped not, but it was looking bleak.

"Can you cancel the event?" Lucas asked now.

I pulled the pillow back over my face. "No. And I wouldn't do that anyway. Of course I'm going to do it. I just want to go on record and say I really, really don't want to."

He pulled me into a hug. "I get it. I'll be there to help. And, uh . . ." He paused.

"What?"

"Hazel wants to come help too."

I groaned. "Am I not going to be able to get rid of her now?"

He laughed. "Honestly, she wasn't bad yesterday. Good with the kids, attentive to the cats. I know you and she have some . . . issues to work out, but it wasn't terrible having her there."

"Good to know. That's fine, sure. She can come. It will all be fine, right?" I tried to put my brave face on.

But I couldn't hide how low I was feeling. We weren't anywhere closer to figuring out who had killed Olivia. I was still highly suspicious of Neil Caldwell, but Hazel's story kept tripping me up. If he truly hadn't arrived until the time she saw him, then he couldn't have done it.

So who was left?

According to her own brother, Olivia hadn't been a great person. Although Jason's own reputation didn't seem stellar either. But a lot of what he'd said had aligned with what I'd also been hearing from others, including my own mother. And that could mean a lot of people were unhappy with Olivia, sure.

But who was unhappy enough to kill her?

I was starting to think we'd missed something. That maybe the real killer had slipped off the island and was gone for good.

I threw the covers off and got up. The party was at noon. Which meant I had work to do before then. Better snap to it.

I opened the bedroom door to head downstairs. The dogs bounded past me, eager to greet the rest of the household. As I watched their little butts wiggle their way down the stairs, I caught movement out of the corner of my eye. Expecting Piper, I turned to look down the hall.

And saw a white and gray cat, sitting calmly in the half-open doorway of the bathroom.

Puck.

He met my gaze without blinking.

*Oh*, I thought. *You're here.*

I don't know why it didn't surprise me. I supposed I could've twisted myself into a knot, wondering if I was just so tired I was seeing things. Or admitting I'd seen him but spiraling on what it meant. Instead, one thought spoke out over all that noise: maybe this wasn't over.

Then the dogs barked downstairs, the moment passed, and I turned away.

When JJ and I got to the cafe, though, Harry and Grandpa were already there. They were doing a little cleaning and a lot of talking. They both paused when I came in.

"There she is," Grandpa said. "My reckless little investigator." Grandpa hadn't been happy with me when he'd learned I'd gone off and confronted Jason without even telling him. He'd thought I was still at the party keeping an eye on things with my mother.

"I wasn't reckless. I brought Adam with me," I said.

"You forgot to mention to anyone else where you were going," he pointed out.

"I didn't forget. I just didn't want to be distracted." I watched as JJ went over to check on the kittens. We had a new batch coming in once the Jetsons went home with Tess's friends next week. JJ loved to babysit the babies.

"You got some good information, though," Harry said, ever the peacemaker.

"Did I, though? We're right back at square one," I said.

"But we were able to verify his story about him and Helen," Grandpa said.

"You were able to check the cameras already?" I asked.

"I had someone take a peek for me before the cops got it," Grandpa said. "Make sure you give Bones a good bonus this year."

"You called my web guy?" I was mortified. "How did you even know how to reach him? Never mind. Dumb question," I said, holding up a hand.

"He's a nice guy. Doesn't say much," Grandpa said.

"Moving on. How's Mom today?" I pulled a broom out of the front closet and started sweeping up litter.

"She's okay. Your dad is angry. I don't blame him. I'm not sure what he's going to do about it, but I expect our chief of police might get some backlash on this one when things settle."

"Don't they have to solve it first?" I muttered. I propped the broom against the couch, abandoning any semblance of pretending to care about cleaning. "What about Caldwell? He's the loose end here. He's been nosing around this thing from the beginning. Why? There has to be a reason. And lots of people seem angry with him already, right?"

"The restoration project is a whole other discussion," Grandpa said. "He's slimy for sure, but it has nothing to do with Olivia. That doesn't mean it isn't serious," he added. "It just means that the two things aren't related. And the town has to handle that one."

"But you already said you had concerns about him relating to Delia," I persisted. "What if Olivia was connected? What if he did do something to Delia and was afraid Olivia had found out?"

Grandpa held up a hand. "Maddie. I said I had questions, not proof. I never got anywhere close to even articulating a theory on that. Would it have been something I looked at if I wasn't shut down? Yes. One hundred percent. But it never went anywhere. Plus, that young woman's timing, if she's right, means he arrived at Olivia's after the fact."

I wanted to protest, but he was right. I was reaching. Because if we didn't have Caldwell, who did we have? And worse—if everyone else was satisfied with that answer, why did stopping now feel like the most dangerous option of all?

# Chapter 42

*Monday*

Piper's birthday party day. The last day the McAllister clan would be under our roof.

Tess had confirmed that she was taking Piper back to Florida to live near Tess's father, and that Dean was going too. She'd avoided my questions about whether she planned to return, or how involved in the investigation she'd be from here.

I wasn't sure what to think about that.

But all we had to do was get through today, I kept telling myself. Then maybe things could somewhat go back to normal.

Maybe if I said it enough, it would actually happen.

Tess seemed different today, though. Lighter. Maybe some of it was because her daughter was clearly delighted with the party planning. Her dad had also arrived, and I think that brought her some comfort as well. And maybe now that she'd gotten her lies off her chest to Mick, she was able to sleep better.

We'd all worked hard after the cafe closed at noon to set up an experience as close as possible to the original Purr-Day Bash Olivia had described to me. Harry had spent an hour hanging fairy lights from the ceiling and around the cat perches, on a ladder that made me hold my breath the whole time, as Adele shouted directions to him from below. After Grandpa's unfortunate ladder experience over the past winter, I had a little PTSD about that kind of thing.

My mom had created a "forest floor" layered with texture: she'd gathered washable rugs in mossy greens and soft grays, and with Hazel's help had scattered them like stepping stones through a garden path. Between them sat oversized floor cushions and low stools, giving the kids places to perch while keeping everything cat-level and cozy. The walls were covered in pink fabrics with sparkles, and there were balloons and pink-frosted cupcakes that Ethan had made.

Hazel, for her part, seemed happy to be there and seemed to be staying out of trouble, so there was that.

Piper wore a sparkly pink dress with a little tiara, and somehow, Lucas had found matching little bow ties for all the cats' collars. JJ had not been interested in a pink bow tie. Tess seemed to be of the same mind. Instead of a party dress, she wore jeans and a simple pink sleeveless sweater.

I'd almost forgotten it had been Tess's birthday celebration too. Their actual birthday had been Wednesday of last week, the day before all this insanity began. At least she and Piper had been able to spend one last official birthday with Olivia.

"This place looks amazing," Dean said when he came in. It appeared, from the armful of presents he had with him, that he'd been out shopping. He deposited them all on the gift table, save for one small box that he kept in his hand.

"Thanks. I think so too," I said.

"I mean it. I really appreciate everything you've done for us," he said, turning his serious gaze on me. "My family has been through a rough time, and you've really helped. It's been so good to be under the same roof with my daughter again. Honestly, I think it's even helped me and Tess."

"I'm glad. You should thank Grandpa Leo," I said, nodding in his direction. He stood with Harry, watching the two of us. "He is very kind about opening the house."

"I'll do that," Dean said, but he made no move to do it now. He was juggling that little box from one hand to the other, nervously, I thought. His eyes kept moving from me to Tess.

His ex-wife had just gone to the door to greet her friends. Shea and Carrie had obviously gotten the memo. They were both wearing dresses like Piper's. Shea's was a bit more sparkly, which fit. And she had a matching tiara, which delighted Piper to no end.

Unlike the other day, when Tess had seemed still in the fog of the murder and its aftermath, today she seemed fully present, exclaiming over their outfits and bringing the cookies they'd brought over to the table to set them up with the rest of the food.

"She seems better," I commented to Dean. "How's she holding up?"

"She's tough," he said. "Once she's away from here and able to put all this behind her, she'll be okay."

I glanced at him. "You think she'll be able to do that? With everything . . . unresolved?"

"Why not? The police know what they're doing . . . hopefully. It's not up to her to figure it out." He turned to his daughter as she ran up to grab his arm.

"Daddy! Auntie Shea and Auntie Carrie are taking the kittens home," she announced excitedly. "That means I get to see them!"

"It does," he agreed, kneeling to her level. "That should keep you busy until you get your own kitty, right?"

Her eyes grew big as saucers as she processed that. "My own kitty," she breathed. "Like Puck?"

Dean looked confused for a second. "Who's Puck?"

She sighed. "My kitty from Grandma's. Mom finally went and got him for me. He's right there!" She pointed to the food table. Under the pink tablecloth that draped over the sides and front, I could see the white and gray cat. Sitting calmly, just like when I'd seen him in the doorway of the room I'd found Olivia in.

"He's white, so he matches my pink," she added proudly, still pointing.

There was no mistaking where she pointed. There were also none of our cats over by the food table. I also had no white cats in the cafe now, so there would be no confusing the two.

Dean humored her, following her pointing finger. He squinted, then tilted his head to peer lower. Puzzled now, he shook his head. "I don't see a cat there. But I see plenty of them around the rest of the room!" He waved his hand to encompass the rest of the cats lounging in various places.

She frowned at him. I could see she was about to argue when the door opened and a few party guests came in.

I'd been a little worried that some of Piper's friends might not show, depending on what their parents had heard about the McAllisters' drama, but all ten of the original invites were confirmed. Tess had personally called each kid's parent and sorted out the reschedule.

No one wanted to say no to a family who'd just experienced a tragedy.

Tess came over to Piper. "Go say hi to your friends," she encouraged.

As Piper ran over to greet them, Dean stood. "You didn't tell me you got her a cat," he said.

Tess glanced at him, the smile fading. "I didn't."

"She just told me you did."

"Well, I didn't," she said, an edge creeping into her voice now to match his. "She thinks a stray that she saw around . . . the house was hers."

"So you didn't go pick it up and bring it here?"

"Of course not," she said incredulously, glancing at me as if to implore some help.

"I think she really just wants a cat," I said, hoping to defuse the situation.

"I know. I'm going to address it when we get home," Tess said. "But for right now, I'm going to go make sure she has a good time at the party." Avoiding Dean's eyes, she slipped away and headed to the door, where Adele was greeting more attendees and making sure no one was holding the door open so any cats could get out.

Dean watched her walk away. For a moment, I thought he might follow her. Instead, he stayed rooted where he was, staring toward the door like it had personally betrayed him. His jaw worked, but he said nothing.

"You okay?" I asked.

He startled, then nodded too quickly. "Yeah. Just . . . can never seem to say the right things with her."

Before I could respond, I heard Tess's voice carry over the hum of the room.

"You made it!"

We both turned toward the door in time to see Tess throw her arms around a man who stood just inside the threshold. He was taller than Dean. Broader too, like he spent a lot of time in the gym lifting weights. He held a pink gift bag with tissue paper erupting out of the top.

"Come in," Tess said, looking positively giddy. "This is Mark," she told Shea and Carrie, who watched with interest. "I told you about him."

Her mystery man. I guess now that she'd told the police

as well as her friends, she was done with any attempt to hide it. Also what could be making her appear lighter.

But next to me, Dean had gone completely still.

Mark bent down to Piper's level, introducing himself, handing over the bag. "You can open it now," he said with a wink. "I won't tell anyone."

Piper accepted it solemnly, like a queen receiving tribute, then immediately tore it open, flinging the tissue paper in the air in her excitement. "Mom! He got me cat socks!"

Tess laughed. "He did! That's amazing!"

Shea and Carrie came over, all smiles, leaning in to meet this mystery man, the five of them huddled together like their own private party.

I risked a glance at Dean. He stared at them, his face unreadable. The little box he'd been holding slipped from his fingers and hit the floor with a soft, hollow sound.

And then it all clicked into place.

# Chapter 43

I tried to catch Grandpa's eye across the room, but he was deep in conversation with my mom and not paying any attention to me. I refocused on Dean, bent, and picked up the box. As I did, I opened a text message to Mick and hit voice record.

"What's in it?" I asked, trying to keep my voice light.

"A necklace," he said, a little robotically. "With her favorite stone. Emerald."

"Tess's," I confirmed.

He nodded, once.

"You were hoping to get her back," I said.

"Them," he corrected, still not looking at me. "My family. We never should have split in the first place."

"Why did you?" I asked. Trying to keep my tone curious, but not urgent.

"Why did we," he repeated, tucking a chunk of his curly hair behind his ear. "That's a great question. Tess could probably articulate it better than I can, but she'd only be repeating what her mother told her."

There it was.

"Olivia," I said quietly.

"Yeah. Olivia. My dear, sweet mother-in-law. Actually,"

he said with a laugh, "my ex-mother-in-law. She would very definitely remind me of that if she were here."

I watched the party unfolding around us: the kids playing with the cats, Adele hovering watchfully to make sure no tails were being pulled, adults clustered around talking. Tess smiling, the first real smiles I'd seen from her. Her dad, chatting with the new boyfriend. It all seemed so utterly normal. I sent a quick, silent prayer that we were left alone in our little corner for a few minutes more.

"Do you know what happened to Olivia, Dean?" I asked. "Did you go see her on Thursday morning?"

He still watched his daughter, snuggling with JJ now as she chattered with her friends. Shea crouched next to them, laughing at something they were saying. Dean looked at me, as if considering whether to answer, then made the decision. "I did. I just wanted to talk to her. Tell her to please reconsider making Tess move out here. I didn't want my kid to be so far away, you know?" His eyes pleaded for understanding. "I know she felt the same way when Piper wasn't nearby. I thought I could appeal to her. I really did."

"Why did you wait for Tess to leave?"

He blinked. "I didn't. Didn't even know she'd gone. I was going to have the conversation with her, I hoped. I thought since she'd had me come out here for the party maybe she was ready to come around, you know? Start talking like real people again. Like real parents . . ." He trailed off, shaking his head.

I waited, not daring to speak.

"But Tess wasn't there. Piper was out back playing. Olivia let me in, but she was dismissive. Gave me five minutes of her time and then told me she didn't think we should be talking without Tess. That Piper was resilient and would be fine, and that Tess had made her choice. About me, and about where she'd live. And it was *disingenuous* to go behind her back." He barked out a laugh. "Disingenuous. Like everything she did wasn't disingenuous."

The soft, almost apologetic tone was gone, replaced by a sharp, angry one.

"Then she told me to leave. And went upstairs to that stupid little office she'd been spending all her time in."

"But you didn't leave," I said.

He shook his head. "I didn't. Pathetic as it was, I thought I'd try one more time to see if she had any empathy left. So I followed her up and pressed her again. And you know what she said? She just laughed at me. Told me she'd won. That if I really loved Piper, I'd let her have a better life with someone more suitable. Then she turned around and just . . . dismissed me."

I was holding my breath. I could guess what happened next, but I needed him to say it.

But he didn't speak for a long time.

"Dean," I said finally. "Can you tell me what happened?"

He looked around the room as if looking for a way out. Not just out of here, but off this whole island. Away from the whole nightmare.

"I just . . . lost it. Maybe I even blacked out. But part of me felt so calm. Calmer than I'd felt in a year, since Tess and I split. There was this mermaid statue on the table near the door to that room. An ugly bronze thing. I picked it up and I hit her. Over the head. She went down hard." He exhaled, as if he'd been waiting to say it. "Didn't even make a noise. Almost like a mannequin, you know? And then I had a moment of, *I gotta get out of there before anyone realizes.*"

"Piper was right outside," I said.

He covered his face with his hands, his shoulders crumpling. "I know," he said, his voice muffled. "I'm horrified about that. I would never do anything to hurt her. But I guess intent doesn't matter, does it. I figured out how to shut the door. Hoped that maybe no one would ever find her in there. Silly, right?" He let out a breath. I could see his hands shaking. "I didn't actually know what I was doing in that moment. Oh God." He looked around the room again. "I'm screwed, aren't I."

I didn't say anything. My phone was still clenched in my hand, still recording. I hit the send button without even looking at the screen.

# Chapter 44

*Two weeks later*

"Okay, one more take," Helen Holloway commanded.

I sighed inwardly but obeyed the tiny dictator in front of me. We were in the cat cafe, and Helen and I were doing a TikTok collaboration on Puck the Ghost Cat.

Once the story had broken about Olivia's true killer, her former son-in-law, Helen had reached out to ask me if Puck had made an appearance that day. I'd been tempted to lie, but wouldn't that be the antithesis of everything Puck stood for? So, I'd come clean and told her he'd been there, overseeing the end of that dramatic incident in the island's history.

And since no good deed ever goes unpunished, I was now doing a TikTok series.

My social media person, Clarissa, couldn't have been more excited when I told her, though. She was convinced I was going to find a whole new audience by being more visible on TikTok, especially with this kind of content.

"Be more dramatic this time," Helen instructed. She was making me tell the story, since she had not been here when Dean confessed, much to her chagrin.

"I'll try," I said. I was trying to temper the drama with the reminder that real people's lives had been torn apart.

After I'd sent Mick the recording, he'd shown up and quietly arrested Dean, outside so as not to completely traumatize Piper. Tess hadn't even realized what was happening around her until much later. The realization that her ex-husband had killed her mother because of her role in separating them had, understandably, been excruciating for her. Her dad had taken her and Piper off the island the next day.

I wondered about her boyfriend, and if she'd ever come back here. My gut told me it wasn't likely.

But Dean's confession wasn't the only truth that had come out in the McAllister drama. Mick had been working behind the scenes with Helen, whom he'd connected with earlier in the investigation. Helen had come clean to him about her real reason for wanting access to Delia's house. It had gone far beyond just wanting a historical win behind her legacy. She'd been convinced that Delia had documented something leading up to her disappearance all those years ago, and that she'd had it hidden in the house all this time.

It had taken her and Mick some time to uncover the journals, but they were under the floorboards in the secret room, hidden away in a hole that hadn't been touched in four decades. The journals told a story of how Delia had uncovered falsified data grant money obtained illegally by Caldwell & Emmett during her time with the firm.

Delia had figured out that the fraud wasn't just financial—it was physical. Environmental impact reports had been altered to greenlight projects that never should have passed review. Sediment tests rewritten. Ecosystems damaged beyond repair. And Caldwell & Emmett had kept cashing checks and collecting accolades.

The deeper Delia went, the more one name appeared in the margins: Thomas Emmett, Caldwell's partner.

She didn't mention Neil Caldwell at all. While he was

out being the face of the firm, Emmett was the one pulling strings behind the scenes, signing off on projects and reports late at night. The one pushing deadlines. The one who hadn't realized that Delia was a better scientist than he'd ever be.

She wrote about realizing she'd made a mistake confronting him directly. About a meeting she agreed to because she thought she still had leverage. It was the day she quit the firm. But not her quest to expose them.

For the next nine months, Delia had worked quietly and alone. The journals tracked her efforts with relentless precision—lists of agencies she'd researched, names of former regulators who might listen, notes about which offices were too closely tied to Caldwell & Emmett to be trusted. She rewrote summaries of the data again and again, refining her case, anticipating the questions she'd be asked.

She was careful. Careful about where she went. Careful about who she spoke to. But she also wrote about the toll it was taking: the isolation, the paranoia, the creeping fear that Emmett hadn't let it go.

In the later entries, she mentioned running into him "by accident" more than once: a parking lot, a coffee shop, a stretch of shoreline near one of the contested sites. She didn't believe in coincidences anymore.

The final pages weren't panicked, but they were urgent.

She'd finally secured a meeting with a federal investigator willing to look at her evidence. She planned to bring copies—never the originals—and had arranged to meet at a site she believed was neutral. Public enough to feel safe. Remote enough to talk freely.

She never made it. The journals ended there.

The rest came together only this week.

When construction crews began work on a long-abandoned Caldwell & Emmett access road—one Delia had flagged repeatedly in her notes—they uncovered human remains buried deep beneath compacted fill. DNA tests confirmed they were Delia's remains. The evidence, combined with the journals, was overwhelming.

But Emmett had been dead for years.

Neil Caldwell had spent most of the last week at the police station—with attorneys, of course—being questioned relentlessly while still playing the role he'd perfected over decades. He maintained what he'd always claimed: that Emmett handled operations, that he trusted him implicitly, that any wrongdoing had been concealed from him.

But eventually, he told Mick that he'd always wondered about his partner and Delia. But not enough that he'd ever tried to find out. It was incriminating enough, however, to get funding pulled on his latest restoration project, which the fishermen had been overjoyed about. And his name was now inseparable from the investigation.

That same day, Caldwell announced his retirement and the shuttering of the firm.

His publicists moved quickly, polishing the story into something almost noble: a respected figure stepping aside after a lifetime of service, bearing the burden of his partner's sins for the good of the island he loved. A man choosing grace over self-preservation. It was a tidy narrative.

I couldn't help wondering how Olivia's family—what was left of it—would receive the news. Whether they would honor the story of the woman they'd allowed to remain a mystery for decades. I imagined it was a lot to handle, on top of what had happened to Olivia.

For her part, Helen had told me that she was writing a book about what had happened to Delia, using a lot of her own words from the journals. I thought that was a fitting tribute.

Helen finally signaled that she was satisfied with the

final cut. "Thanks for doing this with me," she said finally. "Now make sure you keep it up on the cat cafe page."

"I can help too with the TikToks," Hazel offered. She'd been watching the filming the whole time. In fact, she'd been hard to get rid of since I offered to let her work with me. She, Ellen, and I had sat down for a serious conversation. I'd offered to mentor Hazel if she really wanted to stay on the island and work with cats, but with certain conditions and the reminder that Katrina and her taser were only a phone call away.

Both of them had agreed to my terms without question. I was taking a chance on her for sure, but I was also going with my gut. And my gut was telling me she was a troubled kid looking for a safe place to land.

And if I could be that for someone, why not?

"Thanks," I told her. "I'll take you up on that. You can work with my social media manager, Clarissa."

Hazel beamed at that.

Helen still didn't make a move to leave. She kept looking around the cafe, like she was waiting for something.

"I don't think he's here," I said. "You're looking for Puck, yes?"

She gave a tight nod. I don't think she wanted to admit that she hadn't yet seen him for herself.

"You know what," I said. "I think when you tell Delia's story, that might be when he shows up. That's probably the bigger story that he's been hanging around for."

She acknowledged that with a tiny, spunky smile. "Well then," she said. "I suppose I'd better get to it and stop wasting his time."